Could you fall in love with a stranger?

Because that was what it felt like.

It was wrong to succumb to the tide of longing that Owen made her feel. She barely knew him. And she didn't know herself at all.

"I must be clinging to my rescuer," she murmured. "It's making me feel attached to him. That's got to be part of the explanation for why I..." She was afraid to say the words out loud. As if that would make the feeling more real than it already was. *That's got to be why I feel as if I'm falling for him,* she thought, unable to entirely wash away the forbidden thought.

"Owen...I wish I'd met you under different circumstances," she murmured wistfully.

Dear Reader,

Winter's here, so why not curl up by the fire with the new Intimate Moments novels? (Unless you live in a warm climate, in which case you can take your books to the beach!) Start off with our WHOSE CHILD? title, another winner from Paula Detmer Riggs called *A Perfect Hero*. You've heard of the secret baby plot? How about secret *babies*? As in *three* of them! You'll love it, I promise, because Ian MacDougall really *is* just about as perfect as a hero can get.

Kathleen Creighton's *One More Knight* is a warm and wonderful sequel to last year's *One Christmas Knight*, but this fine story stands entirely on its own. Join this award-winning writer for a taste of Southern hospitality—and a whole lot of Southern loving. Lee Magner's *Owen's Touch* is a suspenseful amnesia book and wears our TRY TO REMEMBER flash. This twisty plot will keep you guessing—and the irresistible romance will keep you happy. FAMILIES ARE FOREVER, and *Secondhand Dad,* by Kayla Daniels, is just more evidence of the truth of that statement. Lauren Nichols takes us WAY OUT WEST in *Accidental Hero,* all about the allure of a bad boy. And finally, welcome new author Virginia Kantra, whose debut book, *The Reforming of Matthew Dunn,* is a MEN IN BLUE title. You'll be happy to know that her second novel is already in the works.

So pour yourself a cup of something warm, pull the afghan over yourself and enjoy each and every one of these terrific books. Then come back next month, because the excitement—and the romance—will continue, right here in Silhouette Intimate Moments.

Enjoy!

Leslie Wainger
Executive Senior Editor

Please address questions and book requests to:
Silhouette Reader Service
U.S.: 3010 Walden Ave., P.O. Box 1325, Buffalo, NY 14269
Canadian: P.O. Box 609, Fort Erie, Ont. L2A 5X3

OWEN'S
TOUCH

LEE
MAGNER

Silhouette®

INTIMATE™MOMENTS®

Published by Silhouette Books

America's Publisher of Contemporary Romance

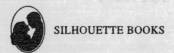

SILHOUETTE BOOKS

ISBN 0-373-07891-9

OWEN'S TOUCH

Copyright © 1998 by Ellen Lee Magner Tatara

Printed in U.S.A.

Books by Lee Magner

Silhouette Intimate Moments

Mustang Man #246
Master of the Hunt #274
Mistress of Foxgrove #312
Sutter's Wife #326
The Dragon's Lair #356
Stolen Dreams #382
Song of the Mourning Dove #420
Standoff #507
Banished #556
Dangerous #699
Owen's Touch #891

LEE MAGNER

is a versatile woman whose talents include speaking several foreign languages, raising a family—and writing. After stints as a social worker, an English teacher and a regional planner in the human services area, she found herself at home with a small child and decided to start working on a romance. She has always been an avid reader of all kinds of novels, but especially love stories. Since beginning her career, she has become an award-winning author and has published numerous contemporary romances.

Chapter 1

Without warning, blistering white headlights suddenly blinded her. The huge truck they belonged to hurtled around the mountain bend with an eerie roar and the grim face of certain death.

The driver slammed his fist down on the horn and his foot on the brakes, filling the cool night air with grating, awful sounds. The huge eighteen-wheeler kept on coming at her, its glistening, reptilian gaze unblinking, its trailer beginning to slide across the highway, unable to stop in time.

Her heart stopped. Her breathing, too. In that unending fraction of a second, she knew there would be no escape from what was about to happen. Visions of happy moments skimmed before her stunned and horrified eyes. Thirty years wasn't long enough, she thought, numb with fear. After all she'd been through in the past year, to think she'd die in a freak accident on some isolated mountain road...

She was squeezed between a stony wall that rose for hundreds of feet on her left and a steep plunge through dense underbrush on her right. Beyond the underbrush were trees, and lower still, the wildly rushing river in the canyon below. But straight ahead of her was the huge truck sliding into her at close to fifty miles per hour. No matter how good the brakes were, it wouldn't stop in time. It was certain death to stay on the road, and the fishtailing truck would crush her against the side of the mountain if she swung into the left lane.

She had only one faint chance of escape. In a heartbeat more, it would be too late even for that. This was countryside that could swallow a car wreck whole, and it was about to have the opportunity to gobble up hers. Oh, God...

The truck's horn bellowed harshly. There was a teeth-jarring grinding of gears and an agonizing squeal of brakes being asked to do the impossible. Tires smoked, and ugly black streaks marked the pavement, but still the truck slid on.

Blinded by the looming headlights, half paralyzed with fear, she jerked the steering wheel toward the right in a desperate effort to escape the fatal collision. She lifted her foot off the accelerator and pressed hard on the brake pedal. And she prayed.

Smoking snake eyes hurtled by her. The force of the beast shook the ground beside her like an earthquake. The truck grazed the car, biting off the edge of her left rear bumper, ripping it from the car like a dry piece of bread crust.

She screamed, but the sound was drowned out beneath the shattering crunch of her front fender against the metal guardrail and the mournful howl of horn and brakes.

She felt her front tires soar through air. Pure terror sucked the air from her lungs. She was too shocked to scream. Her mouth opened but no sound came out. Her knuckles whitened as she clutched the steering wheel with all her strength.

Down, down banged the car as it plummeted over the steep embankment and bounced unevenly down the rugged mountainside. Her headlights briefly illuminated different bits of hillside. Glass shattered. One headlight went blind. The other sent light dancing wildly from one spot to another ahead of the car's crazy descent.

She was flung forward and instinctively crossed her arms in front of her face, trying to protect her eyes.

Her car tilted and tossed, twisted and bucked. It was shoved up hard, then slammed down onto its right side. Then it was skidding...down, down, splitting young saplings, smashing wild-flowers, uprooting hardy mountain shrubs. Branches and leaves whipped at the windows like desperate hands. She was tossed around hard.

A blow to her left shoulder jabbed agony into her. Her seat belt bit into her chest, leaving a band of pain where it held her fast. Then, suddenly, the belt released her. A sharp pain lanced through her forehead as she bashed it against the steering wheel. She was slammed up against the windshield, then against the far side of the car, finally onto the ceiling as the vehicle tumbled over and over.

Pain and darkness warred with her frightened thoughts, but she was too scared to let herself pass out. She struggled to stay conscious, to save herself, to do whatever she could to survive. Out. She had to get out. To escape this battering.

Sounds. Dim, but she still heard them. She clung to them like a lifeline. The car was still sliding. Grass and shrubbery scratched at the metal as it scraped by. How much farther? she wondered desperately. There was a river at the bottom of the mountain. It was fierce, fast moving. Cluttered with boulders and rocks.

I will not die...I will not die....

A jagged pain bit hard into her neck, then worked its way quickly down her back. Another vicious tooth sank into her side.

The car slowed in fits and starts, until, finally, it smacked into something too big to be smashed down or knocked out of the way. She was thrown forward and to her left as the wet gravel and mud torn loose by her runaway car now pelted it with a brutal shower of stones and dirt.

Will I be buried alive? she wondered, struggling to remain conscious. But hard as she struggled, consciousness began to slip from her panicked grasp, floating away from her. Coldness crept into its place, numbing her mind, dulling her senses. Pain receded until it was almost too far from her to feel anymore.

Am I dead? Paralyzed?

A trickle like sand running over rock was the last thing she heard. Then there was nothing but oblivion, swallowing her whole.

Rocks and underbrush ripped loose during the crash spilled down the mountainside ahead of him as he scrambled down toward the wreckage. His flashlight skimmed over the area, searching for the car. Where the hell was it? He squinted and wiped the drizzle off his brow. Something glinted a little farther down. He pointed the beam toward it. There. Barely hanging on. Ten more feet and the car would have gone into the gorge.

He heard an explosion farther down the mountainside, somewhere close to the river, and turned in time to see huge orange-and-yellow plumes stab into the blackness.

For a few moments, the entire area around the explosion was as bright as day. Birds flew pell-mell out of the canyon to escape the inferno, and animals raced through the scrubby forest, frantically fleeing the unexpected disaster. A few plaintive cries of creatures injured or dying pierced the night.

Grimly, he turned toward what was left of the car. He heard no cries there.

He could see the lights turn on in the ranger station on the far peak, about half a mile down the river. They'd obviously seen the fire already. The truck's tanks were burning like a huge torch. Help would arrive as soon as it could be mobilized, probably by air, since helicopters were often used in mountain disasters around here. Well, that was one piece of good news, he thought grimly. Now, to see whether the silence coming from the car was good news or bad...

Sliding down the slippery slope, half on his knees, half on his feet, he reached the battered vehicle within moments. The car was balanced on something underneath the chassis, and its nose pointed toward the gorge below. He moved around it gingerly, using the flashlight beam to make a quick check for leaking fuel or smoldering parts. He sure as hell didn't need to be blown to pieces.

He crawled onto the car. Very carefully. It rocked as it took his weight. Sweat dampened his back. Hell, they might both end up in the gorge, he thought grimly.

He wiped the rain from his face and shone the light into the car through the shattered hole that had been the passenger's-side window of the badly damaged car.

Folded in an awkward heap on the front seat was the form of a woman. He swore under his breath. The car began to teeter again. He held his breath. It stopped.

She was a crumpled figure, lying against the driver's door and wedged beneath the steering wheel. She was covered with finely crushed glass. There was blood all over. He couldn't tell whether she was still alive.

He gingerly moved off the metal and bent down, running the flashlight under the belly of the car to see what was propping it up. Her salvation had been the gnarled thigh of an old pine tree and the broad shoulder of an ancient boulder poking up from beneath the mountain's dirty face.

But would they be enough to keep the car from sliding down into the gorge if he climbed inside to get her out? He ran a critical eye over the car. Then he cautiously rocked his weight in two different directions, testing the stability of tree and stone. The car moved a little, but only when his weight shifted the center of gravity over to the passenger's side of the car. If he tried to get her out by keeping off the car as much as possible, working through the driver's-side door, he thought it just might hold.

But it would be a gamble. Her life...and his...would be the stakes. Maybe he should wait until help arrived.

A creaking sound caught his attention, and he swept his flashlight across the boulder and the tree again. The boulder seemed loosened but holding its own against the weight of the car. The tree, however, was losing its grip, apparently. He could see the huge roots slowly but inexorably pulling out of the shallow, rocky soil. The car was winning the battle.

He swore softly.

He couldn't even hear sirens or helicopter rotors yet. While he sat here watching, the car would slide down the mountain, and it would take her with it, to certain death.

He struggled with the jammed driver's-side door until he finally managed to force it open. He eased himself inside the tangled wreckage a little, but the car rocked and he stopped, holding himself suspended half over her limp form. The movement stopped. The boulder-and-pine moorings were holding, but not for long.

He braced himself against the dashboard and the seat back and took a closer look at her. He lifted her damp, tangled hair away from her delicate face and throat. Her eyes were closed. She was either out cold or dead.

He adjusted himself so one hand was free to feel for a pulse in her neck. The blood on her made it difficult. His fingers kept slipping. He couldn't find a heartbeat. Damn.

Then he put his palm in front of her lips and waited tensely. Come on, come on, he thought fiercely. If you die here...

There! He felt something. A light, feathery something. Her breath across his warm, damp palm. She was breathing. Yeah, he thought, allowing himself an unexpectedly triumphant sigh of relief. She was alive! There was something about her that stirred his desire to protect, in spite of himself.

His relief was interrupted by the rhythmic beating of an approaching helicopter's rotors. They were coming fast. He looked up and thought he saw lights in the sky. Considering how bad the visibility was, that chopper had to be pretty damn close. He frowned fiercely at the woman's unconscious form.

He ran his hands over her, trying to see if he could find the source of the blood, but it was no good. Even with the flashlight, he couldn't see well enough. He didn't see any pulsing rivulets, though, so he figured no arteries were cut. At least, none that were bleeding on the outside of her.

He grimly looked toward the rescuers who'd begun to hover cautiously over the hillside, searching for signs of her wreck. They had found the truck already. That twisted, blazing wreckage had been easy to locate.

She moved a little. Moaned. Struggled to lift her eyelids.

"Don't move," he told her firmly.

Her eyes opened, and she tried to find the face that went with the voice. It was hard. Everything was blurry at first. And it was dark, except for the thin wand of light he was shining over her body.

He was leaning over her, staring at her. She blinked. Her vision cleared a little. Enough to make out his form and to see that he was looking down at her.

"Help is coming," he told her softly. "Hang on."

"Help...me...." she whispered, trying to reach out to him.

He caught her hand before it could move far and he clasped it. His grip was firm. Strong. His strength flowed into her, as if he was willing her to stay alive.

"I'll help you," he muttered tightly. "Just be quiet and don't move. You'll be okay." He damn well had no idea if she'd be okay, but if he could get her to believe that, maybe it would make a difference, he thought grimly. Unfortunately, he could feel the car slide again. They had to get out of it. Fast.

"Do...I...know...you?" she whispered, confused.

"No. Don't move. Let me try to slide you out of here. Can you tell if anything is broken?"

Something in the way he was staring down at her connected with her in a very personal, very intimate way. Then it was gone. As if a steel door had slammed down and hidden part of him away.

She struggled to get his face in focus, but it was impossible.

"Everything...hurts...." she whispered.

"Does your neck hurt?"

"Yes." She tried to move her head.

"Don't move! You might do more damage!"

"I think my neck's okay," she said in a thin, thready voice. She felt the car slip a few inches, and she saw the fierce, grim expression in his face. "Pull me out before it goes..." She swallowed. "Or get out yourself...you don't have to be a hero...." The pain throbbed everywhere. Scrapes, bruises, deep aches where she was unaccustomed to feeling hurt. Darkness swirled around her. She smiled a little. "Thanks for...trying...."

He stuck his flashlight into his hip pocket, ripped off his canvas jacket and carefully slid it under her head and shoulders. He pulled her out as slowly as he could, tugging steadily on her clothes and his jacket, trying to minimize moving her body whenever he could.

Ultimately he had no choice; he had to lift her out of the car to get her to the ground. The car tilted up just as he was pulling her free, and the side of the vehicle hit them as it suddenly turned up and slid down the mountainside with an agonizing scraping of metal against stone.

"Don't move," he said. His voice was clipped and gravelly.

She didn't. She clung fiercely to his hand. And she held the sound of his voice as close to her heart as she could. *I'll help you...I'll help you....* The world was spinning. She felt half-dead.

"Hang on. Help is almost here. They'll get you to a hospital in no time," he assured her.

She almost smiled. He had a warm, soothing, reassuring voice. She believed him, in spite of the agony she was in. In spite of the cold sinking into her body. In spite of the terror she was facing.

She tightened her grip on his hand.

"Don't let go of me," she whispered. No matter how much she blinked, she couldn't see him. Everything was badly blurred. Her eyes began to feel gritty and slick. "Don't let go," she pleaded weakly.

He shifted his hand, closing his fingers around hers gently but firmly.

"I won't let go." He wondered whether it was a promise he would have to keep for very long. She looked pretty badly injured.

Hearing the helicopter landing on the highway, he fished the flashlight out of his back pocket and waved it in the direction of the emergency-rescue team. As they scrambled down the mountainside, he turned to look at her. A slight grin lightened the grimness of his expression for the first time since coming down the hillside after her. "I won't let go, if you don't."

"That's a deal," she whispered, trying to smile but too weak to succeed this time.

He saw her eyelids close and watched her slide into unconsciousness. Still, he held her hand. Right up until the paramedics pried her fingers loose and loaded her into the medevac helicopter a short time later.

"Hold on," he said, leaning over her as they carried her to the waiting helicopter. He thought she might have heard him.

As they began to close the helicopter door, one of the paramedics gave him a critical look.

"Are you sure you don't want to come, too? Just to make sure you're okay?"

He shook his head.

"I think the police want to talk to me," he explained. He glanced down at himself and saw why the paramedic was worried. "It's all her blood. I didn't get a scratch. Go!"

The helicopter door closed, and the pilot wasted no time lifting off. Within moments the aircraft was a distant sound in the night.

There were several state police cars, county police cars, a fire truck and an ambulance crowded along the roadside overlooking the crash. Lights flashed, looking eerie in the deserted mountain landscape. Mist from the river below was working its way up the hillside, casting a ghostly blur over the hulk of the burned-out truck.

Someone spoke into his walkie-talkie. No one down by the truck had any hope of finding the driver alive. It was too dark to be sure he was still in the truck, of course. If he'd been thrown out of the cab on the way down, his body could be anywhere.

"Well, start searching," the officer in charge said grimly. "And ask that news helicopter to shine its lights down the crash path. If anybody sees anything resembling a person, yell out."

The county police sergeant on the scene came over to the woman's rescuer then.

"How are you feeling?"

"A hell of a lot better than either of the drivers are."

"Any of that blood yours?"

"No."

"I'd like to ask you a few questions while things are still fresh in your mind. Then we'll get you to someplace warm and dry. Take you to the hospital, if you want."

He nodded and wiped the rain from his face. The drizzle was returning. It was light but persistent.

"What's your name?" asked the officer.

"Owen Blackhart."

"Is that your car parked over there on the shoulder, Mr. Blackhart?"

"Yes."

"So, you weren't in the crash yourself, then."

"That's right, Officer."

"Did you see what happened?"

"No. By the time I got here, they'd both gone over the side. I heard the sounds, but by the time I came around the bend, the truck was halfway to the ravine and the car was teetering on a rock and a tree. I got to it just before the tree gave way."

"Lucky for her," the policeman observed, shaking his head. "It's amazing you came along when you did. By the way, which way were you coming down the road?"

"Eastbound. I was a few minutes behind the truck."

"Do you have any idea what could have caused the crash?"

"I didn't see it...."

"Was the truck weaving any time you saw it?"

"No. He passed me back up the mountain, though, and he seemed to be in a hurry. Took a couple of turns pretty fast. But like I said, I didn't see what happened."

The officer nodded. His men were already putting flares along the roadside to help to assess the tracks, and to look for evidence to explain the deadly mistake that had been made that night.

"Do you know the woman?"

"No."

"Did she say her name or anything?"

Owen resisted the temptation to laugh.

"We didn't have time to exchange pleasantries."

The officer grunted and nodded.

"We haven't found any identification for her yet," he explained. "But once we get the tags on the car, look around for debris, maybe find her purse or something, we'll have a name for her, too."

"She's a Jane Doe for now, then?" Owen asked softly.

"Yep."

Blackhart frowned and turned to stare down into the ravine. It would be hard to find anything tonight in the dark, especially with the drizzle and the mist. Anything that had fallen into the river probably would be washed downstream by daylight.

"Maybe someone will call her in as a missing person."

The policeman nodded.

"Maybe so. Well, if you want to get into your car and get warmed up, why don't you do that now, sir. If you want to follow us down the mountain to the hospital, we can see to it you're cleaned up and put up for the night or get you to a telephone."

"That's nice of you," Owen said, a little surprised.

The policeman grinned.

"Up here in the mountains, we believe in treating people in a neighborly way. This isn't the big city."

"I can see that," Owen said dryly. "I think I'll get in the car and try to towel off."

"You've got things with you?"

"Yeah. I was on the road this week, so I've got luggage with me, and a change of clothes."

"When you're ready to go, I'll send my corporal along with you. He'll get a few additional details—your address, phone number—and buy you a cup of coffee."

"Thanks, uh...?" Owen gave the officer a questioning look.

"Sergeant Buddy Lefcourt."

"Thanks, Sergeant Lefcourt."

Owen turned toward his car. He wondered what was happening to the woman he'd pulled out of the wreck. Was she still alive?

He tried to shake off the memory of holding her in his arms during that interminable wait while the emergency squad scrambled down the mountainside, but he couldn't quite escape it. The feel of her body was still with him. And the soft, anxious look in her unfocused eyes as she searched to make out his face in the darkness.

Damn it, he thought. Forget about her. She wasn't his problem. He didn't even know the woman.

He stripped off his blood-smeared shirt and slacks beside his car, uncaring if anyone cared to watch. There were a couple of uniformed women on the scene now, but they were busy elsewhere. Owen opened the trunk of his car and dropped his wet, dirty clothes inside. Shoes and socks, too. He pulled out some fresh clothes from his suitcase and carried them into the front seat to avoid the rain. He dried himself off with a clean T-shirt and put on jeans and a white turtleneck shirt. By the time he'd pulled on socks and laced his athletic shoes, the corporal arrived at his car window, wearing a bleak smile.

Owen rolled down the window.

"Any word from the hospital on how the woman's doing?"

"She made it to the hospital alive. Last we heard, she was being wheeled into emergency for X rays, maybe surgery. Sergeant Lefcourt said we should help you find a place to stay."

"I guess I'm not going to get much farther tonight," Owen said with a sigh. "Any help with the local motel people would be much appreciated, Corporal."

"The name's Morrison Hayes, sir." He grinned. "Follow me down the mountain. I'm going to stop at the hospital first, but I'll talk to Madge about holding a room for you at the Mountain Mist Motel tonight."

"Much obliged."

"Don't worry, none. Madge hasn't been full up this time of year since the governor stopped in unexpectedly forty years ago."

Owen grinned.

The corporal tipped his finger to his hat and strode over to his marked police car, got in and pulled onto the highway.

As Owen followed him through the misty night, his thoughts drifted back to the woman. Was there someone out there waiting for her, wondering why she hadn't arrived?

That was hell, waiting and not knowing where your friend was, not knowing what had happened to her, if she was all right...or in pain...or hurting and in need of your help...or worse.

Owen's jaw tightened, and his eyes narrowed in remembrance.

Time barely dulled the memory of that kind of pain, especially if you never learned what happened to the one you cared for.

He saw the lights of a small city glistening in a valley up ahead. A few more twists around the mountainside, and they'd be driving straight in.

"Give them your name, mystery woman," he muttered under his breath. "Tell them who you are...." Before it's too late, he thought grimly.

The county police car pulled into the emergency entrance of the hospital, parking in the area marked off for police and emergency squad use. Owen pulled into the regular lot and parked his car. The policeman stood by the entrance and waited for Owen to join him.

When Owen reached him, the corporal gave him a reassuring smile.

"I called Madge on the radio on the drive down here. She says you're welcome any time you can get to her place. She's saving a room for you. And some hot soup and coffee, if you want it."

"Thanks."

He followed the corporal into the emergency room and stood nearby as the policeman talked to the nurse handling triage.

"So they've taken her up to surgery already?" Corporal Hayes asked.

"Yeah, Morrison. They know they've got a couple of problems, but they aren't sure what they'll discover when they've opened her up."

"But it's just broken bones or a concussion or internal bleeding?"

"It's too early to say. They have called Dr. Halifax...."

"The neurologist? The guy who just joined the hospital last month?"

"In a town this size, Morrison Hayes, you know very well there couldn't be two neurologists, let alone with the same name," the nurse teased.

"Or who both hold the record for fastest receipt of the 'worst-personality award' from the hospital staff?" he added, chuckling.

Great, Owen thought irritably. The girl had no one to go to bat for her, and she's in a hospital with a neurologist even the staff disliked. He could only hope that the doctor's professional skills were superior to his social skills.

Corporal Hayes flipped open his notebook and pulled out his pencil. He began jotting down some facts, getting the exact time of admission from the nurse, along with the diagnosis on admittance and the names of the people attending her when she was discharged from the helicopter.

"So they think there's brain damage?" Hayes asked.

"They're not sure yet. They'd expect it, though, from the kind of trauma she experienced."

"Guess you don't need a medical degree to know that," Hayes conceded.

The nurse nodded.

"Any other specialists being brought in that you know of?"

"The ophthalmologist."

"That's eyes, right?"

"Yes. It looks like she's got damage to the corneas from the glass that shattered, but they want a consultation from Dr. Evergreen, just to be sure they don't miss something crucial."

"Hmm. She's been practicing longer than I've been alive," Hayes said wryly.

"And she sure knows her stuff. The patient is very fortunate to have her."

When the corporal had finished, he turned toward Owen and smiled.

"Come on. I've got what I need. Let's get you over to Madge's and put some hot soup and coffee in you. You look pretty beat, yourself, if you don't mind my saying so."

"It's been a long day." Owen hesitated. "When will the woman be out of surgery?"

Hayes looked over at the nurse and raised his eyebrows. She'd been listening to them and had heard the question. She gave Owen a comforting smile, one intended to empathize without offering unrealistic hope.

"That depends on how badly she's hurt," she replied gently. "I'm sorry I can't give you something more definite than that. Is she a friend of yours?"

Owen shook his head. "No. I never met her before tonight."

"She was very lucky that you were there," the nurse said warmly. "The paramedics told us how they found the two of you. It's a miracle she's alive."

Corporal Hayes grinned.

"Come on, Mr. Blackhart. Let me give you a hero's escort to Madge's."

"I'm not a hero, Corporal. I was just there. That's all."

Hayes lifted his brows and shook his head. Seeing the closed expression settling over Owen Blackhart's face convinced him not to pursue the comment.

Owen followed the police car to the Mountain Mist Motel, lost in his own thoughts. The accident had thrown his plans off. However, if he left early tomorrow morning, he could still get to the lawyer's office in time for the appointment. He'd tell Corporal Hayes where he could be reached in case the police needed anything further from him later. Although he couldn't imagine what they'd need from him. The accident pretty much spoke for itself, from what he'd seen of it. So he'd give the cops his lawyer's address and phone number and forget about the matter.

But two hours later, he was lying in his bed at the motel, staring at the ceiling in the dark, remembering the woman he'd pulled from the wreck seconds before it had rolled into what would have been her grave. He kept feeling the press of her hand against his as he told her to hold on, the curve of her hurting body, damp in the rain.

Was she alive? Was she critically injured? Was anyone missing her? Worrying about her? Looking for her? There for her?

He threw off the covers and swore. He wasn't going to be able to walk away from this. Not yet.

Chapter 2

The lawyer closed his briefcase and stood up. Smiling, he held out his hand to Owen. Owen shook it.

"I think that should take care of everything, Mr. Blackhart," he said. "If you have any questions, or if any problem should arise, please contact my office." He pulled a business card from the inside of his suit jacket and extended it to Owen.

Owen pocketed it and nodded. "Thanks."

Averson Hemphill, Esq., smiled broadly and followed Owen out of the office onto Main Street. A car pulled up, and Hemphill got in. He leaned across and kissed the driver, a casually attired redhead. Since there were two children dressed in soccer clothes bouncing up and down in the back seat, Owen assumed the driver was Hemphill's wife. Owen stifled a jaundiced laugh. The last lawyer he'd seen had gotten into a car, too. But it was the back seat. And the woman waiting for him had been poured into her dress. She hadn't looked like anyone's mother.

Owen sighed.

He wasn't living in New York anymore, obviously. It kept coming as a shock to see normal people living average lives, lives not consumed with crushing the competition or getting ahead socially.

He watched the Hemphill family drive away, the kids bickering in the back seat now. Their father, looking exasperated but resigned to a bout of sibling rivalry, struggled out of his suit jacket and loosened his tie. Then the station wagon turned a corner and disappeared from view.

Owen strolled down Main Street, reacquainting himself with the modest town he'd be calling home for now. A bookstore owner stepped out onto the sidewalk in front of his shop and settled a sign beside the door. When Owen reached him, the bookstore owner smiled.

"Say, I don't believe we've met," the man said.

"No, we haven't."

"Well, welcome," the shop owner exclaimed, offering his hand. When Owen reciprocated, they shook hands. "I'm Seymour Rushville. I own the one and only decent, full-service bookstore within a sixty-mile radius." He laughed heartily. "And modesty has never been a problem for me."

"I can see that," Owen said, amused. "I'm Owen Blackhart."

"Blackhart? Say, aren't you the guy who inherited Portia Willowbrook's place out on Algonquin Road?"

"As a matter of fact, I am." Owen looked at the man a little more narrowly. "How did you know that?"

"Oh, well, we've been gossiping about you for months," he explained, sporting a totally guilt-free grin.

"Really?" Owen lifted an eyebrow, encouraging the man to expand his comment. "How fascinating."

"Oh, yeah. People around here haven't had much new to gossip about, so when poor Portia passed away, naturally there was lots of speculation about what would happen to her property."

"Naturally. What kind of speculation, exactly?"

"Oh, there were some who thought the land would be sold to a developer and we'd have one of those huge discount-outlet malls plopped down in our midst. Others thought she'd donate it to a university or a museum or some such. She was always having soirees in New York with the high and mighty, so we figured they'd weaseled into her affections, and her pocketbook.'' Seymour laughed heartily. "Were you a relative or something, Owen?''

"No.''

"Where'd you know Portia from, anyway? She traveled a lot, and frankly, Averson hasn't been talking to anyone about the transfer of that property. Said the information he was privy to wasn't any of our business.'' Seymour laughed again. He obviously didn't hold a grudge against the lawyer for being close-mouthed with the town gossip mill.

"I knew Portia from New York.''

Seymour's face froze, and for a moment he looked a little uncertain of himself.

"Don't tell me you were one of her soiree attendees?'' the bookman exclaimed, rolling his eyes in concern.

"Not exactly. I attended a few over the years, though.''

"Oops!'' Seymour grimaced. "Well, I stuck my foot in it this time, didn't I? Look, let me get you a cup of coffee down at Rafael's Café. He makes the best coffee I've ever had, carries a great selection and he's got fresh-baked pastries and breads. Why, everyone in town says it's the best on the continent.''

Owen resisted the urge to grin. You couldn't be irritated with a man like Seymour, he decided. The bookman shot off his mouth with abandon, but there was no real malice in anything he said.

"Some other time, maybe, Seymour. I've got a couple of things to take care of right now.''

Seymour smiled sheepishly. "No hard feelings, I hope?'' he said.

"None. Forget it.''

"Then you just let me know when you're ready for that trip to Rafael's, okay? It's on me.''

"Fine. I'll stop in at the bookstore someday.'' He glanced through the window and read the titles of some of the magazines on the rack near the door. "I'll probably drop by to pick up something to read occasionally.''

Seymour beamed. "Say, I like you already, Owen!" Then, on a more confiding note, he added, "You know, people were relieved that the place went to someone who was going to live in it. That much we did twist out of Hemphill. That's true, isn't it?"

"Yes." It sounded like the townspeople should consider becoming private investigators, Owen thought in amusement. He wondered what torture they had visited on poor Hemphill and his family to pry loose the two pieces of information they had.

Just then a newspaper truck screeched to a halt in front of the bookstore, effectively interrupting their conversation. The driver, a long-haired, lanky young man, swung down from the cab, went around to the back of the truck and slid open the rear door. Within moments he was carrying stacks of newspapers into the shop and piling them next to the cash register.

"That's the evening paper," Seymour explained apologetically. "I've got to sign for them."

"Say, could I buy one from you?" Owen said abruptly. When he glimpsed the front page, a headline in the lower right quadrant caught his eye.

Seymour handed him a newspaper with a grin.

"It's on me, Owen, compliments of The Well-Read Bookshop."

Owen took the paper. "Thanks."

Seymour turned to talk to the deliveryman about the invoice, and Owen walked away. After he'd gone a couple of blocks, he turned down the side street where he'd parked his car earlier in the afternoon, before going to the lawyer's office. When he reached the car, however, he paused to read the article that had drawn his attention.

The headline read Who Is This Woman? The opening sentence stated, "Mystery woman in critical condition at Cleary Hospital."

She hadn't regained consciousness long enough to tell them who she was, he thought. And according to the article, her identification had not been found yet. Whatever she had with her name on it must have been washed away, lost or destroyed after the accident. He wondered why her car hadn't provided a solid lead.

Owen grimly stared at the description of the woman that the hospital and police had provided in an attempt to learn who she was. Young woman in her midtwenties to early thirties, about five feet four inches and 115 pounds, dark red hair, green eyes. Anyone knowing who she might be was urged to contact the county police and speak to Sergeant Lefcourt.

Owen closed the paper and folded it.

This wasn't any of his concern. Unfortunately, he couldn't get the thought out of his mind that somewhere, someone might be wondering what had happened to her. Someone might want to help her, but didn't know where she was. No one was calling to notify them that she was badly hurt.

Grimly, Owen Blackhart climbed into the front seat of his car and turned on the engine. His telephone service was being connected sometime before 5:00 p.m. Maybe he could call the hospital and ask how she was doing. Then he would try to reach Lefcourt and see whether the newspaper had generated any new information for the police.

Yeah. That's what he'd do.

That's *all* he would do.

At five minutes past five o'clock that evening, he lifted the receiver and got a dial tone. The first call he made was to the police station.

The operator put him through, and the police sergeant's voice boomed over the telephone.

"Lefcourt!"

"This is Owen Blackhart."

"Blackhart? Oh, yeah...the guy who pulled the Jane Doe out of the car last night. Sorry if I sounded like a cannon. Uh, we've been a little busy here this afternoon."

"Another accident?"

"Naw, nothing like that. There's a leak in our ceiling, and we're trying to get it fixed before it rains tonight. That rain last night opened it up, and our files are getting soaked," Lefcourt explained in exasperation. "The electrical system is acting up again, too, so we've been waiting on the county electrician who handles our electrical repairs to get down here and see whether we've got a fire hazard or anything.''

"This isn't your day, is it?''

"No, sir. It sure as sugar isn't,'' the sergeant agreed. He sighed in resignation. ''But, hey, never mind about our headaches. What can I do for you, Mr. Blackhart?''

"Has anyone come forward to help identify the woman?''

"No, but it's a little early to expect that. They may not know she's missing yet. She could have been on a trip or something. Maybe no one is expecting to hear from her yet.''

"What about her car? Couldn't you identify her from the registration papers or the license tags?''

"Well, her car was so badly mangled that we haven't been able to get into the glove compartment to search for registration papers. The car rolled down onto the truck, and it was an inferno, so if there were papers, they probably are burned so bad we may not get anything off them. And the metal tags, well, they melted down in the fire. Can you believe that? It must have been one hellishly hot fire. Anyway, we can only make out a couple of numbers. To be honest with you, we're not certain we can be sure of those.''

"What about tracing her through the engine identification number?'' Owen asked sharply.

"That's trickier, but we'll give it a try if no one comes forward by the time we figure out what that ID number is. And I'm not sure when that'll be,'' he said regretfully. ''You see, the engine was so badly burned in the fire, and so badly damaged in the fall off the mountainside, that some of those numbers may be pretty much impossible to read, too. This case is a pip, isn't it?''

Owen exhaled slowly. This couldn't be happening. He'd never believed in fate, but this situation was eerily reminiscent of another tragedy that had touched him years ago, leaving a wound that had never completely healed. He'd buried the wound so deep inside him that he'd almost managed to forget how badly it had hurt when it was inflicted. But now the memories were coming back. Flashbacks. A girl's smile. The flash of perfect white teeth. Welcoming, warm lips. Laughter like carefree birds playing in a soft spring rainfall.

"Uh, Mr. Blackhart? Are you still there?"

"Yeah. I'm here."

"Are you okay?"

"Yeah. I'm fine. Have you talked to anyone at the hospital today about her?"

"Yeah."

"I read in the paper that she was in critical condition."

"Yeah. It's a pity, isn't it? They're doing what they can for her, but..."

"Do they expect her to live?"

"It's hard for me to say, Mr. Blackhart," the police sergeant said diplomatically. "A lot of times they call patients critical when they're pretty sure they're going to do okay. 'Course, other times I've seen 'critical' become 'poor' and 'poor' become 'deceased' in mighty short order."

"Will they talk to me if I call them?"

"Let me call someone I know over there in the administration offices. Under the circumstances, maybe they can tell you something. Nothing really personal, of course."

"Of course."

"You just want to know how bad she is, right?"

"I want to know what her chances of recovery are."

"Sure. I understand. It's real decent of you to take an interest. Lots of folks just go on with their lives when something like this happens, you know? It's right nice of you to care what happens to her. I'm sure Jane Doe'd appreciate it, if she knew."

Owen's jaw tightened. *Jane Doe.* He hated the name. It sounded like it belonged on a corpse at the morgue instead of an unconscious, living and breathing woman in a hospital bed. It wasn't the policeman's fault that they didn't have the woman's real name to use in discussing her, however. So Owen swallowed his irritation.

"It's no effort, Sergeant. By the way, my telephone is connected.'' Owen gave him the phone number again and said good-bye.

About fifteen minutes after they'd hung up, the sergeant called back.

''It's all set. They put a note in the patient's record about who you are and that a little information could be shared with you, since you saved the woman's life and are interested in her welfare. The nurses are worried about her not having anyone coming to her bedside. It sounds to me like they'd be happy for you to come and visit her, even if she's unconscious.''

Owen frowned. That didn't sound like any hospital he was familiar with. They usually restricted visits to family and close friends when someone was in critical condition.

''Why are the nurses worried?''

''Something about the patient's agitation. She's delirious or comatose or something. She's not making any sense, doesn't really see anyone or know what's going on around her too clearly. But she keeps holding out her hand, like she wants someone to take it. And she's saying something every once in a while. Mumbles something they can't quite make out. The head nurse on the floor swears she's calling for someone, wants the person to hold her hand. When they try to hold her hand, she pulls away and gets worse. I dunno. Sounds like she's just delirious to me. Having nightmares or something. Who wouldn't, after what she's been through, huh?''

''Yeah. Who wouldn't.'' Owen frowned fiercely. He remembered holding the woman's hand after he rescued her from the car, telling her he'd stay with her, wouldn't let go.

But he had let go.

Could that be what she was agitated about? In her wounded state, was she trying desperately to cling to the last source of human comfort and help that she'd known?

''Thanks, Sergeant. I'll call the hospital.''

''Good luck, Mr. Blackhart. Keep in touch.''

Owen hung up the phone and stared at the empty house around him. He had a sleeping bag for a bed, and a few pieces of furniture scattered around the place. The heat was on, and so was the water. The curtains were still up. They were some of the few furnishings that had remained in Portia's house after she left it to him in her will. The rest of her antiques and art had been put on the auction block. That was fine with Owen, since his taste hadn't run toward Portia's bohemian decor. Besides, he had his own furniture.

Unfortunately, it wasn't going to be delivered for another week.

He picked up the telephone and dialed the Mountain Mist Motel.

"Madge, this is Owen Blackhart.... I'm fine, thanks, and you?... Good... No, I got here in plenty of time. That personal business is all taken care of.... It's nice of you to invite me back. As a matter of fact, I'm calling to make a reservation. Do you have any rooms left tonight?... Great. Could you save it for me? I'm coming back to see how the mystery woman's doing. I should be there in a few hours... No, I'm not sure how long I'll be staying. I may need the room for more than the one night, though. Will that be a problem?... No? Good... Uh, no, Madge, I'll eat on the way. No need to heat up the soup... No, the soup was just fine last night. I really appreciated it, since I missed dinner in all that confusion on the highway. I'm eating before I leave here— I won't be hungry this time. I'd appreciate a thermos of your coffee, though, if that wouldn't be too much trouble... Great. Thanks, Madge. I'll see you later tonight. Bye."

Hospitals were all different, and yet, in some ways, they were all the same, Owen thought. Late at night, they were ablaze with lights. Staff members hurried down wide corridors, administering medications and observing patients. The scent of medicine and antiseptics clung to the air. The sound of rubber-soled shoes squeaking softly on the bare floors echoed eerily throughout the long hallways.

Cleary Hospital had carpeting in a few places, but mostly it was bare floored. Here in the mountains of eastern West Virginia, money for such things was dear. The hospital's board of directors preferred to put its cash into staff salaries and modern equipment. So Owen's tread was not muffled when he stepped out of the elevator and out into the hospital wing where he'd been told the mystery woman's room was.

The nurse at the nursing station nearest Jane Doe's room glanced up as Owen approached her. Her starched white cap was settled securely on her trim dark hair. Her eyes did not waver as she watched him over her reading glasses.

"I'm Owen Blackhart. I was told it would be all right to stop in and see the woman who was hurt in the accident. I believe Sergeant Lefcourt spoke to someone here about it?"

"Oh, yes. Jane Doe..." The nurse produced a cool smile.

Owen's jaw tightened. Jane Doe. Jane Doe. Why the hell did they keep calling her that?

"Dr. Darbyson mentioned that you might be coming." She gave him an interested look. "He said you weren't a relative or a friend—"

"That's right."

"You were the man who saved her...."

"Yes." There didn't seem any way to sidestep that question, so he dealt with it as quickly as possible. "Can I see her?"

"Just let me finish what I'm doing. It won't take long. I'll be with you in a moment." She turned back to filling out the patient record she had in front of her, writing quickly.

Owen looked around, wondering where the woman was. There were a dozen rooms opening onto the corridor. One of them was hers. He glanced at the nurse impatiently. He'd come a long way. To be this near and cooling his heels did not come naturally to him. Of course, visiting a hospital didn't come naturally, either. He removed his jacket, slung it over his shoulder and waited.

The nurse soon clicked her ballpoint pen closed and slipped it into the breast pocket of her tailored, snow white blouse. Then she stood up and walked around the counter, joining Owen in the deserted corridor. She pulled on a beige-and-red sweater, smiling crisply at him. Weathered skin wrinkled near her eyes.

"Do you ski, Mr. Blackhart?" she asked curiously.

"I beg your pardon?"

"Do you ski? We have a lot of winter sports in this area. I just thought you looked like a man who enjoyed athletics." She looked him up and down with a critically approving eye.

"Is that a professional opinion?" he asked dryly.

"Professional and personal," she unhesitatingly admitted. She smiled. "Don't worry, Mr. Blackhart. I'm a fifty-year-old married woman."

He gave a short laugh.

She gave him a sly look. "It's a little far to come back here, isn't it?"

"Could be worse."

"She must have made quite an impression on you."

"She'd have made an impression on anyone. Seeing someone that near death leaves a mark on you."

The nurse nodded. "Yes. That's very true," she said. Her smile softened in empathy.

Opening the door, she led him inside.

The hospital room was large and square. A single bed, centered along one wall, contained the only occupant. In the bed lay the woman, heavily bandaged and hooked up to the various pieces of equipment that surrounded the bed. The whir and click of monitors were the only sounds audible. The woman lay still, unmoving.

"Can she hear us?" Owen asked quietly.

"Sometimes, I think she can. We're not sure if she understands or not. Her responses to direct questions are...ambiguous, at best."

"Has she said anything?"

"Nothing that has made any sense. She has mumbled a few times, but we can't make out what she's saying. We aren't even sure she is trying to actually communicate. It could just be random impulses somewhere inside her mind, things that have nothing to do with her surroundings."

The nurse walked over and touched the unconscious woman's hand, lying limply on top of the sheet that was covering her.

"Can you hear me? If you can, move your hand. Your finger..."

The nurse lifted the limp hand. Waited. Then gently put the woman's hand down again. She looked at Owen and shook her head, then she walked around and checked the readings on the monitors.

Owen shoved his hands into his trouser pockets. He felt helpless, a sensation he disliked intensely at any time, but especially now. Why the hell had he come? What did he think he could do here, anyway?

"You have no idea what her name is?" he asked, frowning. "She didn't say anything? Not anything at all? Even part of a name? Hers or someone else's?"

The nurse blinked.

"No," she replied, sounding distracted. "Would you mind speaking again, Mr. Blackhart? Anything. Say anything."

"What do you want me to say? And why do you want me to say it?" he asked, wondering why she was staring at the blood-pressure and cardiac monitors.

"When you spoke, her readings changed," the nurse explained. She glanced at the patient, then over her shoulder at Owen. "Talk some more, Mr. Blackhart. Talk to her." She indicated the unconscious woman. "It may be coincidence, but let's just experiment a little...."

Owen took his hands out of his pockets and walked closer to the woman's bedside. Her head and eyes were swathed in white. Her body looked frail and bruised beneath the pale print of the hospital gown and the stark white of the bedsheets. Her hand was scraped and covered with recent cuts.

She looked all alone in the world. Weak and defenseless. On the edge of eternity. Needing only the slightest excuse to release her tenuous hold on the slender thread of life.

He stopped near her bedside, wondering what he could say that might penetrate the depths of her comatose state. What could pierce that heavy veil? What could connect with some fragile remnant of her wounded mind?

"Do you remember me?" he asked in a low, quiet voice. "We met last night. In the rain and the darkness. I pulled you out of your car...."

The nurse whirled and looked at him. Excitement was gleaming in her eyes. She motioned for him to continue talking.

"I came back to see how you were doing," he explained. "It looks like they've done a good job of patching you up." His voice softened, and he smiled slightly. "You've got to help, though. Give them some sign you're trying to stay with us. People want to hear from you. Everyone's pulling for you to get better. Did you know that?"

The nurse motioned for him to keep speaking, and she hurried out of the room, turning in the direction of the nurses' station.

Owen pulled up a chair and sat beside the bed. The injured woman looked sickeningly still to him. The monitors might be showing some interesting activity, but her body looked like it hadn't moved a muscle. Not so much as an eyelash, if he could have seen her eyelashes beneath all those bandages.

"They've put an ad in the paper," he said. "They're hoping someone will recognize your description and tell us your name. Did they tell you that? It seems your identification's not been found yet, so they don't know who you are." He half laughed. "Hell, I don't know what to call you. I'd just as soon not call you anything until we know your real name. So, I won't call you by any name. Not yet, anyway."

The nurse returned with a woman and a man. They were wearing white lab coats and had stethoscopes draped around their necks. Their names were on plastic tags and identified them as physicians.

At their urging, he continued a quiet monologue with the unconscious woman while they studied the readings on the monitors, touched her and observed the patient's reaction to Owen.

When Owen stopped and looked at them with a clear question in his eyes, the physicians glanced at one another. The young man deferred to the woman, who seemed a little older, but still young to be in charge, from Owen's point of view. Physicians were getting younger every year, apparently. Or he was getting older.

"I'm Dr. Kelway," the woman said. "I'm with the neurology department here at Cleary Hospital...."

Owen thought she seemed young but experienced. She didn't look like she was thirty yet, but her calm and professional manner impressed him.

"When you talk to the patient, she appears to respond. We see changes in her pulse, her respiration and her blood pressure."

"Is that good?"

"It's wonderful. It means she's connecting with us, instead of sinking into depression or deeper into the coma. As I understand it, you didn't know her before the accident."

"That's right."

"That's unusual." The blond doctor stared at him for a moment, then looked thoughtfully at her unconscious patient.

"What's unusual, Doctor?" Owen asked, annoyed by her cool observation. Did they think he was lying about knowing the woman? He pressed his lips into a hard, flat line and stared at the three medical people.

"It's just that I would have expected that if *you* could reach her, *we* should be able to reach her, get the same kind of reactions that you are. But we don't. She hasn't been responding to any of us, as far as we can tell. You are the only one to get a response from her. Now, if you were a close friend or family member, that would make a certain amount of sense. Emotionally we all connect at a deeper level, a different level, with those we know well or love. But you say you're a stranger—"

"I *am* a stranger," he interrupted pointedly.

"Yes. I'm not arguing with you, Mr. Blackhart," she said, trying to soften her words with a somewhat apologetic tone and a conciliatory smile. "It's just an unusual occurrence. But it's one I'm very happy that we have. We can work with it."

"'Work with it? We?" Owen asked sharply.

The physician motioned toward the door.

"Perhaps we could discuss this down at the nurses' station," she suggested. She glanced toward the patient, still unmoving in the hospital bed. "At this point, we need to assume that Jane Doe can hear some, if not all, of what we say...or at least, what you say. It might be wise to have a frank discussion where our comments can be considered before we say them in front of her."

Owen shrugged and got up. They walked out of Jane Doe's room and reassembled at the nurses' station. Several other staff members were there now, busy with other cases. They were too absorbed in their own duties to pay any attention to the four people huddling to discuss the comatose woman with no name.

"To cut to the chase, Mr. Blackhart," said Dr. Kelway, "could you keep talking to Jane Doe?"

"For how long?"

"For as long as it takes. Or as long as you can. Until she comes back to us and can communicate with us herself, or..."

"Or?" Owen lifted his eyebrows questioningly.

"Or until she dies." Dr. Kelway's expression softened.

The comment hit him like a body blow. And the request for him to stick around indefinitely hadn't been much easier. Owen frowned.

"She may die, then." He spoke without noticeable emotion.

"Yes."

"Let me think about it," he said grimly.

"Of course. If there's anything I can say to your employer that might help buy you some time..." Dr. Kelway offered cautiously.

Owen laughed harshly.

"That won't be necessary, Doctor. Believe me."

Chapter 3

She was adrift in the depths of a sinister sea.

There was no direction. No up. No down. And yet, she intuitively grasped that she was sinking ever deeper into its mysterious Hadean embrace.

She was dangerously tempted to slide into those deathly arms. To relax. To put an end to the struggling. To let go. She was hanging on to the last of her strength by a very slender thread.

But a primitive urge stubbornly kept welling up within her, forcing her to resist that hypnotic, nearly irresistible attraction. Somewhere in the innermost depths of her mind burned the memory of a happy young woman. A woman with dreams and hopes for the future. A woman with a wrong to avenge. And sometimes a man's chilling smile lanced through her jumbled thoughts, tearing her emotions apart and spurring her to battle harder to survive.

But then, just before she could find the key to it all, remember everything, pull away from the whirlpool that bound her, the suffocating waves of that darkling sea rolled over her once again. Thundering, it pulled her down into its bottomless depths.

She screamed for help, but no one heard. The ocean smothered her words. They rose like faint bubbles through that deep sea of coma, and when they reached the surface, they sounded garbled, even to her own, deafened ears.

If only she had someone to cling to. Someone to touch, to give her hope. Someone warm to melt the bone-deep chill that was freezing her.

She reached out with her left hand, stretching her fingertips until they were as far as they could go. She strove to break through the surface of the abyss. Surely she could find him again, if only she could reach out far enough. He was there somewhere. He had held her, saving her from death's jaws once before. But she had fallen back into its horrible maw after he had let go of her.

Many times she had tried to find him, only to have cold touch her palm. Or something sharp and hard. Things she recoiled from instinctively.

She vividly remembered the touch of his hand, and the low, reassuring timbre of his voice as that burning dragon had roared and tried to swallow her broken body whole. He had saved her then. And if she could reach him again, surely he would pull her from this cold, wet shroud.

But it was so hard to concentrate, to focus on finding him. And a relentless, aching pain kept pounding inside her head. She was weak and confused. Was she reaching in the wrong direction? She choked on a half sob born of frustration and despair.

"Help..." She struggled to say the word aloud. Forced her lips to move, wondered at the strangeness of the sounds.

Then the miracle happened.

She felt his hand grasp hers. Warm and strong. Hope flowed into her, just as it had before.

"Hang on," she heard him whisper.

He sounded a million miles away. She strained to hear the rest.

"I won't let go," he added, his voice gruff and gravelly sounding, but louder now.

She felt the softening around her face, in spite of the horrendous pressure of the sea as it pounded on her head from every direction. Relief. She'd found him! She'd found him at last. A sigh feathered across her lips. The slightest hint of a smile touched their soft, still lines.

"Don't...let...go...." she struggled to say. It was so hard to form the words. So very, very hard. She couldn't be sure what they sounded like, either. She feared they weren't coming out right. But the man gently tightened his hold on her hand, and she relaxed. He'd understood her. She knew he'd understood her then.

Tears burned in her eyes and seared the bandaged skin of her face. Her fingers tightened in mute thanks.

Please don't let go, she thought fiercely, struggling against a growing terror of the oblivion enveloping her. Hold on to me...please, don't let me go....

Coherent thought began to splinter, and the world disintegrated around her. The last sensation she had was of hearing a man's low, reassuring voice and feeling the firm, solid touch of his hand holding hers.

With him nearby, it seemed less dangerous to drift into the small death of sleep.

Owen felt her fingers relax. His gaze snapped up to the monitors. He held his breath, fearing the worst.

"It's all right," said the nurse. "She's just fallen asleep."

"I thought that's all she's been doing," Owen observed dubiously.

"Well, with the coma, it's trickier to identify semisleeping states and normal sleeping states," she conceded easily. "It's just my opinion, of course, but the readings seem like normal sleep to me."

Owen felt relieved. He respected the nurse's judgment.

"I'll take your word for it," he said.

The nurse left. When she returned, she was finishing up before going off her shift. After she'd noted the readings on the patient's chart, she replenished the intravenous bag hung beside Jane Doe's bed. Then she came around to the side of the bed where Owen half dozed in the chair. His hand still covered the unconscious woman's.

"Mr. Blackhart?" the nurse called quietly.

His eyes opened, pinning her with an uncannily alert gaze that startled her.

"I thought you were asleep," she said, taking a step back in surprise.

"I was. I'm a light sleeper."

"Oh. I see. Well, I was just getting ready to leave. There will be someone new coming in to check on the patient for the next shift. And the doctors are due for morning rounds soon."

Owen checked his wristwatch. The sun would be up soon. He looked over at the woman whose hand lay so still and cool in his. She was still breathing regularly. And he thought the color of her cheeks looked a little better than it had last night. Or maybe he was just getting used to the stark white bandages contrasting against her pale, clear skin.

"You've been holding her hand for hours, Mr. Blackhart. Wouldn't you like to get some rest? Or at least stretch your legs a bit, get something hot to drink?"

"I'll take a break in a while. Don't worry about me." He smiled slightly. "I'm a hell of a lot more comfortable than she is, I expect. If she can take it, I suppose I can."

The nurse didn't look too persuaded.

"I'm sure that Dr. Kelway didn't intend to glue you to the patient's bedside when she asked you if you could stay with her, talk to her for a time. She would have been pleased if you'd spent an hour here, talking to the patient or touching her hand. Why, you should have seen the doctor's face light up when she came by the nurses' station on her way home a little while ago. She walked down the hall far enough to see you sitting in this chair, holding the patient's hand, and she looked as surprised as I've ever seen her. She was delighted that you stayed at all, believe me, Mr. Blackhart. You know, she'd be the first to tell you to pace yourself, to take a break from this as often as you need to."

"Does Dr. Kelway get this involved in all her patients' cases?" he asked curiously.

"Yes. She's very dedicated. But we all get...especially involved with a case like this."

"What do you mean?"

"Well, most patients have families or friends who come to their assistance when they're hospitalized or unable to speak for themselves. Others...aren't so lucky."

"Like..." Owen looked at the nameless woman's delicate hand lying in his.

"Yes. Like Jane Doe. She needs us, not just as nurses and doctors but as people who'll try to look out for her best interests until she can look out for herself again. It's...an act of charity," the nurse explained, laughing a little uncomfortably. "My, I didn't mean to sound like I'm sermonizing."

"You weren't."

She looked at him curiously.

"Why are you doing this for her, Mr. Blackhart? If...I may ask?"

"Consider it an...act of charity," he answered.

"Remember to take a break, Mr. Blackhart. If she wakes up, you shouldn't look like Rip Van Winkle."

"Why not?" he asked, grinning slightly. "She doesn't know what I look like."

"People form an image of what someone looks like from the sound of their voice," the nurse countered sagely. "And you have a very...attractive voice, Mr. Blackhart." The nurse smiled broadly. "Take time to shave if you stay the day, hmm?"

Owen snorted his disdain.

"I didn't say I'd be here long enough to get a five-o'clock shadow," he stated.

The woman's hand moved, and he turned his full attention to her.

"I think I'll be seeing you tonight, Mr. Blackhart," she announced with a shrug.

"Really?" he said, his voice sharpening with annoyance. He

hated it when a perfect stranger could anticipate him so accurately. He was tempted to leave, just to prove her wrong. But the hand moving in his quelled that thought. "Maybe so," he conceded softly. He moved his fingers, wrapping them gently around Jane Doe's in silent reply to her questing. "Maybe so..." he whispered to himself.

He dozed off again without much effort. He was accustomed to sleeping in planes and trains and waiting rooms all over the world. The hospital chair wasn't the most comfortable place he'd ever spent the night in, but it wasn't the worst by a long shot.

His grip loosened as he slept, but he never lost contact with Jane Doe's hand. Footsteps eventually roused him from his slumber, and he opened his eyes as three doctors and a male nurse walked into the room a couple of hours later. They looked at him briefly, then they turned away and began discussing the patient among themselves. So he closed his eyes and dozed off for another couple of hours, her hand firmly in his.

He was awakened next by the touch of a hand on his shoulder. It was the male nurse, and he indicated that they were moving Jane Doe. Reluctantly, Owen withdrew his hand from hers. Her fingers tightened on his, and he bent close to her, murmuring reassurances.

"You've got to go on a little trip. I can't go with you. But I'll be here when they bring you back. Hang in there. This won't take too long."

She reached up, her hand seeking the sound of his voice.

Owen was startled. So startled that when she touched his cheek, he didn't know what to say. So he caught her hand with his and pressed it to his roughened and unshaved jaw.

"You must be feeling better, lady," he said in that gravelly voice he always had in the early morning before that first swallow of coffee. Then he comfortingly squeezed her hand and firmly laid it back down on the bed again. "They won't let me go with you. But I'll be here when you get back. I'm still waiting to hear your name, you know."

She didn't move, but he thought she heard what he was saying. Something about the softening of her lips made him think she was smiling a little. Maybe she'd even understood him.

The nursing staff rolled her out of the room and wheeled her bed down the hallway, heading toward the X-ray department. They were going to take new views of her head. Owen rubbed his neck, stiff from the uncomfortable sleeping position he'd been in, and wondered whether the radiographs would bring good news or bad.

Just then a teenage girl stopped in the doorway and glanced doubtfully at Owen. She was wearing the brown-striped apron and buttermilk white clothing that was the uniform of the hospital's volunteer corps. In her hand, she carried several pieces of paper, obviously notes and messages accumulated from various sources around the hospital, all in the process of being delivered.

"Mr. Blackhart?" she asked uncertainly while nervously fingering the envelopes and notes.

"Yes."

"I have a message for you. The operator took it and asked me to deliver it since I was coming up to this floor for a while." She looked at the messages, fumbling through the pile to locate the one intended for him. With a small, triumphant smile, she handed him a pink piece of paper torn from a telephone answering pad. She smiled at him sympathetically, obviously thinking he was a friend or relative of a patient, and then she hurried down the hall to delivery the other notes.

The message was from Sergeant Lefcourt. He wanted Owen to call him as soon as possible.

Owen frowned. Had Lefcourt learned the woman's identity? He went straight down to the lobby, located the phone banks and slipped into a quiet corner location to dial the police officer. The police operator put him straight through.

"Sergeant Lefcourt? This is Owen Blackhart. You wanted me to call you?"

"Yep. Thanks for gettin' back to me so quick."

"Have you discovered who the mystery lady is?"

"Uh, actually, I was hopin' she might have said something by now that could help us figure that out. I guess she hasn't mentioned her name or anything like that?"

"No, Sergeant. She hasn't said an understandable word."

Lefcourt's sigh was eloquent. The policeman was frustrated.

"Haven't you come up with anything from the physical evidence at the scene of the crash?" Owen asked impatiently. "How long does it take to identify a car's registered owner, even if you haven't completely made the tags?"

"It varies. From 'not very long' to 'never.'"

"That's great," Owen muttered.

"Look, we aren't a bunch of backwater hillbillies, if that's what you're saying!"

"I don't believe I was."

"We've made progress in tracing that license tag, but we only got three numbers off it. That's not enough to ID the car, unless someone's reported it stolen and we get a physical-description matchup off the computer search we've sent out. Otherwise, we've got a lotta legwork to do to try and trace it down. Hell, I can't even get the damn doctors on the phone at the hospital there to call me back and tell me whether the patient's said her name! And they're in the same town as me! How'm I gonna light a fire under the police in some other jurisdiction, askin' them to drop their cases to check out mine in a hurry?"

Exasperated, Owen ran a hand through his hair. That explained why Lefcourt was calling him for information about Jane Doe, he thought. In spite of his own irritation at the delays, Owen felt a bond of sorts with the policeman. They both had stumbled into this woman's problem and wanted to get her connected with her family again. Lefcourt was a decent man trying to do his job. Owen respected that. So he brushed away his irritation and reached for his self-control. There was nothing to be gained by the two of them arguing.

"Look, Sergeant, I apologize for implying that you and your department aren't up to this job. It's not your fault you don't have more evidence to investigate."

"Well, apology accepted." Lefcourt cleared his throat awkwardly. "I, uh, guess I owe you an apology for the way I spoke to you. I got a little touchy because, well, we don't have the money or the manpower that we need to do what has to be done. So we don't get results as fast as we'd like. And it's pretty frustrating. I shouldn't have let that get the better of my professionalism, though."

"Forget it. Let's call it even."

Lefcourt hesitated.

"Look," the sergeant said. "I feel real sorry for this woman. I bet she's a good-looking lady when she isn't covered in mud and her hair all tangled with underbrush, her face scratched and bloody from flying glass. Back up on the mountainside, when I saw her in your arms, I thought she was the kind of woman that turns men's heads when she walks into a restaurant. You know what I mean? I'm not being disrespectful of her or anything. But that's what I thought. I'll be damned if I know why, 'cause she sure looked a mess."

Owen understood.

"I keep thinking that some guy out there must be involved with her. A husband or a boyfriend or something. She surely has to have a man in her life somewhere. So why isn't he raising Cain with some local police department and filing a missing-persons report?"

Lefcourt fell silent, musing. Then suddenly he asked, "Say, do you know if she was wearing any jewelry? I asked the hospital that hours ago, but no one had an answer. And at the time, we all were busy with other things...the doctors working on her, and me working on the accident investigation. So I kind of forgot about it. Is she wearing a wedding ring, an engagement ring, a bracelet with an identifying inscription?"

"There's no ring on her left hand." Since Owen had been on fairly intimate terms with her left hand for most of the night, he was absolutely sure about that. "I can't say about the right. I haven't seen it. It's on the other side of the bed, and I haven't been paying any attention to it. I don't remember seeing any bracelets on her except for the hospital ID tag. I'll check when she gets back, though."

"Thanks. Back?"

"From getting her new set of radiographs taken." Owen added, "I thought most hospitals remove jewelry and check it in somewhere. So even though she's not wearing a wedding ring now doesn't mean she didn't arrive at the hospital with one on her finger."

"That's the way it's supposed to work, I guess. Would you ask the nursing staff about that? And ask them to call my office and give someone a description of any jewelry they took off her, especially anything with names or initials on it. I've got to go back to the scene of the accident and make sure we got everything done we need to do for the investigation before we turn it over to the highway department for repair of that side railing. Otherwise, I'd be down there now rattling their stethoscopes."

"I'll ask. And if I hear anything useful, I'll call it in personally, Sergeant."

"Thanks."

"And, Sergeant?"

"Yes, sir?"

"I'd appreciate it if you'd call me as soon as you've got any news about her."

"Sure thing."

"Thanks."

Lefcourt added, "We already sent her tag numbers along with the description of her car to the Maryland state motor vehicle department. A quick computer search turned up thirteen cars that might be a match. They've assigned somebody to contact the owners and find out if their car's missing."

"But so far nothing?"

"That's about the truth of it."

"You don't sound optimistic."

"That's because all thirteen cars that the computer spit out at us are registered to men. We're not getting any female names for our Jane Doe...."

"She could be the wife or daughter or sister of a male owner," Owen advised.

"Yeah. But we won't sift through that till we talk to each of those thirteen owners."

"Maybe you'll get lucky," Owen said dryly. "You could always hit paydirt in the first few calls you make."

"I just don't think we're gonna have that kinda luck in this case," the policeman said fatalistically.

"Why's that?"

"Well," the policeman explained grimly. "We already got some bad news about one of the registered owners."

"What happened?"

"The owner was found dead in a motel halfway to Maryland from here. No word yet on the current location of his car, the one that's a partial match to Jane Doe's."

"Dead? What happened?" Owen asked sharply.

"They're not sure yet. The local police are waiting for the medical examiner to tell them the cause of death before they say anything official," Lefcourt drawled tiredly. "But they're treating it as a suspicious death."

"Meaning?"

"Could be a suicide...or a homicide. And there's always a chance it was an accident."

"Interesting coincidence," Owen muttered.

"Yeah. That's what I thought."

Her head throbbed.

And it felt leaden. Numbed.

She could hear the medical people around her talking. Gradually the words fit together into coherent patterns. Some of the time, anyway. Like a picture going in and then out of focus. Then the words would suddenly fade out into incoherent babbling far, far in the distance. Only to return again, clearer and in longer stretches.

"...better than the last ones..."

"But it's still potentially a problem...."

"That bleeding may have damaged..."

"...no swelling. That's really good. So why don't we keep her on the same series...."

"Yeah. She certainly seems to be holding her own."

"Ever since he got here. She really responded to him. He's got the magic touch."

A chorus of laughter and chuckles erupted around her.

"Maybe we should hire him."

"Yeah. Touch therapy. My favorite."

"No way. The billing department doesn't have a code for it, and the insurance companies would never agree to pay."

"Well, medicine's been around longer than either of those."

Dry, cynical laughter scattered around the room.

"Okay, let's wheel her back down to her room. Let's see how that 'hands-on' therapy works now. It looks like she won't be going up to surgery today, after all."

"Honey, you are one lucky lady. Tell me, who's your guardian angel, huh? I sure could use that diligent one myself...."

Sound fluttered in and out of her awareness. Elevator doors closing. People murmuring. Doors opening again. A distant voice floating in the air, calling for some doctor to pick up the nearest phone. She felt the vibrations as the bed she was lying on rolled down the hallways. But she couldn't see anything. Her face felt strange. Something was wrapped around her eyes. Around her head.

Panic set in. She needed to know what was happening to her, what had happened. She didn't know why she was so afraid. There was a reason. But what was it? She couldn't remember. She couldn't remember, and that just made her more anxious. There was something important, lost in her mind. But what was it? Lord, what was it? And why was she so scared? Every loud noise made her want to jump out of her skin.

Someone raced by, the fast approach sending a hot flush of alarm through her. She opened her hand. Felt nothing but air. Oh, yes. He had told her he would be waiting for her. That he couldn't come with her on this trip.

She relaxed a little. She could remember that much. That helped. Enough to keep the panic at bay. She moved a little, experimentally. Both arms did what she asked of them. Legs, too. When she tried to move her torso, dull pain washed up through her abdomen. Sharper pain pressed across her collarbone, ribs and back.

Better not to do that, she realized. Maybe it was easier to stay in the fog. It hadn't hurt so much there.

No. Easier had never been her kind of choice. She focused on listening. As sharply and as broadly as she could. Training her mind to focus on what it could hear. That didn't hurt. And it did help her form a picture of where she was and what was happening to her.

She sensed when she was being wheeled back into a room. The acoustics changed. The place was more intimate than the open halls. Less populated than the crowded elevators.

And he was there.

She heard him ask the others a question. She turned her head a little, straining to hear his voice more clearly, but a nurse spoke.

"...so she's doing very well, all things considered. She still may need surgery, of course, if there is any bleeding. But right now, it looks like it's just a bad concussion. And she's recovering from the surgery yesterday. She has a hairline fracture on her collarbone and another on her rib. Some bruising around her vertebrae. The abrasions and cuts are mostly minor. Her eyes—"

"Her eyes?" he asked steadily.

"We think they're going to be all right, but the doctor is coming by this afternoon to take off the bandages and see how she's coming along. They can tell a lot by examination."

"If she's not comatose."

"Well, yes. That kind of complicates assessing her vision. But we'll just have to see what things look like to the doctor this afternoon. Are you going to be staying?"

She listened as hard as she could.

"Yes."

She exhaled softly, concentrating hard, forming the word carefully. ''Th...ank...s.''

She felt him draw near, bend close to her, cover her hand with his.

''Did you hear something?'' he asked.

She knew he was asking someone else, not her. Her lips softened in a smile. One so faint he probably couldn't see it, she thought.

''No. Why?''

''I thought...'' He pulled up a chair beside her and gently picked up her weakened hand, settling it comfortably in his again. ''Nothing. It was probably just the wind outside.''

''Hmm.'' The nurse uttered the sound without much curiosity. ''Well, if she says anything, pull the string to get someone at the nursing station back here right away. That would be a very good sign.''

Exhausted from concentrating so hard and so long, she no longer had the strength to stay awake, struggling to listen to everything around her. As her energy ebbed, she slid toward the brink of sleep. Rest. If she could just rest awhile, everything would be fine, she told herself groggily. She'd recoup her strength. And then...

What then?

Black waves of sleep swallowed her, wiping away the question before she could panic again. Before she could remember.

She hadn't been wearing a wedding band.

The nurses told Owen that no jewelry had been removed from her and bagged for safe keeping, except for a watch that they had taken off her wrist. It had a delicate black cord and tiny diamond chips embedded in the white gold of its small oval face.

Her clothes, still muddy and blood spattered, had been allowed to dry and then put in a plastic bag. The police had picked them up that morning, hoping clues to Jane Doe's identity might be lurking among the folds.

Owen swallowed the last of his orange juice and finished reading the *Wall Street Journal* that he'd picked up at the magazine stand in the hospital foyer.

Lefcourt had called him at the motel that morning to trade what little information they'd acquired since they'd last spoken.

Unfortunately, it wasn't much.

And Jane Doe was still without a name of her own.

By the time Owen reached her bedside, she'd been bathed and rebandaged, and fresh linen had been laid on the bed.

But when the woman lying there turned her head slightly at his approach, he knew things had changed profoundly.

"Is that...you?" she whispered.

He stopped in midstride, too thunderstruck to reply at first.

"What?"

"Is that you?" she repeated, with a great deal more doubt in her voice than the first time that she'd asked. She reached out her left hand, raising it slightly from the bed. "The man who...helped me...." she explained, her voice shaking with the effort to get the words said, and said clearly.

Owen came to her bedside and took her hand in his.

A slow smile illuminated her still partially bandaged face.

"Who are you?" she whispered.

"Owen Blackhart. And...who are you, mystery lady?" he asked softly.

Her smile faded. Her mouth opened and closed a little.

"I... I'm..." she stammered. "I'm... I don't know," she whispered in shock. "I don't know...my name."

Chapter 4

Suddenly, her breath couldn't fill her lungs. Her fingers tightened on his, as if she might retrieve her vanished thoughts through him. It did stabilize her panic. Unfortunately, no memories returned.

"I can't remember," she exclaimed shakily. "Who *am I?* Oh, please, *who am I?*"

Owen exhaled very slowly. For several days, he had entertained a fantasy that she would wake up, tell them her name and the next of kin to call for help. Then he was to have walked out of this hospital—and her life—without a second thought. Naming her would have snapped his sense of connection to her. He could have patted her on the hand, wished her well and gone on with his life.

But this... No. This hadn't been part of the plan. The doctors had said that she might die. That she could be permanently disabled. That her brain might have been damaged. Sure. But he'd never considered the damage might be to her memory. He had feared that she might remain comatose, unable to speak at all. But he had never contemplated the possibility that she could wake up and still be a Jane Doe, without a name or a family to call her own.

"You don't remember your name?" he asked slowly, not eager to verify the problem.

"No."

"Not at all?" He frowned. "Nothing?"

"Not a syllable. Not a sound. I...I... It's just blank."

There was a faint sense of hysteria in her last words. Owen instinctively squeezed her hand and leaned closer to her.

"It'll be all right. Take it easy...." he murmured.

She looked stunned. Her breathing was unsteady, and there was an irregular catch now and then that sounded suspiciously like a stifled sob to him. He felt something in his chest tighten.

"Look, it's probably just temporary," he said.

When in doubt, punt, right? he told himself grimly. What did he know about amnesia? He intensely hoped it was going to be temporary. This kind of problem wasn't his forte at all. He ran a hand through his hair and glanced around. Where had all the nurses gone, anyway? Like taxis, they were never in the neighborhood when you needed them, he thought in exasperation.

"Temporary?" she said in surprise. "Are you a doctor? I hadn't thought..."

"No, I'm not a doctor. But most injuries heal, don't they? And sometimes we all have problems with memory. After getting banged up like you did, it's probably not unusual to forget a few things. What do you bet?"

"I haven't forgotten a few things. I've forgotten *my name! Who I am.* I mean, isn't that a pretty major thing to have misplaced?" She half laughed. "You remembered your name. It was...Owen, right?"

"Yeah. But I didn't go tumbling down the mountainside in my car."

"Is that what happened? It's all so confused. I can barely make sense of it. It's like an incoherent nightmare."

"Yeah. Your mind probably just needs some time to recuperate from the accident."

"Time..."

"They say that time heals," he said gently.

"I hope they're right." She sighed.

"Say, I'm surprised you don't have a room full of doctors and nurses," he said, trying to get her to focus on something less depressing.

"Why?"

"You're talking! For days they've been telling me to call them right away if you said anything. So when your big moment came, they must have filled the room with applause. What happened to everybody afterward, anyway? Did they go out for a champagne breakfast to celebrate?"

"Uh..." Her face fell and she stared at him in dismay, although he couldn't see that so clearly, with all the bandages over her eyes.

"Wait a minute. You did speak to them? Didn't you?"

"Um, no. Just to you, Owen."

"Just to me?" He stared at her in amazement. "You waited for me?" That's what it had sounded like she had meant. But it seemed too ludicrous to believe, so he asked her to verify it.

Which she did.

"Yes. You were like a lifeline to me. And it was easier trying to focus on you when I was trying to find the words and get them out." She hesitated. "Um, I tried to talk yesterday, but no one seemed to understand a word. I thought I was losing my mind. People just ignored the sounds."

"No one could understand them," he said, trying to sound calm and reassuring. *Reassuring* wasn't hard. *Calm* was a stretch.

"Yes. Well, it was very frightening. I mean, when you're screaming as loud as you can and no one can make out a word that you're saying..."

"Believe me, that's not a problem any longer."

She grinned.

"That's progress, then," she said, the smile warming her voice and lifting her spirits.

"Yeah. So keep that in mind about this name thing, okay? You got your voice back. You'll get your memory, too."

"That's why I tried talking again when you got here just now," she said softly.

"Why?"

"Because I thought you were my best chance."

Owen grunted.

"Do you always do that?" she asked curiously.

"Do what?"

"Back away when someone tells you that you saved them from oblivion?"

"I don't know. I never saved anyone from oblivion before," he said dryly.

"Really? I would have bet you've had lots of experience."

Owen frowned. Now, why would she have guessed that? He wasn't stupid enough to ask her. He didn't want her to speculate on an answer.

"Well, when you remember your name, I'll see if I can remember some of my life experiences," he teased. He leaned over and buzzed the nursing station. "Now, let's see if we can get the rest of these highly trained, overworked and marginally paid medical professionals in here to admire your newly exercised vocal cords."

He moved away from her, relaxing his grip on her hand, but her fingers clung to his until he was almost beyond her reach.

"Thanks," she whispered, her voice low and filled with emotion. "I don't think I would have made it without you. Not on the mountain. Not here."

He tightened his fingers one last time. Then he let her go. This time she didn't cling to him.

"Say..." she blurted out, having just thought of it. "I don't know you, do I? I mean...did we ever meet before this happened?"

"No. We never met before. You don't know me from Adam."

"That's what I thought." She forced a rather unconvincing smile. "At least some of my senses are still working."

Owen laughed.

And then the nurse appeared in the door.

"Well, well! Look who's awake and talking! We have a lot of people waiting to speak with you...?" The nurse hesitated, waiting for the patient to take the cue and provide her with a name.

The woman on the bed stared blindly through her bandages in the direction of the nurse's voice.

She desperately tried to hold on to her composure, but the nurse's question brought back the brutal reality. She didn't know who she was or what she was doing at the time of the accident. She fiercely wanted to be able to handle all this herself, but she was wounded in a way that made that very difficult.

"I feel like an alien who was just dropped onto the wrong planet without a guidebook," she said, forcing an unconvincing laugh. "You see, I..." She swallowed hard, fighting against the fear welling up inside her. "I..."

Her voice wavered with emotion. She turned her head in Owen's direction, holding on to the thought of his encouragement, of the solid strength of his hand holding hers for so many hours.

"It seems we have a little problem, nurse," Owen said. "Our mystery patient has forgotten a few things."

"Such as...?" the nurse asked, eyebrows arching.

"Her name, for one. And just about everything else, apparently."

"I see," the nurse exclaimed softly. A look of pity filled her eyes. "Well, let's call in the doctors and see if any of them can help with that, shall we?"

Jane Doe smiled gamely.

"Let's hope they can," she murmured. "And thanks, Owen," she said, breathing a sigh of relief. "I don't know why it was so hard to say it out loud in words. Gee, I keep saying thanks. You'd better come up with a way for me to repay you for all this help you're giving me."

Owen grinned slowly. She was down, but she wasn't out.

"I'll think about it."

She laughed weakly. "Just don't ask for anything risqué, all right?" she said.

Owen laughed softly. "It's a little late to be throwing in conditions," he commented.

"It's never too late for that," she replied.

She was smiling in his direction as the doctors arrived.

"I've got to go," he said. He wasn't a member of her family, after all. This wasn't really any of his business, he reminded himself. "I'll call you tomorrow to see how you're doing."

Was it bewilderment he saw settling over her face? She covered it with a reasonably convincing smile before he could be sure.

"Watch out for the traffic," she said. "Especially the trucks."

He laughed. He liked her spunk.

"Yeah. I'll do that."

He sensed her bandaged, unseeing gaze on him as he turned and left the room. It stayed with him on the long drive home that evening, like the pleasant aftertaste of a good wine.

Who the hell was she? he wondered. And why couldn't he just forget about this, anyway?

He fell asleep still not having found the answer.

As he had promised, he called her late the following day.

"I thought you forgot," she said, rushing through the words nervously.

"I don't have that many things to remember," he teased. "I didn't want to interrupt the hospital routine."

"You're a highlight of that," she said with happy candor.

"I'm more fun than needles and examinations and people coming in day and night to check on every personal need you have? Am I supposed to take that as a compliment?"

"Yes, you are," she said, laughing softly.

He felt a shiver scamper down his back. Her laughter was light and sparkling, like a gurgling summer river on a clear, bright day. He swallowed and shook off the feelings she had unexpectedly touched in him.

"Owen? Are you still there?" she asked, sounding puzzled.

"Yes. I'm still here. It was a...surprise hearing you laugh. Guess it just startled me."

"Oh." She paused, as if waiting for him to give her a little more insight into his thoughts. When he didn't, she continued. "Well, they've examined about all there is to examine on me, and they think I'm doing pretty well, I guess."

"That's good news."

"And the lady ophthalmologist, Dr. Evergreen..."

"What about her?"

"Well, she's going to remove the last bandages from my eyes this evening. They're off for good, if the corneas are healed."

"Now, that's great," he said, his voice rich with warmth.

"Yes." She hesitated. "They think my eyes will be okay."

"But...?"

"But they aren't so sure about the memory thing."

"Isn't it a little soon to make any predictions about that?"

"It didn't stop you," she argued.

"True. But I can't be sued for saying something optimistic that doesn't pan out."

"Oh. That's...true."

"Hey, I didn't mean it the way it sounded. I *do* think you'll catch hold of your memories. I just meant that doctors are very cautious about what they say to patients now. They're afraid their words will be used against them by a disappointed patient's lawyer. So, they promise little. They avoid giving firm dates for recovery or promising full recovery at all. It's safer to give a gloomy forecast, qualifying it with all the things that can go wrong that they can think of. Then when you get better, you think they're geniuses, having saved you from all those possible bad endings."

She giggled.

"You sound a little negative yourself," she noted.

"Yeah, I guess so," he conceded, grinning slowly. "Well, they don't have crystal balls, they can only give you an opinion."

"I suppose you're right," she murmured. "I just wish..." She fell silent, keeping her fears to herself. Her silence was more eloquent than anything she could have said.

"You wish you knew who you were," he supplied softly.

"Yes. It's awful not knowing where I belong…what I'm doing with my life…who my friends are…my job—" Her words caught in her throat. "I don't know if I'm married, divorced, widowed or single. So I can't even fill out the hospital admission forms," she said with a shaky laugh. "What if I have kids? What if they don't know where I am?"

"Do you think you have kids?" he asked, frowning. Somehow, it had never occurred to him that she might. He wondered why it hadn't.

"Well, actually, no. I'd remember that, wouldn't I? I mean doesn't mother instinct, her love for her child, override anything else?"

"I don't know. Maybe."

"Well, I don't feel like I have children somewhere waiting for me…but it would sure help if I knew that was true."

She fell silent, and her pain was palpable across the miles to him. He didn't have to see her to know she was struggling with the agony of not knowing what her responsibilities in life were.

"I just wish I knew what to call you," he muttered in frustration.

"They call me Jane or Janie D. or Ms. Doe…."

"I will *not* call you Jane Doe!"

"Okay, okay!" She smiled at his vehemence and brushed away a tear that had trickled down beneath the bandage lightly covering her eyes. "I'm not all that fond of the name myself," she conceded.

Owen heard the wobble in her voice and wished he were sitting by her bedside where he could hold her hand while he was talking to her. Funny how he'd gotten used to the feel of her slender fingers in his. Of course, it was his own fault that he wasn't there. He'd come back to check on his mail and to give her and the people at the hospital a chance to work together on her problem. He'd thought his most important job was done. And he thought that he might retard her improvement if he stayed with her too much now. Leaning on him might slow her down.

But maybe he'd been wrong.

Maybe he'd left too soon. Maybe she still needed a psychological crutch to lean on just a little while longer.

"Owen?" she asked hesitantly. "Are you still there?"

"Yeah. I'm here. Just thinking."

"Well, think out loud, huh?" She cleared her throat and said, a little awkwardly, "Are you thinking that calling me was a mistake?"

"No. What made you think of that?"

"Well, I know you have your own life to get back to, and spending all this time holding my hand here at the hospital probably didn't help you any. I mean, you probably need to catch up on your work...."

"I'm taking a...leave of absence. I haven't missed anything."

"Well, then there's your family...."

"Not an issue."

"But your wife must be wondering when you'll be getting home for dinner on a regular basis."

"Are you asking me if I'm married?" He'd heard the curiosity in her voice.

"Well...yes. No one around here seemed to know for sure," she admitted a little defensively.

"I'm not married."

"Well, your girlfriend...?"

"I don't have one anymore."

"Oh. I'm sorry."

"No need to be. Anything else you'd like to know about me?" he asked, beginning to smile. He could almost see the blush running up her cheekbones. The sharp intake of her breath had given her away.

"No."

Then he realized he couldn't ask her those same questions, not even to tease her. She wouldn't be able to remember the answers. His heart twisted a little in pain.

"Hell, what can I call you?" he said with a sigh. Then he remembered. "The doctor said your eyes are green."

"Well, that's nice to know," she said wryly. "Every shred of fact about myself is something to build on."

"So I'll call you Green Eyes."

"Oh." Her voice floated off into a sigh of surprise. "Green Eyes. Well, that sounds more interesting than Jane D—"

"Don't say it!" he growled.

She laughed again, and the spring sun shone lightly upon him as if the sound had illuminated the barren room he was standing in.

"Will you be busy tomorrow?" he asked abruptly.

"No busier than usual, I guess," she replied. "They seem to want to keep me in the hospital for a few more days. I'm still getting over the surgery they did when I was admitted...something about fixing some internal bleeding and some injury to my spleen."

"So if I dropped in to hold your hand again for a while, you'll be receiving visitors?" he drawled.

She laughed again, and this time she sounded more relaxed.

"I'll receive *you* anytime, Owen."

"I'll stop by during late-morning visiting hours tomorrow, then. All right?"

"Are you sure this isn't going to...?"

"Inconvenience me? No. You want me to come, right?"

There was a long pause as she wrestled with her own pride, which had suddenly reasserted itself with a vengeance. Pride lost.

"Yes. I would love to see you again. You're the closest thing I have to a friend right now," she admitted.

"Then I'll be there," he said softly. "See you tomorrow."

"Owen, I hope I can repay your kindness someday."

"In a way, you're doing that now," he said reluctantly. "So don't worry about it. Besides, what man wouldn't jump at the chance to hold a good-looking woman's hand?" he teased.

"I look like a mummy!" she exclaimed in mild disgust. "And it is a big inconvenience. The nurse says it takes hours to drive from where you live to the hospital. You had to stay in a motel, they said. That costs you money...."

"I like to drive. And my furniture still hasn't arrived here, so it was more comfortable sleeping in the motel anyway. Look, don't worry about it."

He said it as dismissively as possible. He really didn't want to explain about the other woman he'd known who'd disappeared from his life. It had a depressing ending. This lady needed stories of hope, not despair. And he had the distinct feeling that she would be digging in that direction next, asking him why helping her was repaying him for anything at all.

"See you tomorrow," he said firmly.

"Yes. I'll see you tomorrow. Bye, Owen."

She smiled as she said it. She really would see him when he came. For the first time since the accident. And maybe this time, she'd make him out clearly, see a well-defined face to go with his swashbuckling name and his soothing, masculine voice and his reassuring touch.

Averson Hemphill called Owen later that evening. He did not have good news. Owen, who'd been fixing a leak in the plumbing, put down the wrench in his hand and exhaled slowly in surprise. For a moment, he felt speechless, astonished by the information that the lawyer had just shared with him.

"No one knew that Portia had any blood relatives who could contest the will," Hemphill went on to say, trying to explain.

"So why should you believe that this person *is* her nephew?"

"Because he's presented legal proof of it. A birth certificate properly authenticated, indicating that he is the lawful child of Portia Willowbrook's late brother. And he's hired a lawyer to contest your ownership of Portia's estate. He says his father grew up on that land, and he has a rightful family interest in it."

"But Portia never mentioned him. I don't think she knew he existed," Owen argued, frowning.

"I tend to agree with you there. She certainly never mentioned him to me, and I specifically asked her about blood relatives when we were writing her will. It's a good idea to mention people who might claim they were overlooked. That way you can prove you gave them exactly what you intended for them," said the lawyer, sounding resigned to the newly complicated situation that had presented itself to them.

Owen was bitterly tempted to laugh, but the potential seriousness of this new legal problem made that impossible.

"So I should be prepared to go to court over this. Is that what you're saying?"

"The short answer is...yes," Hemphill reluctantly admitted. "But I'll try to discuss this with the nephew's attorney. We still may be able to come to some sort of mutually acceptable understanding without dragging this to trial."

"Good. I hate trials."

Hemphill sighed.

"As a matter of fact, so do I," he conceded. "I much prefer mediation. Especially when it comes to family matters."

"I suppose you'll need a retainer to work on this?"

"Yes." Hemphill mentioned the amount needed.

"Consider the check in the mail," Blackhart said.

"By the way, I read in the paper that the mystery lady is awake and talking."

"Yes."

"Has her family come to see her?"

"Not yet."

"Hmm. That's odd. She has family, I assume."

"Most of us do."

"I'm sorry...I thought you were, uh, sort of involved with her recovery. Am I poking my nose in where I shouldn't?"

"Yes."

There was a moment of silence while Hemphill waited to see if Owen might offer any more enlightenment on the condition of the formerly comatose lady.

When Owen did not, Hemphill continued. "Well, tell her we're all glad she's recovering. By the way, what's her name? I haven't seen any more in the paper about her except that she's recovering."

"I don't believe I got her name," Owen said. The finality of his tone was clear.

"Uh, yes. Well, I'll be getting on with that other matter. And I'll let you know when we have some progress to report."

"Good."

"Goodbye then."

"Goodbye." Owen hung up the telephone and shoved his hands in the back pockets of his jeans.

Great. A lawsuit from a disinherited, greedy relative. Just what he needed, Owen thought in irritation.

Well, who would have thought Portia would have forgotten the one living relative she had on the face of the earth?

Owen swore under his breath and went back to work on the leaking pipe under the kitchen sink. That had to be fixed before he left to see Green Eyes, or he and the unexpected, litigious nephew would be squabbling over a pond where once a lovely old home had stood.

Owen arrived at Cleary Hospital the following day around noon. He checked in at the motel, agilely evading Madge's steady flow of questions about the "mystery lady," as everyone in town was beginning to refer to her. He dropped his one piece of luggage inside the door of his room, closed and locked the door and firmly strode back to his car.

"Well, nice talking to you," Madge said with a shrug. "Maybe next time you'll talk to me," she suggested with a hopeful twinkle in her pale eyes.

Owen grunted noncommittally and got back into his car. Madge stared at him as he drove away, and he had the distinct feeling that she was plotting new ways to dig out information about the mystery lady.

At least Madge was a warmhearted curiosity seeker, he thought. He just hoped some of the more callous and self-serving ones kept away from Green Eyes until they could figure out where she

was from and who her loved ones were. On the long drive back
to the mountains, a disturbing idea had come to him. What if
someone decided to take advantage of her loss of memory? They
could manipulate her for their own purposes, telling her she was
someone that she was not, or deceiving her into believing things
that were not true. Green Eyes would be very vulnerable to that
kind of deviant. She'd have no way of knowing she was being
lied to...unless someone did a very thorough background check
on anyone claiming to know her.

Owen's eyes narrowed thoughtfully as he pulled into the hospital parking lot and took a parking ticket from the automatic
dispenser at the gate.

The police could help her, he told himself. He could already
hear Buddy Lefcourt pointing out how limited everybody's time
was to do something like that...especially in other jurisdictions,
where they had their own problems and probably rarely needed
to trade favors with the tiny hamlet where Lefcourt and Morrison
Hayes took care of most of the police work that needed doing.

So she could hire a private detective, he argued as he locked
up his car and walked into the hospital, resisting the obvious
solution to Green Eyes's problem with every stride he took. She
could if she had money. Which, at the moment, she certainly
didn't. She was as broke as a person gets. Not a dime to her
name. Not even a name, he reminded himself grimly. No credit
rating. No assets, except the bloodied and torn clothes that had
been on her back the night of the accident.

Owen Blackhart swore to himself and punched the elevator
button.

Well, he could help in a limited way, he begrudgingly conceded
to himself. Just so long as she didn't get overly dependent on
him. He wasn't taking that kind of responsibility for a woman,
not again. He was done with that. Absolutely, positively, forever
done with that.

Grim faced from his dark thoughts, Owen stepped out of the
elevator and into the hospital corridor leading to Green Eyes's
room. A woman in a hospital gown was walking away from him.

She appeared to have been walking around, getting some exercise. A nurse followed along, chatting amiably and looking pleased at her patient's progress.

Owen recognized her immediately. And this time, there was lots of that beautiful, dark red hair showing. The bandages were off. He couldn't see her face, because she had her back to him. He walked toward her, and as his footsteps approached, she stopped and turned.

Their eyes met.

"So they are green," he said softly, stopping a couple of feet away from her. He scanned her pale face and throat and looked her over slowly. Finally, his gaze returned to the dark green eyes that had never looked away from his face. It was the little streaks of chestnut that made the green so dark, he decided. Unusual color, those green eyes. Like the lush forest at the end of spring and the beginning of summer.

She walked toward him and held out her hand uncertainly.

"I didn't know how to picture you before," she said, still a little stunned at the first sight of him. She smiled wryly as he took her hand and gently squeezed it in greeting. She wanted to hug him, but she didn't know him. He might take it the wrong way. So she just shook his hand, aching to be thanking him with her whole heart for what he had done for her. What he was still doing for her. Even though he was a total stranger. And yet...when she was with him, she didn't feel that they were exactly total strangers. She blinked. Maybe it was the head injury she'd had. It was making her fanciful, excessively romantic or something.

She smiled and looked him up and down, as he had done to her. They released each other's hand and stepped back a little, as if thinking along the same lines: not too intimate...keep things businesslike...this is a peculiar situation...ignore the feelings. This isn't exactly normal.

"The nurses tried to describe you to me," she confessed, turning to walk slowly back to her room. Owen walked alongside.

She tilted her head and looked at him askance. "They said you had a face filled with character."

Owen laughed and lifted an eyebrow.

"Is that so?" he said, casting an amused glance at the nurse discreetly trailing along on the other side of the patient. "Is that a polite way of describing a broken nose, an eyebrow cut by a scar and a face that's wiped up its share of floors in bar fights?"

"Oh, no! I'm sure they were trying to say you were a hand-some man but not pretty like some male models," she explained, laughing.

When she reached her bed, she sat down and stared at him for a long moment, as if she would memorize his features.

"They're right," she mused. "Your face does have character."

"Be careful, Green Eyes," he said softly. "You don't know me. You don't know anyone right now. Keep your defenses up."

"That's good advice," said a voice from the doorway.

They turned to see Sergeant Lefcourt, and with him, another man.

Chapter 5

"Uh, ma'am," Sergeant Lefcourt began, "this here's a gentleman who might know you. Could we come on in so's he can see you, see if you're the lady he thought you might be?"

She stared at the man standing beside the sergeant. Nothing about him seemed familiar. He was gaunt. About fifty. Thinning hair, streaked with gray. He was staring at her, frowning a little, as if he wasn't sure who she was, either. He seemed nervous, too, rubbing his hand slowly against his brown suit jacket. Back and forth. As if to dry a sweating palm.

She swallowed and glanced at Owen.

Owen met her gaze and began to frown. She was afraid of being left alone with the man who claimed to know her when she didn't know him from squat, Owen thought. She was totally vulnerable. She wouldn't know if he was telling the truth about her or not.

"Ma'am?" Sergeant Lefcourt prompted her courteously. "Could we come in and talk to you?"

"Can you stay?" she asked Owen. She tried to be levelheaded and to sound calm. She didn't want to act like a child. But...why did she fear being alone with a stranger? A glimpse of a memory almost surfaced. Then it slid beneath her grasp and was lost. But the fear remained. Fear of a man. A man with an evil smile. A man whose features and appearance she couldn't quite recall. She swallowed hard and looked deeply into Owen Blackhart's eyes as he weighed her request of him.

He nodded and walked around her bed to the far side, sitting down at the chair in the corner of the room. He stretched out his legs and crossed them at the ankles, the picture of a thoroughly relaxed man. He smiled slightly at her.

"Sure. I'll stay," he said softly.

"Thanks," she said, her voice brimming with gratitude. Something about Owen Blackhart gave her courage. She would have hugged him then, if she'd known him better.

Owen slid his gaze back to the nervous man standing next to Lefcourt. Green Eyes turned her attention to them, too.

"Come in," she said, smiling as best she could. "Here," she added, indicating the chair next to her bed, where Owen had sat for so many long, patient hours holding her hand. "Sit down, Mr....?"

"Kelton."

"Mr. Kelton," she said.

He shook his head slowly.

"No," he said quietly. "My first name is Kelton."

He seemed to be waiting for her to respond, as if that should mean something to her. She couldn't imagine what, though.

"Oh. I'm sorry...Kelton."

The man leaned forward a little hesitantly, as if afraid to offend her by coming too close. He was studying her face, her hair, her general appearance. She was still wearing hospital clothes, but the gown and the thin cotton robe left him with a clear impression of her build.

"Do you know me?" she blurted out, guessing from the sympathetic expression in his eyes what his answer was going to be.

"In a way," he replied. He searched for the right words. "We have met several times in the past six months. At a meeting." He paused and watched her expectantly.

"I don't remember," she said with a sigh. "What meeting? Where?"

Kelton glanced at the other two men in the room.

"I can't really discuss this with her while you are in the room," he said.

Owen raised his eyebrows.

Sergeant Lefcourt looked resigned and rolled his eyes heavenward.

"Look, we already talked about this, Kelton," Lefcourt argued. "This is a missing-person case. She's missing and can't remember where she belongs. We need to get her back to her own home, her own friends and relatives. This anonymity thing has to take a back seat to the police work."

"You already talked about what, Sergeant?" she asked, perplexed.

"What anonymity thing?" Owen interjected, beginning to become suspicious.

Kelton looked at her seriously. "What I know about you is private. We know each other from a place where everyone swears to honor the privacy of the other people there. I can't talk about you in front of these two men unless you say it's okay for them to hear about it."

"Good heavens," she murmured. "I mean..." She gulped. "What kind of place was it?"

Increasingly bizarre possibilities flew across her mind. Some sort of group therapy? Maybe a peculiar hobby group? A criminal fraternity of some sort? Parole counseling sessions? A kinky...? Well, her imagination was too energetic, she told herself.

Sergeant Lefcourt held up his hand.

"Just a minute," he said firmly, a frown of authority settled on his face. "You're here at my request, Kelton. You saw the photo of her in the newspaper and called my office. I made this appointment with you. You're here seeing me." He stared pointedly at Kelton. "Now...do you recognize this woman?"

"Yes." Kelton slumped a little in the chair and looked apologetically at Green Eyes.

"What is her name?"

"I only know her first name."

"Why's that?"

"We only give our first names at meetings," he explained.

"What meetings?" the lawman asked.

Kelton looked at Green Eyes.

"Look," she said. "Whatever it is, I'll have to face it. Right now, I just want to know who I am. So, tell us…what meetings. It's okay. Sergeant Lefcourt and Mr. Blackhart have been doing everything they can to help me. They've…saved my life," she said desperately, with a wave of her hand to underscore the fact. "So, what meeting did we attend?"

"AA."

She blinked.

"Alcoholics Anonymous?" she said.

"Yes."

"I'm an alcoholic?" she asked, confused, waiting for that to ring true. She felt nothing. Not the ring of truth or the dissonance of a falsehood.

"I…don't actually know." He looked unhappy. "I'm not supposed to share what you said with outsiders. I could tell you, while we're alone, what you said at the meetings, and if you want to tell them, well, that's up to you."

She stared into his eyes. He was looking back at her. He seemed tired and worried, but absolutely clear about what he was saying.

"What's my name?" she asked softly.

"Mary Ann."

"Mariann…" She exclaimed. Her eyes brightened. "Yes…" Then a frown crossed her face. Maryann…Mariann…Mari…

"Does that sound familiar?" Sergeant Lefcourt asked hopefully.

"Yes."

"But?" Owen injected.

"It sounds right and yet, not right," she blurted out. She clasped her head in her hands and closed her eyes. "Why does it sound right and wrong at the same time?" she murmured in frustration. "I feel so near...and yet so far from the truth."

Owen turned to Kelton.

"Do you have any proof of what you're saying, Kelton?" Owen demanded bluntly.

"Well," the man said cautiously. "I could talk to some of the regulars at the next meeting. A couple of them could tell you the same thing. They saw Mary Ann there a few times."

"Is there any other proof?" Lefcourt asked.

"Like photos or tape recordings or signed papers or something? Well, no. We don't photograph our little meetings and we don't tape-record them, either. I mean...the whole idea is to have someplace where you can be honest with other people and not worry about it coming back to bite you later on. So first names and anonymous get-togethers work pretty well for us. Course...sometimes people are friends outside the meeting...." He looked at her sympathetically. "You drove in from outside. I don't think anyone in the group ever knew you outside of the meetings."

"When was the last meeting?" Owen asked.

"Sunday evening."

"They're held every Sunday evening?"

"Yep."

"Where do you meet?" Owen pressed.

"An old church vestry room in the next county over."

Owen looked at Lefcourt. The lawman was thinking the same thing that he was, Owen realized. They both looked at Green Eyes, newly anointed with the name of Mary Ann. She stared back at them blankly.

"What is it?" she asked.

"You were heading in that direction on a Sunday evening when you had that accident," Lefcourt said.

"Oh." Her eyes widened. Was that where she'd been going, then? she wondered. She struggled to find the memory of that trip. An incoherent collage of faces and sounds burst into her mind's view. The mountain highway. The driving rain. The white lights of the huge truck. A woman's silhouette. A pay phone in a narrow hallway...

A pay phone? Inside a building? Now, why would that have surfaced? she wondered. Why could that sliver of recollection pierce the veil still covering her memories? And the woman? Was it her? No...someone else, she thought. But who?

"Mary Ann?"

She looked quickly at Owen. It was the first time he had called her by that name. It sounded tentative on his lips, as if he was unsure whether the name really belonged to her.

"Are you all right?"

"I was just lost in thought. Not any thoughts that will solve the riddle of my life, apparently," she ruefully replied.

He leaned back in the chair, but the frown on his face remained.

"Take your time," he suggested. "It'll all come back to you. Eventually."

"So you keep telling me," she said with a sigh.

"Well...we've got a name for you," he reminded, raising his eyebrows as if wondering if she'd overlooked that little fact.

"Yes. I guess that is progress," she conceded. She couldn't hide the reluctance in her voice.

Owen frowned. "Something bothers you about the name, doesn't it?"

"I don't know. It sounds right, and yet..." She ran her hands through her hair nervously. Then she shook her head. "Give me a day to get used to it, okay? Maybe I'm just a little rusty when it comes to my own name." She half laughed and turned her green-eyed gaze on Kelton again. "So when did we first meet, Kelton? Tell me all the details...good, bad or unprintable. I want to hear it all. Okay?"

Kelton smiled awkwardly.

"I know what it's like to wake up and not be able to remember the last month," he said candidly. "I've done it often enough. Waking up in alleys...in strange buildings...covered with dirt..."

He shook his head. "But the last time...well, I woke up in a hospital three states away from the address on the driver's license that the police had taken off me when they pulled me out of what was left of my car. It was wrecked so bad that even the junkman had to be paid to take it away."

He swallowed hard at a painful memory.

"I'm sorry," she murmured sympathetically.

"The woman who'd been in the car with me...she barely made it," Kelton explained. "It was nothing less than a miracle that saved her." He looked at her seriously. "And me."

She leaned toward him and comfortingly squeezed his arm.

"Sometimes we get a second chance, don't we?" she offered.

The corners of his eyes crinkled as he smiled. He nodded his head slowly.

"Oh, yeah. We surely do. And I used up a whole raft of them before I finally hit bottom." He sat a little straighter in the chair. "I take every day as it comes. One day at a time. And I thank the miracles that come our way. So, thank the miracle that saved your life, Mary Ann. And that saved me to be here to tell you who you are."

She smiled and nodded. "I'll not forget today, Kelton," she promised him. "It's the first day of the rest of my life."

Kelton grinned, a little abashed. "Well, uh, I didn't mean to get up on a soapbox or preach at you," he said awkwardly.

Buddy Lefcourt cleared his throat uncomfortably. "Well, meaning no disrespect Kelton, but, uh, maybe we could get back to talking about Jane Doe, er, Miss Mary Ann here? She didn't get in that wreck because she'd been drinking. There wasn't any alcohol in her body when they brought her in here that night. She didn't smell of it, either. Course the car was burned to a cinder, so, it's hard to know for sure, but..."

Kelton smiled. "I'm glad she was sober. She has been ever since the first meeting she came to." He fell silent and looked at the green-eyed woman wrapped in hospital garb.

"Then maybe I'm winning the battle with alcohol?" She glanced at Owen, as if he might know. He shrugged, and she immediately felt ridiculous for seeking his opinion. "Well, naturally, you wouldn't know about that, would you, Owen?"

She gave him a tart grin, but it faded almost as soon as it had appeared.

"I don't feel like I'm an alcoholic," she murmured as much to herself as to the others. "It just doesn't seem real. I can't imagine craving a drink or binging till I passed out in some strange place," she said, struggling to discover the truth that lay hidden deep within her. Seeing the men's raised eyebrows, she conceded, "Okay! I'm not in the best condition to know what I have or have not done."

"Right," Owen murmured.

She grimaced and gave him a look of annoyance. "I thought you were here for moral support!"

"Yes. But support has to be based on the truth," he argued. "Reality is the best starting point when you've got a problem to solve."

Well, he was right about that, darn it. She sighed. It was irritating that he was, for some reason.

She stared into his eyes, and for a moment the others faded away. There were just the two of them. Heat flowed into her heart and spread outward in all directions. Suddenly it was very warm in the room. She became uncomfortably aware that she was wearing only a thin cotton hospital gown and an equally unsubstantial cloth robe.

Her cheeks reddened and she hastily dragged her gaze away from Owen, struggling to reassemble her mysteriously shattered composure.

"So where does Mary Ann live?" asked Sergeant Lefcourt, briskly taking charge of the situation and pressing on with the police work. He stuck the tip of his pencil on the pad of paper, ready to jot down an address.

"Someplace east of West Virginia and west of Washington, D.C., I think," Kelton guessed.

"That covers a *lot* of square miles," Lefcourt argued with dismay. "How about narrowing that down? Didn't you have an address for your group members? A mailing address? An emergency contact person? Next of kin? Something? Anything?''

"No. We posted meeting announcements in the church and in the local paper and with a regional information and referral service. AA is an *anonymous* group, Sergeant,'' Kelton reminded him, annoyed at having to point out something so obvious. "You know about Alcoholics Anonymous, don't you?''

"Sure,'' Lefcourt replied. "But I'm conducting an investigation here. I've gotta ask the questions. I can't assume anything.''

"I guess not. I'm sorry, Sergeant,'' Kelton apologized stiffly. "Well, go ahead, then. What else do you want to ask?''

Lefcourt narrowed his eyes and stared at Kelton for a long moment, as if X-raying his brain for any hidden motives for obscuring the truth.

"Kelton, just think for a minute,'' Lefcourt said. "Do you know anything that could help us figure out where she might have been living? Did she mention anything about her travels?''

"Well, I'd say she probably lives east of the Shenandoah Valley and west of the capital,'' Kelton said thoughtfully. "She was pretty familiar with some places around Dulles airport and Leesburg,'' Kelton said. "Someone in the group was talking about a new office building there, and she got quite excited talking about the architecture.'' He grinned at her. "She got real detailed about the glass and the designs and all. Then she just stopped talking about it. I guess she realized she was giving away some things about herself that she wasn't ready to share yet.''

Kelton had shifted his attention from the lawman to her.

The sergeant drew him back. "So how far away would you say she lived?''

"Well, she needed about three and a half hours to get back home after meetings, especially in bad weather. I remember because once we had a bad storm blow through all of a sudden, and she kept checking her watch, fretting over whether to leave early or not. We talked about how long the drive was and whether it was safe or not to take the turns in a hard rain. The mountains are slow going in some places...especially in foul weather, you know.''

"Yeah. We know," Lefcourt said dryly.

The lawman tapped his pencil on the small notebook in his hand.

"You said she mentioned Dulles airport? Did she mention any other places? Streets? People? An employer?"

"Not that I remember."

"How'd she hear about your group?" Owen asked, puzzled. "And why'd she come so far to a meeting? If you're right, she traveled a long way to attend meetings. If she really didn't know anyone around there, why would she do that?"

Kelton shrugged. "I'm not sure why she came so far out of her way to come to an AA meeting. Could have been embarrassed, I guess. Some people don't want to be seen going into AA meetings. Afraid someone they know might see them. It's unfortunate. Keeps a lot of people away who could really use the support. After all, it's an illness. Not a character defect," Kelton muttered.

"How'd she find you?" Owen repeated.

"I think she said she heard about it through some phone-referral program. But I'm not too sure. You know, we just care that people come. We aren't too choosy about how they arrived at that choice," Kelton explained dryly.

Owen looked at Mary Ann. She seemed as unconvinced as he felt. If they knew why she picked that place, they might have a clue to finding her identity, he thought. But it didn't appear that they would be getting any more information on that score out of Kelton. If he knew anything else, he simply was withholding it, Owen decided. Although, Owen was inclined to believe that Kelton was telling them all that he knew.

"Did anyone ever come with her to the meetings?" asked Lefcourt.

"No."

"Did she do anything besides sit in the meeting?"

"Like what, Sergeant?"

"Oh...eat nearby, go to a gas station near the church, stop at a local convenience-type store, take up with anyone in particular in the group afterward?"

Kelton thought for a while. "Well...she did use the pay phone in the church hall. Just about every time she came."

"Do you know who she was calling?"

"I didn't listen in," Kelton said sourly.

"Nobody's saying you did. But anything you can recall could help her a lot."

Kelton frowned and thought hard.

"Was I happy when I was on the phone?" she asked anxiously. "Or sad? Angry?"

"You seemed kind of worried. Preoccupied, I guess. Like there was something going on that you couldn't do anything about but that really mattered to you," Kelton said.

"Did I mention a name...of a person or a place?" she pressed him.

"No..." Suddenly his expression brightened a little. "I do remember something," he exclaimed hopefully. "I was getting a cup of coffee from the church kitchen and I walked down the hall just as you were saying something about some bird...now, what kind of bird was it?" He scratched his head. "Firebird? No. Bird of paradise? No, that's not it, either. Something to do with some old myth."

They all leaned a little toward Kelton, as if collectively willing his memory to produce the details.

Kelton frowned and thought hard, but eventually he had to shake his head regretfully.

"I'm sorry. That's all that I can remember. It's kind of a jumble now. It's been a few months since that happened, you know," he said in his own defense. "And I had the flu that night," he added. "I had taken some medicine and was a little woozy." He stiffened when he saw Sergeant Lefcourt's cynical look. "I hadn't been drinking! I was light-headed from not eating and from taking some cold medicine! And that's the God's honest truth!" Kelton exclaimed irritably.

"All right, all right!" Lefcourt said. He held up his hand to stem the tide of Kelton's indignant protestations. "Don't get touchy, Kelton. I'm a cop. Remember? I get paid to think of alternative reasons and to assume that everyone might be, let's say, shading the truth to put themselves in the most favorable light."

Kelton grumbled.

"Well, I think I need to talk to some of the other folks at that AA meeting," Lefcourt continued. "And I'd like to copy down that pay-phone number. Never know when it might come in handy." He grimaced. "I can't get to it soon, though. I've got some other things I've got to handle the next few days. Maybe someone in that county can help me out with the legwork." He smiled sheepishly at Mary Ann. "I hope this helps jog your memory some," he said. "And if you want to keep talking, why, go on ahead. I've got to get over to the county morgue and check on an accidental drowning. They called me about it just as I was on my way over here with Kelton."

"Go on, Sergeant. I appreciate all your help," she said sincerely.

"I just wish we could have come up with a last name, as well as a first name, ma'am."

She smiled. "Hey...I'm ahead of where I was when I woke up this morning," she stated.

"Yeah. Well...you take care, Miss Mary Ann. I'll be in touch."

The lawman left. Behind them they sat in uneasy silence.

Owen sent her a questioning look.

She guessed his thoughts before he could voice them.

"Yes. I'd like you to stay while Kelton tells me everything I ever said, as close as he can remember it," she said firmly.

He grinned. "Well, for a lady who can't tell me a thing about her past, you do a hell of an impressive job at telling me what's going through my mind at the present."

She laughed. Then she turned to the man seated next to her bed.

"Well, Kelton, when I spilled my guts at these meetings, exactly what did I say?'' she asked, bracing herself for all manner of hair-raising tales.

Kelton chuckled. ''You needn't look like you're about to be martyred,'' he reassured her. ''You said the usual things... especially at the first meeting. That you weren't sure you had a problem, but that you were afraid you might.''

''Did she ever mention a husband?'' Owen asked curiously.

''No.''

''Boyfriend?''

''Uh, no.''

''Did I wear any jewelry?'' she asked. ''Rings?''

Kelton chuckled again. ''To tell you the truth, I don't pay much attention to the jewelry people wear. Maybe a really expensive watch...or a big gaudy ring. Nothing else, though.''

''Never mind,'' she said, brushing aside her disappointment. ''So, what kind of things did I talk about?''

''Oh...you asked questions, mostly. Not the first time...but later, when you came back.''

''When she came back?'' Owen asked, frowning.

''Well...she came and then we didn't see her for nearly a couple months. When she came back, she looked healthier, better rested. And better fed. You know, alcoholics have a lot of problems with malnutrition...drinking kind of interferes with getting three good meals a day.''

Owen looked at Mary Ann. She didn't look malnourished. Even after the accident, she looked basically healthy beneath the bruises and scrapes.

''So maybe I went to a health spa or something?'' she suggested.

''I dunno. But you seemed like a much stronger person. The first time, you'd been so fragile and so scared... Hell, none of the regulars expected to see you come back. You were like a little rabbit, shaking near to death in fear. You never did explain what was eating at you that first time. Later, you kept asking for people to explain how an alcoholic can shake free of the booze. What their friends and family could do to help.''

"Are you sure I wasn't there asking for help for someone else?" Mary Ann asked in consternation.

"Well...if it hadn't been for that first visit, I'd say you might be right. I did wonder if I should send you over to the AlAnon meeting next door...where the family members, spouses and such, share with each other. But I remember that first visit. You looked...well, like you'd had a few the day before. You still looked hungover. Hair kinda unkempt. You looked real thin, like you'd been drinking instead of eating. And you stood up and said you were struggling with a problem and were hoping to find some strength in this program to help you through it."

When he fell silent, the quiet was profound.

"I guess I have a drinking problem, then," Mary Ann said slowly. "What other kind of problem would you drive a couple of hours to an AA meeting in the mountains for?"

Kelton stayed for an hour, but he really had very little more to add. If he'd known he was going to have to remember so much about her, he swore he would have paid much closer attention to everything she'd said and done.

As he left, he handed her a card with his phone number and first name on it. On the reverse he'd written the name and address of the church and the day and time of the AA meetings there.

"Come back and see us when you're better," he said. "And take it one day at a time," he suggested with a wry smile.

"Thanks, Kelton," she said, squeezing his outstretched hand briefly with hers. "Thanks so much for answering that police ad, and for driving down here to see me."

"Others have done much more for me over the years," he replied seriously. "I figured it was my turn to try and do someone else the same kind of good turn. I just hope you find out who you are and where you live. There's something good waiting for you. You just have that kind of air about you."

As if feeling he'd overstepped the bounds by saying that much, he awkwardly turned toward the door. Nodding at Owen and then at her, he hurried away.

She wrapped her arms around her chest and gave Owen an amused look.

"I don't quite know where that leaves me," she admitted with a sigh.

"What do you mean?"

"Well, I still don't know who I am. They...want to discharge me." She took a deep breath. "I'm afraid to look at the hospital bill," she said. She laughed shakily. "I'll probably relapse when I see how much all this cost," she said, waving at the single room and the equipment, most of which had been removed since she was much better.

Owen frowned. "You can't worry about that right now," he urged. "I think the hospital can wait awhile. I doubt that their solvency rests on your writing a check or filling out an insurance form in the next twenty-four hours."

"Maybe not," she said with a shrug. "I hate...not being able to take care of myself." She chewed on her lip. "What kind of job do you suppose I have? I mean...assuming I'm not staying home taking care of a handful of children, I must be working at a job. Even if I am raising kids, I could be holding down a full-time job...."

"And when you remember, you may find that paying the bills won't be a problem," he suggested. "So instead of worrying about that, let's concentrate on figuring out exactly where you were coming from that night. Maybe if you return to some of your old hangouts, you'll recognize something...remember an address...a phone number...a name."

"Or...maybe someone will recognize me," she said thoughtfully.

She raised her eyes to his.

"Maybe," he agreed.

Chapter 6

The hospital social worker had managed to find some clothes for her.

Mary Ann, still uncomfortable with that newly acquired name, was now also uneasy in the ill-fitting, donated clothing she was wearing. In one hand, she carried a paper bag full of her own clothes, still dirty and torn from the accident. In her other hand, she clutched a thick envelope containing the multipage bill for her stay at Cleary Hospital. They had saved her life, for which she was deeply grateful. However, when she saw how much it had cost to care for her, she thought she might spend the rest of that life paying them back for the favor.

"Now I know how a bag lady feels," she murmured to herself. She had no identification, no keys, no decent clothes and no place to go. No job and no immediate prospects for one. "Well...things could be worse," she told herself optimistically. Although right off the top of her head, she couldn't imagine how.

She stood in the hospital foyer, waiting for Owen, who'd promised to drive her back to northern Virginia. Everyone was hoping that familiar surroundings and escape from the hospital atmosphere would facilitate her recovery. Maybe she'd see something that would jog her memory...and then...presumably...everything would be just fine again.

She tried not to put all her hopes on that. The doctors wouldn't predict how long it would take her to regain her memory, although all of them felt that most of her memories probably would return. Eventually.

Eventually. She sighed. What in the devil could she do until then? If her friends and family didn't find her, she'd be on her own. Penniless. Without a roof over her head. The social worker had volunteered to help her find a place to stay and some sort of employment...although the lack of a social security number would be something of a problem. Without that, she wouldn't be able to apply for most jobs, even if they could figure out what kind of work she was capable of doing. Still, the social worker had assured her that anytime she came back to town, social services would try to help her get on her feet.

Mary Ann appreciated that. It seemed odd being on the receiving end of charity, she thought. She wondered if that was a clue to her past. Maybe she had been self-supporting. She liked that idea.

So, maybe people involved with her work would be missing her soon and begin searching for her. Owen had suggested once that she might have been on vacation or something. Perhaps that was why her picture hadn't been circulated on police missing-persons announcements. If so, then maybe that would be changing soon. And someone would see her and recognize her face and show her the poster and tell her who she was and where she belonged.

Owen, as usual, was punctual. When she saw him walk through the revolving doors and into the hospital, she hurried over to him, smiling happily. It felt good to have a friend, even if he was brand-new.

"You look like a new woman," he observed with a slow-dawning grin. He gave her a careful visual examination. "These clothes are fine, but I kind of liked that hospital gown," he con-

fessed. His grin widened, and the gleam in his eye reflected un-
diluted male amusement.

"Oh, sure!" she teased. "I was drop-dead gorgeous in that
pale, shapeless print, with tubes in my arm and bruises and cuts
all over." She brushed her hair away from her face reflexively.
The sarcasm was a good defense for the uneasy feelings swirling
just beneath the surface. Owen Blackhart made her feel glad to
be alive.

He reached out and touched a healing line of puckered red
flesh. Her skin felt warm and smooth beneath his hand.

"You're healing well," he noted.

"You're seeing the wonders of modern medicine...aided
mightily by modern cosmetics."

"Do you have anything else to do here?" he asked, glancing
at the paper bag and the envelope she was holding.

"Nope. Cleary and I have said our goodbyes. And I told them
I'd give them a forwarding address as soon as I had one." She
grimaced at the reminder that she had no home to return to for
now.

"Let's see if we can find some familiar-looking places and
come up with an address for you, Madame X," he suggested.
"My car's just outside." He waved his arm in front of them.
"Shall we go?"

"As fast as possible!"

They left through the same revolving doors that Owen had
entered just moments before.

If she was nervous about riding in a car after the accident, she
hid it well, he thought. She fastened her seat belt and looked
around with curiosity as Owen turned the car out onto the nearest
main road.

"Gosh...it's pretty in the daylight," she murmured.

"Just keep looking," he said. "Yell if you want me to slow
down or stop for anything...to take a closer look at something."

She nodded.

Owen pulled out onto the interstate and headed eastward, toward northern Virginia and Washington, D.C. And, hopefully, toward something memorable.

It was dusk when they finally gave up.

She was discouraged. She'd tried to keep her expectations low, but apparently, they hadn't been modest enough.

"I wish I could have sensed that something...*anything*...was familiar," she said dejectedly.

He parked at a family-style restaurant on the edge of the town.

"How about dinner?" he suggested evenly. "My treat," he added, grinning.

"Well, we certainly wouldn't eat much if it's *my* treat," she said wryly. She looked at him awkwardly. "I...didn't mean to become an appendage," she said apologetically. "Maybe I should go back and take up the offer of help that social worker made."

He got out of the car and came around to her side. She had already gotten out by the time he reached her, but she wore an air of ambivalence.

"Look...I want to keep track of how much this is costing you," she announced firmly. "Later...I'd like to pay you back."

"That's not necessary."

"Yes, it is."

"No, it's not," he said, lips forming a stubborn, straight line.

"It is for me," she argued passionately. "I don't want to be a charity case. Besides..."

"Besides?"

"Well, people will start to talk."

He laughed and opened the restaurant door for her.

"Let 'em talk," he said with a shrug. "Who the hell cares?"

She frowned.

"I'm a gentleman," he explained. "And you're a lady."

"Well, how do we know that?" she said, worrying.

"That I'm a gentleman or that you're a lady?" he asked, a little irritably.

The hostess, who had been staring at them in surprise, cleared her throat.

"Two for dinner?" the hostess inquired diffidently.

"Yes," Owen said.

"No," she interjected, stubbornly standing her ground instead of following the hostess, who was already moving toward the dining room with Owen sailing along in her wake.

Owen turned and stared at her, eyes narrowing. The hostess stopped in midstride, eyebrows raised in delicate question.

"Yes?" the hostess repeated cautiously. "Or no?"

Owen took Mary Ann firmly by the elbow.

"If you want to pay me back for everything I spend on you, go right ahead," he said, more amused than angry at her independence. "But right now, I'm very hungry. I don't handle frustration well when I'm hungry. I suggest we follow this nice lady to a table and feed me before we argue any more."

"Oh. Well, of course, I wouldn't want to fight with a man weakened from starvation," Mary Ann conceded with a distinct air of innocence.

The hostess looked from Owen to Mary Ann, took a breath and turned toward the table she'd had prepared for them.

"This way, then," the hostess said cheerily, as if these little tiffs were the norm at her restaurant. After she'd seated them, she handed them their menus and then indicated the drink list.

"Perhaps you'd like a cocktail? A glass of wine? Or beer?" she suggested hopefully.

"Yes," Mary Ann said, without thinking about it. Then she caught Owen's gaze on hers and she remembered what Kelton had said. "No. An iced tea would be nice. With lemon."

"Ginger ale with a twist of lemon."

"Certainly. Your waiter will be here to take your order in a few minutes. Please enjoy your meal," the hostess said, her tone almost tentative.

Mary Ann leaned across the table and whispered to Owen, "Remember...I'm paying you back...every penny."

He didn't look up from the menu.

"Fine," he growled. "Now...what do you like to eat?"

She looked at the selections, and her mouth began to water in anticipation.

"Everything," she replied.

"Good. I hate women who pick at their food."

She definitely did not do that. An hour and a half later, she was finishing the last of her tea as Owen watched her, impressed with her robust appetite.

"Didn't they feed you at that hospital?"

"Pudding, steamed vegetables, broiled chicken and skim milk just doesn't stick to the ribs."

"Check that hospital bill and make sure they didn't overcharge you for the food," he suggested, grinning wryly.

She laughed. "Good idea!" She sighed contentedly. "Steak."

"What?"

"Sizzling steak smothered in onions with corn chips and salsa."

"What the hell are you talking about? You're not still hungry, are you?"

"No. I just...was thinking this was great, but my favorite foods are spiced with salsas and sautéed on a grill or a griddle...I can smell the garlic and the Worcestershire sauce...taste the fresh peppers...green and red and orange." She snapped out of the reverie and stared at Owen. "I remember them. Eating them. In a restaurant. With a fountain and soft music. Mexican." She pressed her hands against her cheeks. "It must have been in the Southwest someplace...there's cactus and sandy landscapes, and some arid mountains."

"Where?"

She frowned and shook her head. "That's all. Just a glimpse...with the sounds and scents and flavors. It was so real," she said, biting her lip against the disappointment. "I could almost touch it all. Why couldn't the rest come back with it? Why remember that and not my address or phone number or...anyone I knew?"

For a moment they sat in anguished silence together.

"Well, maybe eating's a key. Perhaps every time you eat, you'll awaken some memory."

"Eating in the hospital didn't stir any memories," she answered dubiously.

"Yeah, well, maybe the hospital atmosphere—not to mention their cooking—couldn't awaken a bear in spring. I think there's a café in this town that's got a Hispanic chef. Maybe if he fixes you some of your favorite foods, your senses will reconnect—and your memory along with them."

"I don't know," she said, unpersuaded by the unorthodox theory of stimulating the memory via the stomach. "It sounds ridiculous."

He laughed. "That's what people have said about all the great ideas down through the centuries," he argued. "Now, unless you're still hungry…"

"Oh, no!"

"Let's go then."

Owen paid the bill, and they went outside to the car. Owen had just unlocked the passenger's-side door when a familiar station wagon pulled up beside them.

It was Averson Hemphill.

He waved excitedly at Owen, turned off the engine and hopped out of his car.

"I've been trying to find you, Owen," he exclaimed. "Ah, and this must be Jane D—"

"Mary Ann," Owen interjected firmly. As the two smiled and nodded to each other in greeting, Owen asked, "Is something wrong, Averson?"

"Uh, not yet."

"What does that mean, exactly?" Owen asked, cynically lifting a brow.

"It, uh, means that you may have a somewhat more protracted battle over the house than we'd originally hoped," he said.

The lawyer's demeanor of mild euphoria was deflating into an impending sense of doom.

"Why's that?" Owen asked pointedly.

Averson cleared his throat and glanced at the redheaded woman standing beside Owen.

"Perhaps you could excuse us, ma'am?" Averson said apologetically. He attempted to draw Owen away for a private explanation, but Owen stood his ground.

"Don't worry about her, Averson. She can hear whatever you have to say."

Mary Ann glanced at Owen. He appeared braced for unwelcome news. In spite of that, there was still a faint hint of dark amusement glittering in his eyes. She wanted to thank him for letting her stay, for making her feel included. Being included in his life, even in this unexpected twist of irritating fate, made her feel more normal, oddly enough. He looked down at her, and for a split second, she thought he understood exactly how she felt.

"Thanks," she said softly.

Owen smiled slightly and turned his attention back to Hemphill.

Averson hesitated, obviously uncomfortable discussing his client's potential legal problem in front of a woman neither of them knew well.

Owen's brows straightened. "Well, Averson?" he prompted.

Averson got the message, even if he didn't agree with it.

"All right," he said, injecting a note of forced optimism into his voice. "Portia's nephew is contesting her will. He believes that he by law should have inherited the house and grounds that you are now moving into. He has retained an attorney who is trying to bar you from living in the old house until a court determines whether a significant portion of her estate...including the house and grounds on Algonquin Road...should legally belong to Portia's nephew instead of to you."

"I see." Owen frowned thoughtfully. "Does he have a case?" Owen asked.

Averson hesitated, gathering his words with care.

"I think they can provide sufficient documentation regarding the nephew's relationship to Portia to get a court to consider the evidence. However, I think that eventually we should win."

"But?"

Averson sighed and patted Owen on the arm. "But you never know for sure until you've tried the case and the judge has ruled...or a jury hands down their verdict."

"How would you rate the odds, Averson?" Owen asked dryly.

"I, uh, I'd rather not put a percentage on it," Averson demurred.

Owen laughed. "That's not very encouraging," Owen observed. He shrugged. "I guess it's just as well that I haven't gotten everything unpacked and moved in yet."

Owen looked at Mary Ann. "It looks like you may not be the only person looking for a home," he remarked dryly.

"Then maybe we should keep looking for mine," she suggested hopefully. "Whoever gets a roof first can share with the other."

He gave a short laugh.

"Deal?" She held out her hand.

Owen grinned. "I assume you've now decided that I'm a gentleman and that you're a lady?"

She blinked. "Well...I'll still be keeping track of how much I owe you," she said hastily.

Owen closed his hand over hers just as she began to have second thoughts and withdraw hers.

"Deal," he declared firmly.

Owen briskly released her hand and turned back toward Averson, who was staring at them in surprise.

"You're taking this all, uh, very well," he said.

"Mary Ann doesn't have a whole lot of options. And this isn't the first time that I've had to hustle to put a roof over my head," Owen noted.

"You've had to hustle?" she said faintly.

"Just a figure of speech," Owen explained with an easy grin. "Portia will be so furious with her nephew for thwarting her will that she'll probably come back and haunt him. He may run out of town faster than his lawyer can withdraw the court papers, after Portia's ghost is finished harassing him."

Averson raised his eyebrows, but he couldn't hold back a chuckle.

"Yes," Averson murmured. "She'd have hated having her will overturned. She was a woman who liked to be in charge of her own life."

A woman after her own heart, Mary Ann thought. She wondered exactly what kind of relationship Portia Willowbrook had had with Owen. She must have been older than he was. Still...it could have been a romantic relationship, she supposed.

"What's the matter?" Owen demanded, seeing her expression.

"Nothing!"

"You're frowning."

"Just...indigestion."

Owen obviously didn't accept her excuse, but before he could pursue the matter, Averson spoke.

"Let's discuss the situation the day after tomorrow at my office. I think we can develop an effective strategy for handling this problem. We might even find a way to settle the dispute before it gets before a judge."

Owen agreed.

Averson glanced at his wristwatch. "I've got to pick up the kids!" he exclaimed in agitation. "My wife took them to her mother's house, but I promised I'd pick them up and get them back home by bedtime! That's right now!"

Averson hurriedly said goodbye while hopping into his car. Within moments, he was peeling out of the parking lot and driving away from them, looking much more harried than when he'd arrived a short while earlier.

"I can get you a room in a local motel, or I can take you back to my house and give you a guest room for the night," Owen said.

"I've run up enough bills!" she exclaimed. She laughed nervously. Being practical about the situation, she reasoned, "Why pay for a motel room when I can sleep for free in a guest room?"

"Why indeed?" he murmured. "Well...let's get back to my house, then, while I still have one."

* * *

She was awestruck when she saw it.

"No wonder her nephew's fighting you for the house!"

Owen walked inside, with Mary Ann close on his heels, her green eyes wide and glowing with admiration.

"This stone must be part of the original building," she said, running her hand over the whitewashed wall.

"Yes."

"This must have been built in the early 1800s," she guessed.

"Close—1796. These four walls were the original house. Now they're the living room. The other rooms were added in 1890 and 1925. Portia remodeled and added an addition in the last twenty years."

"She had the workmanship done in a style that nearly duplicates the original."

Owen looked at her curiously. "You seem very familiar with architectural styles," he said.

"Do I?" She looked startled. Didn't everybody notice these kinds of things? she wondered. Apparently not. She looked around the room, littered with large unopened boxes of furniture.

"Are you sure you don't need to unpack anything?" she asked doubtfully.

"I'm sure," he said dryly. "Why unpack before the court decides whether the property is legally mine?"

"What about that old saying...possession being nine-tenths of the law?" she said hopefully.

"I doubt the local judge relies on 'old sayings' in writing his rulings," Owen answered. "And I detest packing. So I'll just leave my things where they are for now." He led her toward the guest room. "However, I did get a few things out...."

There were two bedrooms, both with beds. One bed was made, and there were towels hung in the adjoining bathroom. That was Owen's master suite. He grabbed an extra set of towels out of an open box and carried them into the guest room.

"I'll find you some sheets and a blanket," he said. He grinned. "This may not provide the level of service you're used to from Cleary Hospital, but sheets and blankets I have."

She wrinkled her nose.

"They were wonderful to me," she said. "But this is a big improvement. No antiseptic smells. No people asking me questions all day. No waking up every few hours to be turned, poked, examined or discussed..." She shook her head and sighed. "As an innkeeper, Mr. Blackhart, you beat the hospital's facility ten ways to Tuesday."

He grinned and went looking for sheets and a blanket.

"I need to get back on my feet," she murmured to herself. "And for that, I'll need money."

When Owen returned with the linens, they briskly made up the bed for her to sleep in that night.

"Do you happen to have a newspaper, Owen?"

He stared at her, startled by the unexpected question.

"Probably. A local one."

"Great! Could I read it?"

"Sure." He frowned a little but he headed toward the living room.

She followed close at his heels.

He reached behind a stack of boxes and plucked the day's paper off the top of a pile of clothes waiting to be taken to the laundry.

"Here it is," he said. He sat on the corner of one large, heavy box and watched her with frank interest.

She flipped through the pages until she reached the Help Wanted ads in the Classified section.

"Reading the Personals?" he teased.

"The...?" She blinked and looked at the Personal columns. "'Single man seeks single woman for companionship and exercise. Free between twelve and two every other Wednesday,'" she read. She burst out laughing. "Why, he's an out-of-towner looking for a no-strings-attached... Er, I don't know if you can even call it an affair!" she exclaimed.

Owen grinned at her outrage.

"I guess you aren't checking out the Personals, then."

"The Impersonals would be a better description of it," she

said. She bent her head down over the paper, searching for the employment ads, which she'd lost in the sea of one-inch ads of the lovelorn seeking companionship.

"At least he's up front about it," Owen remarked.

She glared at him and harrumphed her sense of contempt.

"Some of the others promise idyllic relationships, but they're just trying to bait the hook. Once they've caught the attention of a likely little fish, they try for seduction. And that's usually followed by abandonment not long after."

She blinked and looked at him. "Did that happen to someone you know?" she asked uncertainly.

"Yeah."

"I'm sorry."

"So's she." He shrugged. "She survived. She was a lucky one."

"Well...I'm not looking for social companionship," she assured him.

He laughed cynically. "Neither are those guys," he observed.

"Well I'm not hunting for a mate, either," she said, becoming a little cross. "After all, I may already have a mate...or a serious relationship...or something."

He nodded. "You're an attractive woman," he observed dispassionately. "It seems logical to assume you've got a man in your life...."

Their eyes met.

That warmth slid over her skin again. As it had before. Her cheeks reddened and she swallowed hard. How could she feel this attracted to Owen Blackhart if she had a man in her life already? she wondered. She just didn't believe that was possible. She didn't know a thing about herself, of course. And she wanted to believe that she was free. Unencumbered by a "significant other."

"If there is a man in my life, why isn't he shouting from the rooftops that I'm missing?" she asked irritably.

"Good question."

Owen kept the potential answers to himself for the time being.

If she hadn't thought of them, he wasn't about to rush her into that unhappy list of possibilities. He glanced at the newspaper she was studying with such intense interest.

"So, you're not reading the Personals," he mused. "You don't have any money, so it's safe to assume you're not looking for antique auctions or special sales ads. That leaves...the Want ads?"

He raised his brow questioningly.

"Don't sound so pleased with your powers of deduction," she declared, amused. "You can see very well that's what I'm reading."

"You don't have to pay me back tomorrow," he stated.

"I know. But I'd like to have my own money...even if it's just a little. I don't think I was cut out to be a career deadbeat."

He laughed. "Find anything?" he asked curiously.

She frowned and chewed on her lower lip thoughtfully. "I don't know. I'm sure I can do a lot of things, but who'd hire me? I have no customary identification, no permanent address, no social security card, no references, no work history, no educational transcripts...." She stopped in exasperation.

"That doesn't sound insurmountable to me," he said with a shrug.

"Really?" she said dubiously.

"Really. First thing tomorrow morning, I'll take you to breakfast at Rafael's Café. While you're rolling salsa and Mexicali eggs over your tongue, we'll see what kind of nickel-and-dime work there is in this two-bit town." He grinned at her expression of astonishment. "Hey...lots of people pick up work without papers. If you really want to do it..."

"I do!" she exclaimed.

He grinned. Her skin kind of glowed when she was agitated, he realized. And a soft sheen of moisture glistened here and there on her. He had the almost unbearable urge to press his mouth against that smooth, salty flesh...to kiss the silky skin.

She wondered why he was looking at her like that. But almost as soon as she noticed the look in his eyes, it dawned on her what the expression might mean. And it made her feel very strange indeed. Her breath caught in her throat. Her heart beat in a painfully noticeable way. And she was momentarily bereft of the power of speech.

"I...do...." she managed to repeat, although it took a concentrated effort. "The sooner I'm earning money, the sooner I can support myself. And maybe I'll remember who I am and be able to go back. Maybe doing things...little tasks—will jog my memory."

"Like sensory stimulation did this evening?"

"Mm-hmm." The sensory stimulation that she visualized had nothing to do with the events earlier in the evening. She swallowed hard and stretched over her face what she fervently hoped was a harmless smile.

"Would you like to listen to some music as you fall asleep?" he asked softly.

She stared at him, feeling hypnotized by his voice...that familiar, that so very trusted voice.

"Uh-huh..." she replied.

"I'll put on a CD...."

"That's...great...."

He watched her head off for her bedroom.

And he began to wonder if perhaps he should have taken her someplace else to spend the night after all.

He'd spent so much time worrying what would become of her, it had never occurred to him to worry about what might happen to him.

Owen swore softly under his breath.

He was experienced enough to handle this, he told himself bluntly.

He put on the CD, and he fell asleep to the soulful strains of a New Orleans jazz group.

It felt as hot as the Louisiana delta all night.

Chapter 7

Mouth-watering aromas wafted a delicious welcome over Owen and his green-eyed lady as they entered Rafael's Café for breakfast the following morning.

The uncertain woman at his side surveyed the intimate little restaurant as they walked to a corner table. It was framed by windows on the connecting walls. The sunshine was streaming in invitingly.

A smiling, dark-haired woman wearing a colorful red cotton skirt and a lacy white blouse brought a steaming pot and a pair of gaily painted mugs to their table.

"What can I fix for you this morning?" she asked, smiling at them warmly, and handing them each a well-worn menu.

A half hour later, they were sipping hot coffee and forking delicious *huevos rancheros* into their mouths.

"Taste familiar?" Owen asked her in amusement.

"Mm-hmm," she said, loving the familiar blend of tomato sauce, spices and cheese. "Mmm..."

"Shut your eyes."

"What?"

"It may help you visualize the memories associated with those flavors," he explained. He speared some of the fresh fruit on his plate and popped it into his mouth.

She took another mouthful of the tasty main dish and closed her eyes.

"Relax," he said quietly. "Just taste the flavors...smell the spices...hear the sounds...."

In the background, she was vaguely aware of some lively Mexican music. Energetic violins. A vibrant, mournful trumpet. A man's tenor voice. A deep-voiced guitar.

Then Rafael's Café receded, and instead she began to see tiles. Hand-painted tiles.

With blue borders and dark red designs amid splashes of rich yellows and delicate dabs of green.

There were tiles along parts of the walls. And along the border of a pool. And brick to walk on. A brick-tiled patio. Her mind expanded the view, and she saw a familiar adobe house. With red dirt around it. And cactus. And mountains nearby. A road. With an occasional car. A view of a desert. And in the distance...scrubby trees along a nearly dry riverbed. And a small town. No...not so small. Just in the distance...so it looked not so very big. There were paints...and charcoal...the kind an artist used to draw with...and a potter's wheel. And pots, lined up to go into a kiln. Ready to be glazed.

She froze. Her throat felt paralyzed. She couldn't swallow the food in her mouth. With an effort, she forced herself to remember how, and finished eating what she'd already half begun chewing.

She frowned, and she listened hard. There was a distant voice. Coming closer. A woman's voice. Speaking to her on a phone. She was hearing a woman whose voice was very familiar, and yet, she couldn't quite make out what was being said. Or clearly visualize the face of the woman speaking to her.

Her body stiffened with the effort to break through the unwelcome barrier encasing her mind. The memories were all there...so very near.... She could almost grasp them.... Almost...

"...help me... I can't trust anyone else... Please!...I beg of you..." the voice said. It was a woman's voice, brittle with anxiety and shaking in panic. A little slurred. Thoroughly drenched in fear. "Mariana..."

Her eyes flew open then, and she gasped. She felt as if someone had just punched her in the stomach. But instead of seeing stars, the light came on brightly in the depths of her mind, and a name burst forth that had been hidden from her. *Mariana.*

"Of course," she murmured, deeply shaken. "How could I have forgotten?"

She blinked, and Owen's face came into focus. He was staring at her through narrowed eyes. Like a cat watching its prey, he watched her. Waiting for her to speak.

"What did you remember?"

"My name is Mariana," she whispered. Then, more firmly, with an edge of triumph in her voice and the beginnings of a smile on her lips, she repeated it. "My name is Mariana. Mariana! That's why 'Mary Ann' didn't quite seem right. It's close. But it's *not* my name."

He nodded slowly. "You don't seem...completely happy to have remembered that," he said slowly.

"Something is very wrong. Somewhere a woman is in mortal danger. She's connected to me. She's...a part of me.... I remembered a sliver of a phone call...." She shivered. She wasn't sure why. It wasn't that cold in the café. "It's still coming back to me in broken shards. In bits and pieces. It's very frustrating," she muttered.

Owen poured her some more coffee.

"Hold the mug," he suggested. "It'll warm you up. And a drink of the coffee...black, no sugar...will help put some steel rods in your spine."

She lifted the mug and took a bracing swallow.

"I hate it like this," she said, shuddering at the bitter taste. "I'm strictly a café-au-lait woman," she admitted ruefully.

"This situation isn't for Milquetoasts," he said with a shrug. "There's nothing you can do but try to remember the facts...and then face them."

"Easy for you to say!" she exclaimed, outraged by his cavalier attitude.

He grinned unrepentantly. "Yes. It is. But it's still the truth, and you damn well know it—" he hesitated, "—Mariana."

Her name rolled off his tongue like a warm caress.

Their eyes met, and she felt as if he were putting his arms around her and pulling her close. Her gaze dropped to his mouth. Her throat felt like cotton, and she looked at her mug in panic.

She shakily raised it to her lips and drank more of the bitter brew.

"It does stiffen the spine," she conceded with a grimace.

"Tell me what else you remembered," he said grittily.

"I live in the Southwest somewhere. In a kind of rustic, adobe house...with tile inlaid in the walls and a view of the desert, the mountains and a fair-sized city. There were artist's tools around...and I felt like they belonged in my hands."

"So you think you're an artist?"

"Yes."

"And...the woman in the phone call...who is she?"

"Someone very close to me. She sounds like me.... Except, she's scared to death." Mariana paused and frowned. "When I was knocked down that mountainside and lost my memory, I had some dreams...or maybe they were memories trying to surface in dreams. I remember seeing a face. The face of a man. I was afraid of him. He radiated evil...and danger."

Mariana paused, trying desperately to recall what she could of that threatening, hovering face. His eyes were the features she most clearly could conjure up in her mind. Especially the cold, ruthless expression in them. And the shape of his mouth...thin and hard...and a small scar along his jaw, just a threadlike trail of white.

"Could you sketch him?" Owen asked abruptly.

She looked at Owen in surprise. Thought about it. And grinned.

"Maybe. I think maybe I could."

"Let's get you something to draw with and find out."

Appreciatively she inhaled the warm, inviting aromas clinging to the café air as Owen paid the bill.

"I'd like to come back," she murmured wistfully. "Do you suppose Rafael could use a good dishwasher? I wouldn't mind a temporary job here."

Owen laughed and opened the restaurant door for her.

"We'll call him later, if we still need to. At the rate you're going, you may remember everything and be on your way home by dinner."

She gave Owen a dubious look and laughed uneasily. She couldn't shake the feeling that she, too, was in danger, just like the woman on the phone. For some reason, home didn't seem like a safe place to be right now. Wherever home was.

"Where are we going?" she asked.

"To pay a call on Seymour Rushville. I saw some sketch pads and artist's pencils by his cash register when I was in his bookstore. The store's just down the street."

"Good. I need a walk after that breakfast!" she exclaimed. She linked her arm through his and strode alongside him.

He glanced at her in surprise. When their eyes had met a little earlier, he had felt the small jolt that she had. He'd known why she quickly looked away, frowning at her coffee cup intently while a soft rose color brushed across her cheekbones.

And yet, here they were, walking side by side. Arm in arm. And she was smiling and looking around, more relaxed than he'd ever seen her.

"Mariana," he murmured softly.

"Hmm?" She looked up at him. Her dark green eyes were open and unguarded.

"Just...Mariana," he said. A crooked grin softened his serious expression. "It fits you."

"You have no idea what a relief it is to know my own name," she confessed. "Such a small thing...just a word...but without it, I felt like I didn't really exist...like I was a mannequin in a store window, not a real person."

"I guarantee you, Mariana, that you are a living, breathing, red-blooded person.'' He grinned and looked her over. "Female person.''

She laughed. She was glad he'd noticed that. It might be unwise to feel that way, since they were spending so much time together, and she still had no place to stay, really. Still...it was wonderful to see that admiration in his eyes. Maybe he'd open the shutters and let her see it again, Mariana thought a little wistfully.

Owen told himself he should unlink their arms and put a little distance between them. Physical distance. He should. He inhaled, and the soft scent of her hair filled his nostrils.

He tightened his hold on her arm.

"Watch your step,'' he said gruffly.

She took a long stride over the crumbling curb and continued with him across the street.

He forgot about letting go of her. Hell. He liked her arm where it was, damn it. He liked the feel of her body close to his. The occasional light brush of her hip against his as they walked on the uneven pavement. The scent of her skin and her hair swirling and teasing his senses as the light breeze washed across her and over him.

Somewhere in the depths of him, something stirred. Something very ancient and very male. Something familiar. That he'd felt before. More than once. And yet...this time, it was different.

It wasn't just the first curls of sexual desire emerging from the depths of him, encouraging him to pursue the woman at his side. There was a tenderness mixed in this soft, burning sensation. And an uneasiness...that she might leave a mark on him...a deep, wounding reminder of her presence in his life. Pain and pleasure were a lot alike sometimes, he thought grimly. They could be hard to tell apart, until it was too late.

Owen quickened his pace.

"Are we late or something?'' Mariana asked, stumbling to keep up with him.

"No.''

"You just don't like leisurely walks?''

"Right.''

She glanced at him, her brow furrowing pensively. "You wouldn't be nervous by any chance?" she suggested slyly.

"Nervous?" he exclaimed in surprise. Then he caught a good look at her expression. His jaw tightened. "Don't be ridiculous. I was chasing women when you were still in high-school health classes."

"My, my," she murmured. "Don't get touchy, now."

"I'm not touchy," he growled.

She patted him on the arm understandingly. "Of course you're not," she said soothingly.

He frowned at her, but it had no effect at all on her serene smile. Which only made him feel more off balance than ever. Damn her, anyway. He was relieved to arrive at The Well-Read Book shop.

He briskly untangled their arms and opened the door for her, pointedly allowing her to step inside ahead of him and begin looking over the interior before following himself.

"Seymour, I've brought you a new customer," Owen drawled.

The bookstore owner looked up from the cash register, and Owen proceeded with the introductions.

"Seymour Rushville, meet Mariana."

The bookman smiled broadly and stretched out his chubby hand. "Ahh...this *is* a pleasure! We've worried about you a lot, you know. Everyone's been hoping you'd recover. From the triumphant note I heard in that introduction, you really *have* remembered your name, haven't you?" he guessed slyly.

"I certainly have," she exclaimed with relief. "At least...the first name."

"You're halfway there, then!" Seymour declared with hearty enthusiasm. "Mariana," he said, listening to the sound of her name as it rolled off his tongue. "What a lovely, lilting name. Don't mind me." He chuckled. "I'm a word lover. I even get a little carried away with the sound of them, on special occasions."

Mariana laughed. They were still shaking hands. Seymour Rushville seemed like a favorite uncle she'd never met until today. She wondered if he had this effect on everyone.

"You certainly know how to make someone feel at home, Mr. Rushville," she said honestly.

"Call me Seymour," he boomed with a hearty laugh. "Only the tax collector and telephone salesmen call me Mr. Rushville!"

They all laughed. Owen leaned against the counter and watched Mariana warm to her new friend. Knowing her own name was giving her confidence. It showed in the steadiness of her gaze. She used to look doubtful about almost everything. Uncertain. A little afraid. But now, all that was receding. Not completely gone yet. But going fast. He wondered what she would remember next. What impact would it have on their relationship? What if there was a man in her life? A husband? Or a lover. A serious boyfriend or something?

Owen's smile began to fade.

Maybe regaining her memory would end their acquaintance.

He shouldn't object to that. He'd been reluctant to get involved. Reluctant to stay involved. And yet...

He found the thought of a significant man in her life to be...irritating.

"Is something wrong, Owen?" Seymour asked. He'd been talking with Mariana and had glanced at Owen only to see the peculiar dark expression settling on his face.

Owen straightened his expression into courteous neutrality.

"No. Nothing's wrong, Seymour. Say, we came in to look for some drawing materials. Didn't I see some sketch pads and charcoal or pastels around here the last time I was in the store?"

Mariana, who'd been staring at Owen in surprise, was distracted by Seymour's booming reply.

"Yes, indeed you did! Right over there. Come Mariana...I'll show you. Do you draw?" he asked with interest.

"I think so," she said gamely. "We'll soon find out, I guess."

Seymour chuckled and stopped in front of the stack of art supplies. "Well, *Mademoiselle Artiste,* select what you will. It's on the house. In honor of your miraculous recovery."

Mariana looked at him in surprise. She hadn't expected the

bookstore owner to give her the things. She reached out and squeezed his hand in genuine thanks.

"Someday, I'll return your kindness, Seymour," she vowed sincerely. "You don't know how much this means to me."

He chuckled and gave her that same avuncular smile.

"Is that everything you'll need?" Owen asked.

Mariana looked over the art supplies in her arms and nodded.

"If I can't draw that man's face, I won't be able to blame it on the pastels," she said with a grin.

"Draw what man's face?" Seymour asked, his curiosity aroused.

"Someone she's dreamed about but can't remember," Owen said.

"Hmm. Well, show me the sketch," Seymour said jovially. "If I've ever seen him, I'll remember his name. I was always good with names."

"I wish I could say the same," Mariana said with a rueful sigh.

"It'll all come back to you, hon," Seymour said reassuringly. He patted her on the shoulder. "You just stick with Owen, here. He seems to be on the right track. Whatever he's doing, it's helping get your memory back."

Mariana looked into Owen's eyes. That strange sensation of being connected to him rippled through her heart like a warm embrace.

"I don't know what would have become of me, if it hadn't been for Owen," she said softly.

The emotion in her voice threw Owen off balance for a moment. She still was very vulnerable, he realized. And she trusted him. Implicitly. And he...he was attracted to her in a way that he had never been attracted to another woman in his entire life. It was as if they had already known one another, in some other time or place. This was just the reawakening of some deeply intense and eternal link connecting them. He knew then he didn't want another man to be involved with her. Not in any way at all. It was irrational. He must be crazy, he thought. But...that was exactly how he felt.

He reached out and touched her cheek. They had been looking into one another's eyes for longer than was seemly for mere friends.

Several other people were entering the store, murmuring and browsing and heading back into the store, passing Owen and Mariana.

Mariana dragged her gaze away from Owen. She smiled at the newcomers as she sidestepped by them, gingerly clutching the art supplies to her bosom.

The curious smiles told her everything. They knew who she was. They were wishing her well.

She smiled back and hurried toward the door.

"Let's go home and draw," she suggested.

"Home?" Owen said, surprised to hear her put it that way.

"Your home is my home for now. Isn't that what you said?"

"That's what I said," he admitted. He followed her out of the store. "See you, Seymour," he said as they left.

"I hope so!" Seymour said, chuckling.

"Seymour?" called out a bewildered voice from inside the bookstore. "Where *are* you?"

"Coming! I'm coming," Seymour shouted back. He turned back into the bookstore to socialize with his other customers.

"That's it!"

Owen walked over to Mariana and looked over her shoulder at the sketch. She'd been working on it for about forty-five minutes. At first, she'd sketched quickly, trying to capture some inner vision. Then her hand had slowed on the page. Shading a little beneath the image of a cheekbone. Darkening the eyes. Shaping the ragged brows.

"I think that's him," she said.

Owen frowned thoughtfully. It was a very specific likeness. Someone ought to recognize the man from this sketch.

"What's the matter?" she asked, her smile fading.

Owen stood up and paced across the room. He stared out the large panels of glass that enclosed the summer deck. Beyond it everything seemed tranquil. Ducks paddled calmly across the pond. The year-round resident Canada geese walked across the stubbly winter grass, picking leisurely snacks.

"Owen?" She got up and came to join him. She held the picture in her hand. Her face was now clouded with doubt. "I thought you wanted to see his face. Didn't we agree this was a step in the right direction? I mean, if I could visualize anyone else, I'd be happy to draw them. But this man is the one seared into my memory so deeply that I can get to his image. If we find him, it'll be a lead. It has to be a lead!"

He nodded and looked at her seriously. "A dangerous lead."

She nodded. "Perhaps. If my feelings are right about him, he is very dangerous."

"It won't be easy to identify him without revealing that you are alive."

"If he reads the paper, he already knows that," she argued.

"And if he doesn't read the newspapers...the ones where your photograph has been flashed for weeks...what does he think?"

"Well...who knows? I mean...maybe he doesn't know where I am. Maybe he thinks I'm on a long vacation or missing or hiding out or something." She began to feel exasperated. "You're not suggesting we keep this to ourselves, are you?" she demanded, astonished at the possibility that he was doing just that. "Owen? What's come over you?"

Owen frowned. "Nothing's come over me," he said curtly. "I'm thinking ahead. I'm trying to figure out how we can use this information and keep you safely stashed out of sight."

"Well...so far I've been okay. I could stay—" She was about to motion around the room, indicating Owen's house, but stopped just in time.

"Exactly. You may not be able to stay here, if that court decides to lock me out until the judge has heard the case. Besides, the news media are likely to be crawling around here, once they get wind of the lawsuit. I'm surprised they haven't showed up already."

"Well, the local paper doesn't have a big circulation, surely," Mariana argued.

"I'm talking about the *Washington Post* and the *New York Times* and the *Chicago Tribune*...for starters."

Mariana's jaw dropped in amazement.

"Are you famous?" she asked in astonishment.

"Infamous, my dear, but not, alas, famous," he replied with a grim smile. "Portia Willowbrook, however, was famous. She was well-known in art and cultural circles in several major cities. She kept homes or apartments in three of them for years. It was only in the last years of her life that she drew back, made New York her principal residence." He looked at the landscape again and smiled a little. "But this is where her heart was, I think. Although Portia loved to pretend to people that she didn't have that particular organ in her body."

"I'm sorry I'll never meet her," Mariana said softly. "She sounds like a very unique person."

"She was."

"Someone who meant a lot to you."

"Yes."

"And you must have meant a very great deal to her, since she left this home and land to you," Mariana added, a note of tenderness in her voice.

Owen shoved his hands in his pockets and stubbornly stared out into the landscape beyond.

"Why don't you tell me about her?" Mariana suggested, trying to keep the request casual sounding, hoping Owen would let down some of his armor and let her inside his heart for a little while.

He glanced at her, considering the request.

"At least you *can* remember, Owen. I've shared every memory I've recaptured with you. Would it be so hard to share this one with me?"

He sighed. "You know how to get through, don't you?" he muttered.

"I'm trying," she conceded with an honest smile.

"All right. But it'll take some time. Why don't we go into the living room and sit down on the sofa while it's still ours to use."

When they got there, Mariana curled up on one corner, facing him. Owen stretched out his legs and tried to figure out how to tell her about Portia.

"I had a short childhood," he said. His brief grin was bitter. "My mother died in a neighborhood drive-by shooting, before it became an everyday occurrence. My father decided to take my brother and sister and me to live in the countryside in New York State. It was supposed to be safer. So he thought."

Mariana had a sinking feeling in her heart.

"He discovered that his employment skills weren't in big demand in the little town he'd run to. Within a year, his savings were depleted, my sister ran off with the town's one and only bad boy and my brother was shot dead in a hunting accident."

"Owen! How awful, for all of you."

Owen shrugged. "I kind of liked some of the people there, personally. Especially the local sheriff. My high-school basketball coach. And an English teacher that all the boys were dying to get their senior year."

She was an attractive, well-educated, world-traveled woman. A widow. No children. She'd come back to her late husband's hometown to help care for his parents. But they chose to move south to Florida, into some retirement home, near a niece. So, she put her house on the market and made plans to move out of town, too."

Mariana, riveted by his tale, now began to frown a little.

"You're wondering what this has to do with Portia, I suppose?" He grinned, a little crookedly, and the boyish look of his youth could almost be seen in his face again.

"Right."

"Well, when that lady needed help moving, I volunteered...along with the entire male population of the high school. And she moved into New York City...around the block from..."

He raised his eyebrows expectantly and nodded for Mariana to finish the sentence.

"Portia!"

"Yes. My teacher had been coming to New York City whenever she could get away...on vacations, mostly...trying to find a job there. Not teaching. She wanted to get into international trade, import-export, art...something like that. And she met Portia during a job interview. A friend of Portia's was looking for an assistant in his art gallery. Well, my pretty English teacher had a lot of talents, but alas, not the skills needed for the art gallery assistant's job."

"But Portia Willowbrook took an interest in her," Mariana guessed.

"She did. Portia was like that. If someone interested her, she'd take them under her wing, help them out, steer them along in directions she felt would benefit them."

"A fairy godmother?"

Owen roared in laughter and shook his head. "More like a devilish mentor, I'm afraid. She always made clear she expected a return on her investments in people. She offered a low rent on an apartment she owned to my gorgeous English teacher. And she hired her as her own personal secretary."

"Wow."

"Yeah. The previous secretary had burned out under the exhausting life Portia led. But for a widow who wanted to start a new life in New York City, it was a great deal. So, she took it."

"And did Portia decide to take you on as an apprentice of some sort?" Mariana teased.

"Not right away." Owen's amusement faded. "The life that my English teacher was running away to seemed exotic and exciting to me. I'd lived in cities, but none to compare with New York. I couldn't wait to graduate from high school. I told my teacher to keep her eyes open for jobs in the neighborhood, and to pass them my way. She wrote to me a couple of times afterward. But she kept telling me to go to college." Owen snorted. "College! I was going to be lucky to keep from being thrown out onto the street. My father's fortunes had not improved. My sister had married the jerk she'd run off with and had gotten herself pregnant to boot. Every dime my dad had, he gave to her, trying to get her prenatal care and decent meals.''

"Facing that many problems when you're so young must have been excruciating,'' Mariana murmured, her brow furrowed with worry.

"Yes. But then I met Portia.'' Owen grinned, recalling how it happened.

"You can't leave me dangling, now, Owen Blackhart!'' Mariana exclaimed with outraged amusement as he fell silent. "How did you meet her?''

Chapter 8

"My English teacher became very insistent that I apply to some colleges in New York. She said I had potential." Owen raised his brows in male amusement. "That's what the teachers said when they were feeling frustrated by the way a kid repeatedly shrugged off opportunities. At the time, though, I was flattered that she'd bother to encourage me. I figured maybe she was right. Maybe I did have *potential*."

"What did you do?" Mariana asked curiously.

"I listened. And I did what she asked. I went to a library and dug out some information about colleges. I talked to her about a few of them. She rolled up her crisp, frilly sleeves and helped organize everything and fill out the forms. I kept studying her motives, of course."

"Of course," Mariana murmured, stifling tender laughter.

"I kind of begrudgingly filled out the forms and sent them back to her, in the stamped envelopes she'd mailed to me. She thought of everything, that lady did."

"She sounds very thorough. And conscientious," Mariana murmured.

"She thought like an English teacher," Owen remarked dryly. "She was organized. Punctual. Detail oriented. A very fastidious woman. And determined to have her way. Well, I figured that I had nothing to lose by humoring her. Maybe if college didn't work out, she'd help me find a job somewhere. Anywhere. I knew I didn't want to stay in that damn backwater town after I graduated."

He hesitated, surprised at the strength of his own feelings. Hell. He'd put this behind him years ago. He glanced at Mariana. He couldn't remember ever telling anyone this before.

"What?" she asked, staring at him blankly. "What's the matter? You look...like you don't want to talk about it any more." She couldn't keep the disappointment from her voice.

"It's...a new experience," he muttered. Her dark green eyes were pools of rich color. Darker now, because she was feeling some strong emotion. He wondered which one. His whole body tightened. He shouldn't open up his life to her, he thought. If he were thinking clearly, like he normally did, he'd cut off the flow of information about himself right now. Divert her attention to something else.

"Owen?" she whispered, reaching out and laying her hand on his. "I really want to know you better. I know it's..." She hesitated. Color washed across her cheeks. She swallowed a little nervously. "I know you're going out of your way to look after me and I don't want to take advantage of that...."

He frowned thoughtfully. "You're not taking advantage of me," he growled.

"I just, well, I'd like to hear about your life." She laughed, a soft, hesitant, embarrassed laugh. "You're the only friend I have. And I don't know a thing about you."

He expelled a breath and pressed his lips together. This probably was not a good idea, he told himself. But he couldn't refuse her. It was that look in her face when she pleaded. A woman as attractive as Mariana could not have escaped the notice of his sex. Why the hell wasn't some man raising a storm of inquiry looking for her? Owen knew he would. He reluctantly picked up the thread of his story where he'd left off.

"I went along with her plans, not really expecting anything to come of it. She sent in the applications to the schools after she got them from me, filled out." Owen grinned wryly. "You can't imagine how shocked I was when acceptance letters started showing up in my mailbox! Just when I got over that, I got a letter from a foundation saying that I qualified for a special full scholarship...if I was willing to agree to the obligations attached to it."

"What obligations?" Mariana asked, fascinated.

"That all my weekends and holidays would be spent working in the employ of Miss Portia Willowbrook. Whatever tasks she gave to me, I had to perform. It was stated in writing that nothing illegal would ever be required of me, but that's all. It was a blank check. My education in exchange for being Portia's all-purpose employee."

"Portia had a foundation?"

"She had just set it up. She used it for a variety of educational and charitable purposes, including sending a couple of other young people on to higher education."

"She must have been very wealthy," Mariana observed, as the magnitude of the money involved began to add up.

"She inherited quite a bit from her grandmother, but she invested it well from the time she was a student at Bryn Mawr. Most of the money that she had by the time she died had been earned through her own canny instincts."

"You really admired her, didn't you?" Mariana said softly.

"Yes. She could be stubborn and opinionated, but she was one hell of a great woman." He half smiled, remembering Portia.

"I assume you accepted the deal that she offered? I mean...you look like you've left that starving teenage boy behind long ago."

Owen nodded pensively. "Yeah. I was a little annoyed, though. I was rebellious and independent, or so I thought. I didn't like the idea of being bought like a slave at auction, being an indentured servant of some sort serving the whims of some old high-society lady for five years.''

"Five?"

"Yeah. I had to agree to spend one year and a day in her employ after graduation. I wasn't sure what she was going to get out of it that could possibly be worth a four-year education. I kept looking for the string...the catch."

"Was there a catch, then?" Mariana asked, a hint of concern flickering in her expression.

"Yes. But I didn't see it until years later. I got my education. And I worked my butt off for Portia Willowbrook. I carried furniture. I cleaned bathrooms. I was her delivery boy, her errand man. If Portia needed something picked up at midnight for a Saturday brunch, I hauled my butt out of bed and took the subway across town to fetch it for her on time. That woman got her money's worth out of me, all right,'' he said with an admiring laugh. "At the rates people charge in New York for all that personal service, I was a bargain. I was a doorman when she felt like putting on airs. I was a gardener when she decided to replant the postage-stamp garden behind her brownstone house."

"You learned a lot of trades,'' Mariana observed ruefully.

"True. I learned to work hard. To be dependable. And how to deal with any level of society that crossed her front door."

Owen stopped for a long moment, remembering. "I learned manners from her. Serving her guests seemed like an insult to me at the time, but after a while, I realized I'd learned all the arbitrary rules of etiquette while filling all those crystal goblets with ice water. When she had her literary friends come by for wine and cheese, I met the people that my university professors were talking about with such excitement in their seminars. Actually, I think the education I got directly from Portia was almost as valuable as the one she paid for at the university."

"So, eventually you graduated?"

"Yes.'' He grinned wryly. "With a degree in history and minors in archaeology and criminal justice."

"And paid back the five-year commitment?"

"Yes." He gave a short, humorless laugh. "With pleasure. There wasn't much of a demand for my particular credentials. History majors were a dime a dozen, a fact I had chosen to ignore for four years. In the eclectic company that Portia Willowbrook kept, pursuing your own interests had seemed reasonable."

"But you kept in touch with Portia, after the fifth year," she prompted.

Owen lifted his brows. "Portia wasn't about to cut loose her investment." Owen's mouth twisted in a smile that looked more rueful than amused.

Mariana looked at him curiously. "Are you certain that Portia thought of you as...an investment?" she asked hesitantly.

"I'm certain." He shrugged philosophically. "She'd be incensed to hear it described that ruthlessly," he conceded. "In her own way, she came to think of me as a member of her extended family. But she always felt that I owed her. And that she could call in the favors when she needed them." He glanced at Mariana. "And I did owe her," he said firmly. "She'd opened doors for me that I was only too happy to walk through. I was happy to pay her back. Any way she wanted it." His eyes darkened, however, recalling the final price he'd had to pay.

Mariana wondered what dark memories were suddenly silencing him. From the way he'd fallen silent, it was obvious he wasn't inviting her into that part of his life. Not yet, anyway, she thought.

She cast about, trying to pick up the thread of their conversation again.

"But she left you this house, Owen. Doesn't that seem more like something she'd have done for...a son?" Mariana asked with innocent curiosity.

Owen blinked, then turned to stare at Mariana. Their eyes held the gaze for a long, intimate moment. He was tempted to tell her the rest, he realized. That surprised him. That surprised him a very great deal. He shoved the impulse away and concentrated on answering the question she'd asked.

"Eventually, I was as close to a son as she had, I suppose," he conceded. "But all those years that I worked for her, I felt

more like a trusted, increasingly relied-upon junior business partner. I was a known commodity. She knew she could count on
me. She could assign me any task she liked," he said at length.
"And I would do it."

"And that was all right with you?" Mariana asked, sensing his
conflicting feelings yet unsure what the conflict was about.

"Most of the time. Portia was usually frank and aboveboard
about her plans for people. When she wanted me to do something,
she came directly to me and stated it in plain English. If I wasn't
interested in going along with it, she let it go."

"She was *usually* frank and aboveboard?" she echoed cautiously.

Owen frowned. Mariana was an astute listener, he realized. She
was hearing things he was leaving intentionally unsaid. It was
like she was attuned to him and sensed what he meant whether
he actually said it or not. He felt an unfamiliar surge of self-
recrimination. He didn't normally let people see into his soul like
this. What the hell was happening to his defenses? he wondered.
If only he could lay to rest that old bitter memory, he thought.
Damn Portia and her matchmaking plot. If he kept talking, Mariana would instinctively ferret it out of him.

Mariana watched his face darken and his lips tighten into a flat,
thin, angry line. What terrible memory brought that unhappy
shadow across his expression? Did it involve a woman? Someone
other than Portia Willowbrook? Mariana felt the burning of jealousy in her heart and was startled into silence. She told herself
that she had no right to feel upset about some unhappy love affair,
if that was what made him look so distant and morose all of a
sudden. Still...

"Did you stay in New York, then?" she asked casually, picking absentmindedly at the sleeve of her shirt.

"Some of the time. I'd met a lot of people in a lot of different
businesses while I lived in Portia's home in New York. One of
them was a private investigator who specialized in insurance
fraud. He had more work than he could handle. So, I hired on. I
had to travel a lot for the first six years. That's when Portia be-

came more like a friend than a benefactress." Right up until she started playing matchmaker, he thought. "I'd drop into her soirees and salons when I was in town. She enjoyed hearing what I was doing. And introducing her newest pet projects."

"Portia never had any children, then?" Mariana guessed.

"No." Just protégés, he thought grimly.

Mariana paused. She hesitated to state the obvious twice in less than a minute.

Owen looked at her and raised an eyebrow. "You think she groomed me to be her son."

Mariana nodded.

"Not exactly," he muttered, looking at her morosely. "But...she eventually had some personal agendas for me."

Owen realized the conversation was heading relentlessly into a sea of very bitter memories that he preferred not to dredge up if he could avoid it. It surely could do Mariana no good to hear about the tragedy that had resulted from Portia's matchmaking.

"Personal agendas?" Mariana breathed the question so softly he barely heard it.

But he did hear it.

His expression became distant.

"You're warning me off this subject, aren't you?" Mariana said with a half smile.

"Very astute of you to notice," he said.

"Why?"

"It's not pleasant to talk about."

Mariana looked into his eyes. His shuttered gaze made it difficult to read what he was thinking.

"Maybe some other time..." she murmured. She truly didn't want to pry into areas of his life he didn't want to share with her. She respected privacy. She told herself quite firmly that she respected privacy. But she wondered what had wounded him and left this scar.

"Look, you've heard the story of how I met Portia," he concluded abruptly. He got up and rubbed the back of his neck as if to rid himself of unwanted tension. "Why don't we call Sergeant

Lefcourt and ask if he'd like to see that drawing you made of the mystery man.''

He looked down at her, his gaze serious. "I'd feel better if we knew who that guy was," Owen muttered.

Mariana swallowed hard and rose to her feet. She shivered just thinking about the face of the man in the drawing. But she gamely smiled at Owen and nodded.

"Then we could drive over to Maryland and see if anything seems familiar," Owen offered.

"Fine."

"Owen?"

He kept looking at her, waiting for her to tell him whatever it was.

"What if...?" Mariana lost her breath. She gathered her courage. "What if I never remember any more than I have?"

He wanted to draw her into his arms and comfort her so badly he ached with it. He was drowning in those liquid green eyes of hers.

"You'll remember," he swore softly. "If not everything...you'll remember enough."

"How can you be so sure?" she asked, hating the tremulous sound of her voice. Listening to him talk about his memories had made her ache to recapture her own to share with him.

He moved closer to her and reached out, against his better judgment. He knew he was making a big mistake, but he couldn't seem to hold himself back from it. His hand brushed her cheek, slid across the soft, warm skin of her neck, and he splayed his fingers into her silky hair.

"I can't stand that being between us," he reluctantly admitted in a harsh whisper. "We'll find out who you are, Mariana. I promise you." He bent his head and kissed her cheek. He heard the soft, sighing release of her breath, felt the sweet warmth flutter across his ear. His whole body clenched, and heat flowed through him in waves.

He lifted his head and looked into her half-closed eyes. There were no tears there. Just a confused and uncertain longing.

"Thanks, Owen," she whispered. *And after you've helped me locate my misplaced memories, perhaps you'll let me discover some more of yours,* she thought wistfully.

Sergeant Lefcourt wasn't at his desk when Owen called. He was out with an insurance investigator who'd been combing the wreckage site for evidence related to the truck driver's liability for the crash.

Owen hung up the phone and turned toward Mariana, who was lounging against the kitchen doorjamb and sipping her mug of hot tea.

"It seems they may have found something important up in the mountains," Owen said evenly.

"What?" Mariana asked, her heart beating faster in anticipation.

"The truck's insurance company sent an investigator up there to take a close look at the scene of the accident a few days ago. The investigator used his cell phone this afternoon to call Lefcourt and suggest he meet him at the accident site. It seems he may have found a purse that could belong to you."

Mariana stared at him, holding her breath, hardly daring to let herself react to the bombshell.

"Lefcourt will call us after he retrieves it from the accident site," Owen went on.

"Oh, Owen…" She said his name with all the anguished hope burning in her uncertain heart. She blinked away unexpected tears and laughed tremulously as she hastily wiped them away. "I don't know how I'm going to sleep tonight if he doesn't call!"

Owen glanced at the artist's pastels and drawing paper lying on one of the kitchen counters. He nodded toward them.

"Why don't you work out your frustrations with your talents?" he suggested.

"Draw?" she asked, startled by the unexpected suggestion.

"Yeah." He walked over to one of the unopened boxes and began unpacking it. He lifted out a fax machine and hooked it up. "Maybe more things will come back to you. Meanwhile, I think I'll fax that drawing you did of the man of your dreams to the police.''

"Man of my *nightmares*," she corrected him, looking uneasily at the sketch, which lay with the art materials.

Owen frowned slightly. The hair was standing up on the back of his neck every time Mariana looked at that sketch. He could sense the uneasiness bordering on fear that simmered within her when she thought of the man in the picture. He'd spent many years honing his instincts, and right now, they were all telling him that Mariana's life wasn't all moonlight and roses. Something was wrong. And until she got her memory back, she wouldn't know what that was. Or who was causing the problem. Or just what kind of difficulty she faced.

Mariana saw the darkness descend over Owen's expression.

"You're worried, aren't you?" she asked softly.

"Professional habit," he muttered. He plugged in the fax and punched in Lefcourt's fax number. He fed the picture into the machine, watching as it slowly passed through.

"What profession makes worry a habit?"

"Investigation."

"Insurance investigation?" she asked doubtfully.

He didn't look at her.

"Yes." But it sounded unpersuasive, even to him.

"Are you still working as an investigator? I mean...you've spent so much time with me, it's almost like you don't have a job."

"I freelance."

"What happened to that job you told me about? The one Portia's friend offered you?" Mariana crossed the room and put her mug down in the sink, coming to stand just a few feet from Owen.

"I retired," he said, his mouth twisting in bitter amusement.

"So young?" she asked softly.

"It wasn't my choice. It was part of a settlement. They made me an offer I couldn't refuse."

Mariana frowned slightly and chewed thoughtfully on her

lower lip. What was he being so evasive about? she wondered. What dark secret was he reluctant to share?

The sketch emerged from the other side of the machine, having been transmitted to its destination.

"There. Now Lefcourt can try to figure out who Mr. X is," Owen said grimly. He laid the picture back down. Then he pinned Mariana with a very direct gaze. "Weren't you going to draw?" he said pointedly. "It might jog some memories."

"Yes, but—"

"You know, I think I'd better not wait until tomorrow to see Hemphill," Owen interrupted, derailing any further questions she had planned to ask about his old job. "I'll just drop in on him now. He should be catching up on paperwork in his office at this hour. A few more things occurred to me since I talked to him. They might affect his legal strategy." He slanted a strange glance at her. "I think sooner would be better than later."

"Oh. Of course. That's important," she conceded. Suddenly, she felt guilty. "You go right ahead," she said with a confident smile. "I keep forgetting, you've got a life to keep up with," she laughed, a little embarrassed.

Owen nodded and headed for the front of the house. He glanced back at her, and for a moment, their eyes met and that warm, sultry feeling pervaded every inch of his body.

"I left the answering machine on," Owen said, his voice gravelly with conflicting emotions. He didn't like leaving her alone. But he had to get the hell out of here for a couple of hours. And it wasn't just to take care of his legal problem with the house. "If Lefcourt calls, pick up the phone," he told her, more brusquely than he felt.

"I will." She was surprised that her words sounded so normal. Her mouth felt like cotton. Her body was pulsing with the rush of heat. Owen's gray green eyes and his rich, gravelly voice were creating havoc within her. She felt caressed and kissed and embraced. And he wasn't touching her. May not particularly want to touch her, she told herself desperately. Mariana swallowed and managed a smile of sorts. "Don't worry about me."

"Right," he muttered darkly.

He didn't look as if he was willing to take that advice, she thought. Her heart skipped a beat in pleasure. But he didn't say anything more. Just grunted that noncommittal reply. And turned away and left.

Mariana sagged against the counter, laying her hands palm down and letting her head bend forward as she closed her eyes.

Could you fall in love with a stranger? she wondered, feeling completely stunned by her own question. Because that's what it felt like.

It was wrong to succumb to the tide of longing that Owen made her feel. She told herself it was very, very wrong. She barely knew him. And she didn't know herself at all.

"I must be clinging to my rescuer," she murmured to herself. "It's making me feel attached to him. That's got to be part of the explanation for why I..." She was afraid to say the words out loud. As if it would make it more real than it already was. That's got to be why I feel like I'm falling for him, she thought, unable to entirely wash away the forbidden thought.

She couldn't remember a single, significant event in her own life. Nor any substantive facts. Not her own last name. Not where she'd grown up. Not whether she had a happy life or a sad one. Not a hint of a memory of a parent or a boyfriend or a boss or job. Nothing. Nada.

Tears welled up and pressed against her eyes. One spilled over and trickled down across her cheek. Frustrated, Mariana wiped it away with her fingers.

"Owen...I wish I'd met you under different circumstances," she murmured wistfully.

Her heart swelled and ached when she thought of Owen Blackhart. She could see the corners of his eyes crinkle as he smiled, recall the granite set of his mouth when they disagreed. Even the rhythm of his tread was intimately connected with her nervous system, it seemed. She remembered listening for his footsteps in the hospital when her head was bandaged and she couldn't see him. She'd felt a leap of happiness then. Thinking about it now brought the same, irrational response from her.

She didn't know him. But she trusted him.

"That's fine for me," she lectured herself. "But he doesn't need to get any more involved in my problem than he already is."

He was going out of his way to extricate her from a terrible situation. She owed it to him not to make his life any more complicated than it was. After all, he was bracing himself for a major legal battle with Portia's would-be heir. And he probably had once enjoyed a social life. Before she began taking up so much of his free time, she told herself severely.

The image of Owen kissing some unknown, faceless woman rose up in her vivid imagination. She saw his arms tighten around the woman, watched his mouth move passionately over the woman's lips.

"No!" she groaned, aghast at her own jealous pain and fury. "He isn't mine. I have no right to object. Or to fantasize about him like this!"

Mariana snapped to attention and grabbed for the paper and pastels. She took them with her into the bedroom she was using. First she'd soak in the bathtub in the adjoining bathroom. Then, after she'd relaxed, she'd try sketching.

She could only pray there wasn't a husband waiting for her somewhere. Or a fiancé. Or a serious, significant other. She could not imagine there was someone like that in her life, but if there was, she was going to face a difficult transition back to reality.

A chill of fear rippled over her then. The face of the man in the sketch stared up at her from the pile of paper.

"Who are you?" she demanded fiercely. "Why do you terrify me? And why can't I remember who you are?"

Hours later Owen returned.

He sat in his car in front of his house and wrapped his hands around the steering wheel. He stared blindly ahead of him, trying to sort out his own feelings.

He closed his eyes and shook his head as if that would clear away the conflict within him.

It didn't.

He got out of the car, locked it and grimly walked into the house.

The lights were still on. Everything was quiet.

He went to the kitchen and noticed the blinking light on the answering machine.

Owen went to it and depressed the Play button.

"Owen?" the recording played. "This is Lefcourt. It looks like it was her purse. And we've got a possible identity for her. Driver's license. Address. Even what looks like a house key tucked in her wallet. Everything's pretty wet from being out in the open all this time, but the information's all there. She looks like the photo on the license, so I'd say we've solved the mystery of her identity."

Owen stilled. She would be leaving then. Grimly, he listened to the rest of the policeman's recorded message.

"I, uh, hesitate to tell you the details over the phone. It seems unfair to leave it as a message. And, uh, a little unprofessional, to tell you the truth. The insurance investigator and I are going to drive down to see you tomorrow morning. I'd like to break the news to Mari—uh, Mariana, in person. And both the investigator and I have a few additional questions for her. How's she doing? Okay, I hope. Madge asks about her. So do some of the hospital people. And Morrison, 'course. Uh, by the way, the insurance investigator says he knows you. Anselm Brock's his name."

Owen frowned. Hell. Anselm Brock.

"So we'll be a seein' ya t'morrow morning."

The recording clicked off.

Owen went around the house turning off the lights, checking the windows and doors and contemplating the great good news.

Finally, he came to Mariana's room. The door was half-open. Light was streaming into the darkened hall where he stood in stoic silence.

No sounds came from within.

Then he heard the rustle of bedcovers. Like a person rolling over and finding a more comfortable position while lying prone.

"Mariana?" he called out, softly in case she was asleep.

No reply came.

He stepped into the room, stopping just inside the door.

She was asleep. Lying on the bed amid the sketches she'd done. Her dark red hair spilled across the plain white pillow. She looked vulnerable. And very, very sexy.

She'd put on the pajamas they'd picked up at the mall store near Tyson's Corner the other day. He'd insisted she needed more than one set of clothes. He smiled a little, recalling her tabulating the total as she picked up a few of the basic necessities.

The soft yellow pajamas had looked plain and simple in the package. On Mariana, they looked like shimmering satin. They clung to her body, making the contours only too clear.

He walked closer, hypnotized by her unconscious form.

In sleep, her face was his to study at his leisure, and he did. Her long dark lashes fanned across the pale skin of her face. The elegant shape of her cheekbones sloped softly to the inviting curve of her neck. There was a soft pulse beating tantalizingly in her throat. Owen resisted the unexpectedly strong impulse to bend down and press his lips to that throbbing point. And to slide his mouth down over her yielding feminine flesh.

The bruises and scratches were faded. Only a few of the more serious scars showed their angry red welts. All those were hidden from his view, beneath the satiny yellow of the pajamas.

He ached to take her in his arms. Just once. Owen clenched his hand into a fist, resisting the foolish drift of his thoughts.

Tomorrow she'd know who she was. This wasn't the time to throw caution to the wind and succumb to his intense attraction to her.

He dragged his eyes away from Mariana's sleeping form and forced himself to look at the drawings. There were quite a few. Mariana apparently had exhausted herself sketching them. He lifted the chalk from her limp fingertips, removed the pad of paper from beneath her hand and placed them and the other supplies on the floor where they'd be out of the way. Then Owen gathered up the sketches, slowly examining each one. From the looks of them, Mariana was getting in touch with her memory, whether she realized it or not, he thought.

What had Mariana remembered?

Chapter 9

Mariana rolled her head from side to side on the pillow. Her eyes were tightly closed, and her body strained against an unseen adversary. "No...No..."

She gasped and cried out. "No!"

Mariana opened her eyes and tried to bring the blurry, darkened room into focus. She pushed herself up with one hand until she was sitting in the bed. Blinking wasn't helping, she finally realized.

A figure appeared in her doorway. Owen. Disheveled, barefoot and wearing only a pair of drawstring-waist pajama bottoms.

"Mariana? Are you all right?"

She rubbed her eyes with the back of one hand and tried to clear away the fog from her mind. "I...don't know...."

Owen crossed the room. In a few soundless strides, he'd reached the edge of her bed. He paused for a moment, then somewhat reluctantly, he bent over and gently but firmly cupped her chin with one hand. He tilted her head back a little so that he could search her face. It only took a moment for him to see her half-sleepy confusion. She wasn't fully awake.

"Another nightmare?" he guessed softly. He let his hand slide a little away, intending to let her head fall forward, telling himself to ignore the intense desire he felt to keep touching her.

Mariana covered his hand with hers before he could pull completely away. She gave up trying to get her eyes to focus and closed them with a sigh instead.

That soft sound rippled along the nerve endings in Owen's body like a tantalizing caress.

"Go back to sleep," he said huskily, gently pressing her shoulder back with his unencumbered hand.

Mariana reclined, but as her shoulders sank into the mattress, she covered his hand with hers, too.

Owen was bending over her, one hand trapped against her jaw and the other captured against her shoulder. He pressed his lips together in a grim line. As he gently tried to disengage himself from her hold, he felt her shoulder tremble. He sensed the unsteady breath she took next. When she opened her eyes and looked up at him, he felt as if an invisible net were drawing around him, pulling him inexorably closer to her.

Owen tried to hold on to his badly fraying common sense. He was old enough to resist an impulse like this, he reminded himself. Unfortunately, his body was putting up an increasingly insistent argument to the contrary.

He tried one last time to emancipate his hands.

Mariana's dark green eyes pleaded silently.

His treacherous hands hesitated.

"Owen..." she pleaded brokenly.

His palms touched her shoulders. He slid one arm under her shoulders and lay down beside her, closing his eyes in silent defeat.

Mariana curled into his body and wrapped her arm around him. His scent was comforting. As was the warmth emanating from his well-muscled physique.

Memories drifted gently back into her mind.

"I remember the house where I live," she whispered.

Her cheek was resting against his chest. Her breath felt soft against his skin. Owen sighed in resignation. Sweet torture.

"What's the house like?" he asked, sliding his hand slowly across her back.

"It's adobe. The one I described before. The one that looks over a city."

"I looked at the sketches," he murmured, gently kneading the tension from her shoulders with his fingertips. "A lot of them were in the desert."

"Phoenix," she mumbled sleepily. "I'm sure my home is near Phoenix."

Owen frowned thoughtfully. "Remember that guy from the AA group?" he asked softly.

"Kelton."

"Yeah. Kelton. He said he overheard you remark about a bird of paradise or something like that when he passed you when you were talking on the phone."

Mariana hugged him a little closer and smiled. "Phoenix," she murmured smugly.

"Yeah. The bird that rises from its own ashes." He rested his chin against her head. "Or...a city in Arizona," he added dryly.

"I drew faces of people. I think... I think one of them is a business partner. And my parents... I can see their faces...."

Owen felt her grow still in his arms and turn her face against his bare chest. One tear and then another splashed onto his hot skin.

He pulled her up to eye level, settling onto his side.

"They're dead," she murmured, her eyes dark green pools glimmering with tears. "I remember the funeral."

"I'm sorry," he murmured huskily. He touched his lips to her eyes, gently kissing each in turn. Her tears were cool and salty on his lips.

Mariana sighed.

When she breathed, Owen could feel her breasts press against him through the satiny fabric of her pajamas. His pulse began a slow, heavy pounding, and his body grew heavy with the beginnings of desire. He tried to pull a little away, but the startled, vulnerable look in her tear-dampened eyes cut him to the core.

"To hell with it," he muttered half under his breath. With a ragged sigh, he slid them up toward her pillow and resigned himself to sweet, agonizing torture.

"My memory is coming back," she whispered.

"You don't sound too thrilled," he murmured.

"I'm glad," she said, feeling more focused and less groggy. "But it's strange to have things return in bits and pieces. Like my pet parakeet when I was twelve...or knowing I'm an artist...or remembering sketching desert landscapes for an architect..." She closed her eyes in frustration. "And that stupid image of the Desert Sands Resort! But...with all that, I'm still missing huge pieces of my life."

He slid his fingers through her hair and pulled her face closer.

"Maybe that won't be a problem much longer," he said quietly.

She searched his eyes, finding only somber thoughts.

"Did you hear Lefcourt's message on the answering machine?" he asked curiously.

She looked at him in surprise and shook her head. "No."

"It seems he's found your purse. There's a driver's license. The picture looks like you. Your address and what looks like a house key are in your wallet. He'll be here tomorrow morning with them. He wanted to give them to you, tell you the information, in person."

She lowered her lashes and gazed past Owen into the darkened, still bedroom.

"So, tomorrow, all my questions will be answered," she said in a barely audible, thready whisper.

"Yes." His voice was devoid of emotion.

She wrapped her arms around him and held him tight.

"Mariana," he whispered, a little hoarsely. "I'm not made of stone."

She lifted her head and gazed into his darkening eyes. The gray green was dark like the ocean in winter storms.

"I don't want to say goodbye," she admitted. "And yet, to-morrow, we may have to."

She saw him tighten his jaw and smiled sadly at his stoic acceptance. She could feel his heart beat against her breast. She knew he was attracted to her. And she admired his effort to avoid acting on that attraction under the circumstances.

Mariana had searched her heart and could not believe that there was a husband or fiancé waiting for her. Surely she'd have been wearing a ring and having some sort of dreams about him, wouldn't she?

"This is Jane Doe's last night," she noted in a shaky whisper. She closed her eyes, ashamed of succumbing to her own weakness for him while Owen seemed to be doing such an excellent job of behaving honorably under highly tempting circumstances.

Mariana wanted Owen to kiss her so badly that her lips ached with it. She had no right to invite that. Not until she knew whether there was someone else in her life, impossible as that was to imagine, considering how she was feeling about Owen Blackhart.

So she warred with herself. Kiss him. Don't kiss him. Invite him. Discourage him. Unconsciously, her arms tightened around him, holding on to his strength even as her own seemed to be slowly melting away.

Owen groaned inwardly as he felt the last slender thread of his fraying control unravel and snap in two.

"Come here, then, Green Eyes," he whispered huskily.

The muscle in his arms flexed, and Owen pulled her fully into his embrace. His mouth found hers, and he was kissing her hungrily, as he'd been wanting to for a very long time.

Mariana closed her eyes and let herself fall into the swirling sunlight that enveloped her. His touch was like the rising sun, bringing glorious beauty to everything it caressed. Warmth and fiery pride illuminated every piece of her that it reached.

His hands swept over her in slow, sure motions, leaving behind skin tingling with warmth and alive with wanting.

He lifted his lips from hers and looked into her eyes. The gray green of his eyes simmered with a golden sheen, like the reflection of the midday sun in the summer sea.

He slid his hand up across her midriff, finding the hem of her pajama top. Then his palm was touching her bare skin, moving upward, ever upward, leaving tiny bumps of excitement across her soft flesh.

He closed his hand over her breast and brushed his lips across hers at the same time.

Mariana moaned and reached up to pull his head closer. She felt his smile as his mouth pressed down against hers. His muffled groan of pleasure at touching her made the sun warm her from the inside all of a sudden. Somehow, sunlight was everywhere, heating her, caressing her, warming her with its life-giving, eternal force.

He slanted his mouth against hers, opening to her as she did to him, and sweeping the tender flesh inside with his tongue. Her soft, tender reply shot desire through the center of his body like a summer lightning bolt on a hot, sultry afternoon.

"Mariana," he murmured, kissing her lips, her jaw and that pulsing spot that so tantalized him on her throat. He groaned in pleasure as he felt her hands on his bare skin, sliding down across his back and beneath the waistband of his pajamas.

"What?" she gasped as he hastily unbuttoned her top and lowered his head to her breasts, kissing the heated flesh, running his tongue over the pouting, dark pink nipple. She arched in pleasure as he moved his attention to the other breast, repeating the caresses, circling the taut flesh again and again.

She moaned with pleasure and frustration as the sensation lasered through her, pooling somewhere deep within her abdomen.

He pushed the pajama top off her shoulders, trailing kisses up her throat until he'd found her mouth with his once again.

The taste of him, the warm pressure of his lips, the sound of his increasingly harsh breathing, all made Mariana lose herself more to him. He kneed apart her legs and settled between her thighs, his forearms resting on either side of her head, his hands sunk in the silky wealth of her hair.

"I want you," he whispered. He closed his eyes and rested his cheek against hers. "God, how I want you, Mariana!"

She could feel the coiled tension everywhere in him. Hardened muscles of his chest and abdomen pressed against her breasts and stomach; his taut thighs felt like unyielding sinew against the inner softness of hers. And the evidence of his desire pulsed hard and ready, snugged against the most hidden part of her. Only the frail barrier of their clothing kept them apart.

"And I want you," she whispered unsteadily. With all my heart.

He lifted his head and looked down at her, warring with himself.

Mariana captured his face between her hands, her own deep longing for him playing across her face like a symphony.

He kissed her lips, gently. But the taste of her mouth, the trembling in her lips, broke him. He deepened the kiss, pouring into it all the tortured wanting that he felt for her. All the frustration and desire that he dared not completely unleash.

She slid her heels around his ankles, as if to hold him close, and he flexed his hips, pushing against her in slow, determined strokes.

He pulled one of her legs up around his thigh, then nuzzled her head to one side to find the tender flesh of her ear.

The warm, wet stroke of his tongue against her ear and the coiling tension within her abdomen suddenly connected. She gasped and caught his back with her hands as he pulled her hips toward him and thrust against her hard.

The sunlight burst into fireworks of brilliant colors.

Waves of beauty pulsed through Mariana, but when she felt Owen shudder against her, felt his gasp of pleasure as he buried his face against her throat, she knew she was where she'd always wanted to be. Home was here. In this man's arms.

They lay together, breathing in the experience, not wanting to let go.

Finally, Owen rolled over, pulling Mariana on top of him. His eyes were dark with emotion. He pulled her head down onto his shoulder and slowly caressed her head. His hand eventually drifted down to rest possessively on her hip. He had resisted stripping off all their clothes, although he wasn't sure where he'd found the strength. He'd managed...just barely...not to actually enter her. Yet he couldn't imagine feeling more completely one with her than he did at this moment. The ecstasy they shared had been as profound and as soul-searing as full consummation.

"I hope you don't regret this tomorrow," he reluctantly whispered at long last.

Mariana managed a half smile. "Funny," she replied huskily. "That's exactly what I was going to say to you."

He pressed a kiss to the top of her head and tightened his arm around her.

"I won't regret it," he promised her softly.

She tangled her legs in his, embracing him with her whole body, fiercely wanting this moment to belong to them alone.

He laughed softly. The sound was rich and dark against her ear pressed against his chest.

"No more nightmares," he murmured reassuringly. "Not tonight."

Mariana closed her eyes, falling asleep to the memory of the sound of his dear, trusted voice rumbling beneath her cheek.

The smell of bacon cooking finally woke her up the following morning.

Mariana stretched, feeling the sheets against her bare breasts. That made her eyes open in a hurry. Memories of the night before came tumbling back in vivid detail. She could hear Owen in the kitchen. She had to admit she was grateful she had a chance to get dressed before facing him. She was sure she didn't have any practice at this kind of thing.

She was halfway out of bed when she realized she knew that was true. And what her last name was!

"Owen!" she cried out, grabbing her pajama top and putting it on as she heard him coming toward the bedroom.

He appeared in the doorway. Dressed in black jeans and a light gray sweatshirt. He seemed a little disheveled. He looked straight at her, though. There was no uncertainty or wavering in his straightforward male regard. His gaze went over her from head to toe. And then back to her face.

"Good morning," he said. He lifted an eyebrow quizzically. "What?"

She hastily buttoned the pajamas, looking up at him between holes.

"I remember!" she exclaimed excitedly.

"You remember what?" he asked, smiling at her enthusiasm.

"My name! It's Sands!" she exclaimed. "Mariana Sands!" She'd gotten to the top pajama button, but there wasn't any buttonhole to go with it. She stared down at the front in consternation.

Owen walked across the room. His bare feet made little sound. He stood in front of her for a moment, looking thoughtfully into her eyes.

Mariana lifted her face, awash in the pleasure of being close to him again. Her eyes softened and her mouth parted, but she was unaware of it. She was basking in the sunlight of his presence.

Owen looked down at the pajama top. Carefully, he unbuttoned it. For a moment, the yellow satin hung there, parted down the center of her body. All the soft warmth he'd held in his arms last night lay beneath it.

He leaned down and found her mouth with his. The lingering kiss was tender and sweet. Reluctantly, he lifted his head and sighed. He pushed the buttons through the holes without comment. Only the gleam in his eyes when he was finished and looked at her conveyed what he'd have preferred to have been doing.

"Mariana Sands," he said experimentally, as if deciding whether her name suited him. He nodded his approval and repeated it. "Mariana Sands. Well, that explains all those desert sands you were drawing yesterday," he said whimsically.

She laughed. "Maybe you're right. My artistic subconscious

was screaming my name at me, but my stubborn intellectual memory cells just couldn't make the connection.''

Mariana looked at his mouth and felt the sunlight streaming through her again. She lifted her eyes to his.

"Maybe aromas aren't the only thing that stimulate memory," Owen suggested teasingly.

Mariana blushed and laughed. "Maybe you're right."

But Owen had his self-control back in excellent working order, and he wasn't about to trash it first thing this morning. Mariana needed to reconnect with her life. Then they could see what could be done about their relationship, he promised himself.

"Lefcourt should be here soon," he reminded her. "How about some breakfast before they arrive?" He allowed himself one, fondly reminiscing look at her wearing her rumpled bedclothes. "*I* certainly enjoy seeing you in those pajamas, or out of them, for that matter," he added teasingly. "But if you prefer to change into something else before our friend the sergeant and his insurance colleague ring the doorbell, I won't object."

Mariana smothered a laugh.

"That's very sensible advice," Mariana said dryly.

"I'm not *always* filled with sensible thoughts, Green Eyes," he conceded, his eyes turning smoky with kindling memories.

Owen's jaw tightened and he glanced at his watch.

"It's nine thirty," he told her succinctly.

"I won't be long."

"It's getting colder. Wear a sweater or something," he advised evenly.

Mariana had the impression the sweater wasn't just intended to keep her warm but to cover her up. She covered her mouth with her hand to suppress a giddy desire to laugh.

"Oh, what a glorious day!" she said, smiling happily as she hurried to gather some clothes and take them into the bathroom to shower and dress.

Owen heard the muffled sound of the shower turning on as he stood barefoot in the kitchen, holding a mug of coffee in his hand. He stared out the window, looking at the broad expanse of countryside. A randy young buck courted a doe on the other side of the pond, near the edge of the adjoining forest.

Owen could imagine just how the buck felt. He swallowed the black, unsweetened brew, but his body was still focused on the muffled sounds of the cascading shower. He could imagine the warm water sluicing over Mariana's naked body, her hands lathering her satiny skin with foaming soap.

He clenched one fist and rested it on the countertop, frustrated as his body grew hot and hard just thinking about her.

"Maybe I should have made iced tea for me," he muttered with a fatalistic sigh. "Not that it would do any good," he had to admit. He watched the antlered stag move closer to the doe, watched the white tail flick. The doe became very still; the buck lifted his front legs off the ground to mount her.

Owen stared at them, a wry expression on his face. Maybe it was just the fall mating season that was getting to him and Mariana, he thought.

He looked back in the direction of her bedroom. The shower had stopped. He could imagine her toweling off, stepping into her underwear. Pulling on some clothes. Brushing her dark red hair until it shone like a sunset.

It could just be something in the ancient rhythms of fall that was driving them into each other's arms, like that buck and doe in the throes of reproductive ecstasy. But Owen felt there was something else between them.

He dumped out his remaining coffee and decided not to think about that *indefinable thing* for the time being. He was reasonably confident that he'd figure out what it was eventually.

He looked up as Mariana walked through the kitchen doorway. She was wearing an oversize knit sweater the color of chocolate over a long-sleeved white shirt. The shirt's crisp white collar was open and framing her throat over the boat neck of the sweater. The shirt cuffs peeked out below the sweater sleeves. The sweater blended well with the corduroy slacks, which were predominantly black but softened by the thinnest possible occasional stripes the color of wet sand.

She was wearing women's black cross-training athletic shoes and thick black athletic socks.

And she'd put on makeup. Just enough to bring out the healthy glow in her skin. The luscious curve of her lips. And the sparkle in those fathomless green eyes.

Owen reached for the instant iced tea he'd unpacked a few minutes earlier and pushed the ice dispenser on the refrigerator with his glass.

"I don't think I ever met anyone who drank iced tea for breakfast," Mariana said in surprise as she sat down at the table.

"Yeah, well, it's a first for me, too."

Mariana saw the wry amusement in his eyes and looked at him expectantly.

"Hurry up and eat," he said, not inclined to explain. That might lead them into territory they didn't have time to explore before their company arrived.

Mariana looked at him curiously, but she was too hungry to pursue it for now.

Between bites of eggs and toast and bacon, Mariana did manage to keep up a conversation.

"So, I'm sure the doctors are right. I think most of my memories will return."

Owen watched her silently, sitting across the table from her with his hands wrapped around his tall glass of iced tea.

"I just don't understand why I lost my identity," she said, frowning and tilting her head thoughtfully to one side. "That's really unusual. And I can't seem to recall anything more recent than a few months ago. I don't even know how I got here or what I was doing in this part of the country."

Mariana laid down her fork and lifted her mug of coffee. After taking a swallow of the sweet, hot drink, she looked at him, perplexed.

"I know I lived in the Southwest. I was selling art by consignment through my agent, who was like a business partner to me. I remember a few friends. And my parents, who I told you..."
She felt the pain again.

"Your parents who you told me are dead," Owen supplied softly.

She nodded and got up.

She began clearing the table, feeling it was only fair for her to clean up since he'd done all the cooking.

Owen watched her, enjoying the shift of her back and hips as she bent and walked and lifted and dipped.

"I just wish I knew what I was doing here." She rinsed the dishes and put them in the automatic dishwasher. When she was through, she turned to face Owen. Anxiety shadowed her face. "I have this awful feeling..." she began huskily.

"You have an awful feeling about what?" Owen probed, rising to his feet and coming to stand beside her. He had that urge to soothe away her hurts and fears again. The profoundly intense desire to protect her from pain. He laid his hand along her cheek in a comforting gesture intended to reassure her that he would be there for her while she faced the truth.

"That man in the picture..." she said, searching for her courage. "I'm sure he's the reason I'm here. And...I'm afraid of him. But I still can't figure out why. And that makes no sense. I should remember something like that, shouldn't I?"

"Maybe you will remember, when your mind is ready to let you remember," he suggested softly. He slid his hand up into her soft, thick hair and let it spill over his fingers. He pulled her into his arms and held her close. "Or," he said, "perhaps you knew him very close to the time of the accident, and you simply don't remember things that happened that close to the time of your concussion. That's normal when people have had a severe head injury, I'm told."

She looked into his eyes and nodded slowly. "The doctors said as much to me," she admitted. She smiled ruefully. "I hope they're wrong, in my case," she added. "I hate having my curiosity going unsatisfied."

"Yeah. Lack of satisfaction is brutal," he agreed. He lowered his mouth to hers and gave her a tender, lingering kiss.

When he lifted his head, she was breathing a little erratically and his pulse was noticeably faster.

"Remind me we're expecting company," he ordered her sternly.

Mariana laughed and hugged him, but she stepped back and looked into his eyes as something else occurred to her.

"By the way," she said, "you never told me how you made out with your lawyer last night."

Owen sighed and let his arms fall away from her. He'd better warn her before she got broadsided by the media, he thought.

"Well, as a matter of fact, there are a few things you should probably hear from me first," he admitted with obvious reluctance.

Mariana braced herself but wondered what in the world it could be. Owen looked positively stone-faced all of a sudden.

"I told you that Portia was famous—"

"Yes."

"—that, even in death, things related to Portia were likely to arouse the interest of the media."

Mariana nodded.

"Last night Averson Hemphill told me he's been besieged by calls from several news organizations about the challenge to Portia's will by her previously unknown nephew."

"Oh." Mariana could see there was more. And whatever it was, he was debating exactly how to tell her. She felt a small quiver of uncertainty about Owen for the first time since she'd met him. What was bothering him about this? she wondered.

"There's a New York reporter arriving here sometime this afternoon. She's asked to speak to Hemphill."

"Are you going to let him do that?"

"Yes. Lawyers are reasonably adept at damage control. But the reporter has made clear that she intends to interview people in town about me and about Portia."

"I'm sorry, Owen," she said sympathetically. "When someone has a story to write, they can really trample your private life."

Owen snorted. "Unfortunately, that's only too true. And..."

He hated to think about the mess this could become if the tabloids got hold of it. Again. "She's probably going to try to track me down and talk to me, too."

Mariana stood still. She wasn't sure where that left her.

"Look, Owen, I'll stay out of this, if that's what you want," she hastened to say. She waved a hand as if for emphasis. "But if you'd like to avoid the press, I'd be happy to have you stay at my home." She laughed a little embarrassedly. "Assuming we figure out where that is in time for you to make use of my offer."

"You need to know a few things before you make an offer like that," he said, frowning. "You see, several years ago—"

And at that point, the front doorbell rang.

Owen closed his eyes briefly in frustration and grimly pressed his lips together.

Mariana looked from the living room to Owen.

The doorbell rang again.

Owen walked toward the living room and saw the police car in front of the house. It was too late to tell her,

Mariana had followed him. She wondered what had put that grim expression on his face. She touched his shoulder reassuringly.

"Maybe this will jog your memory," he said evenly, trying to find something positive in the situation.

"We'll know in a very short time," she declared, smiling bravely.

They opened the door and let the policeman and the insurance investigator in. Sergeant Lefcourt greeted Mariana and Owen, then turned to introduce the insurance investigator.

"I understand you two know each other," Lefcourt observed, speaking to Owen.

Mariana watched in surprise as Owen curtly nodded his head.

Chapter 10

Anselm Brock was a gray-haired man with a middle-age paunch and the remains of what had once been a muscular build. He was modishly attired in buff wool trousers, a dusky red dress shirt with white collar and a brown tweed sports jacket of the type commonly seen at local steeplechases. His tie was a unique oblong knit woven of complementary shades of brown, beige and red. His dark brown dress shoes were as highly polished as a new car. He sported tinted prescription glasses with gold wire frames most often seen on the young and flamboyant.

The insurance-investigation business must pay well, Mariana concluded, startled by his unexpectedly dapper appearance.

"I believe I owe you my thanks, Mr. Brock," Mariana said, recovering from her surprise and smoothing it over with a welcoming smile. She politely extended her hand in appreciation.

Brock shook it firmly. His plump, well-manicured hand was calloused and his grip strong, much to Mariana's renewed amazement. And from the way he was enthusiastically pumping the handshake, he was obviously pleased by her response to him.

"I'm glad to be able to help, ma'am," he drawled. "My associate and I were very happy to find your purse."

"Your associate?" Mariana echoed, trying to extricate her hand without immediate success. "Then you don't do your own digging when you go out in the field like this?" she asked.

Brock chuckled. "Not if I can help it. Not anymore," he replied. "We decided that your purse was most likely thrown out of the car when the vehicle first started tumbling down the mountainside, based on where we found it, by the way."

Owen had a vivid flashback of that moment and shot a look at Mariana. He saw her swallow and try to keep her smile bravely in place.

Anselm Brock, unconcerned with their reactions, plowed on.

"You might have even inadvertently dragged it out when you pulled her out of the car, Blackhart. Then the force of the mountain slide itself carried the item away from you, mixing it with leaves and branches and mud. That made it hard for the earlier searchers to find it. Since the rain's stopped, we were able to get into some areas too slippery for the police," he explained. "We were just damn lucky to stumble onto it," he said flatly. "Maybe fate led us to it."

"In any event, she has it back." Owen motioned for them to come farther inside the house. "Let's go into the living room. It's not a hell of a lot more comfortable than standing in the foyer," he said dryly. "But you *can* sit down in it."

They went into the living room and sat down amid the boxes and the few pieces of furniture. Lefcourt handed Mariana the purse.

"Why don't you look at the contents," he suggested kindly. "I take it you haven't completely remembered everything?"

"That's right. Just fragments. But more every day."

Anselm Brock folded his arms in front of his barrel chest and eyed Owen speculatively.

"This must have been déjà vu for you, Blackhart."

Mariana saw Owen stiffen.

The insurance investigator saw the mystified expression on Mariana's face and immediately launched into an explanation.

"I guess you have no way of knowing about that, unless Owen told you."

Owen's stony face became positively granite.

Mariana had snapped open her purse in an attempt to divert the insurance man's comment, but that didn't derail him at all.

"Owen here was as good as engaged to a society girl up in New York some years ago. One of Portia Willowbrook's protégés. But the young woman drove off one weekend and disappeared. Took them years before they finally found her body."

Mariana felt cold all over. She tried not to betray her feelings. It seemed unfair to do that, in front of Lefcourt and Brock. She forced a sympathetic expression onto her face.

"That must have been a terrible experience," she murmured.

Brock nodded. "For a while, there were rumors that she'd had second thoughts about Owen, and he was questioned as a suspect in her disappearance," Brock added helpfully.

Mariana stared at Owen. He was looking thoroughly displeased with Brock's revelations.

"And then the papers started recounting how he searched for her personally, relentlessly, for months after her disappearance. It would have bankrupted anyone else. But you made it a personal quest, didn't you, Blackhart? First he was branded a suspect and then pitied as a desperately suffering lover." Brock shook his head and sighed. "Life can be hell, can't it?"

Owen gave the insurance man an implacably cold look.

"Yes," Owen replied, through barely unclenched teeth. "Weren't you here to talk about Mariana's purse? And her accident?" he asked pointedly.

"Yes, indeed," Brock agreed. "But I thought it was a great twist of fate that you finally had a chance to *save* a young woman. The other lady died, after all. Didn't they conclude that she'd died of exposure? After apparently being carjacked? But the perpetrators had knocked her too hard on the head and then panicked when they realized she needed medical care. Anyway, that was the theory."

"You seem to remember it all very clearly, Mr. Brock," Mariana said.

"Oh, it was big news for months," Brock assured her. "Besides, I knew Owen and his boss by reputation. We all worked the same part of town back then. Like I said, it just strikes me as poetic justice that he could save you and kind of make up for the woman he lost." Brock glanced at Owen. "That other lady was tagged as a Jane Doe, too, wasn't she, Owen? At the county morgue, when they finally came across her body."

"Yes," Owen replied succinctly.

"Well, this Jane Doe has a happy ending," Brock exclaimed, thumping his knee enthusiastically.

Mariana nodded automatically. "Yeah," she numbly agreed. But maybe not as happy an ending as she'd believed a few minutes ago, she thought.

Owen looked at the bleak expression in Mariana's eyes and repressed the urge to angrily toss Brock out of the house. *Hell!* He'd known that Anselm Brock had an uncanny knack for creating problems with his penchant for rambling gossip. If that wasn't bad enough, Brock always had possessed an unerring instinct for setting people's worst nightmares out into public view at the most delicate moments. He had no social tact at all. It helped him tear openings in the masks of people he investigated, which made him highly successful in his field. However, at the moment, Owen was cursing himself for not having told Mariana about this first. He'd wanted to forget about the past. He should have realized that bad news followed you forever.

Lefcourt was watching the conversation with growing interest. However, he glanced at his watch and reluctantly intervened.

"Uh, I hate to interrupt, folks, but I have to get back to the office this afternoon, so maybe we could come back to the present case?" he said with a faintly apologetic smile. "Back to *our* Jane Doe, here?"

Mariana felt a sudden chill at the mention of Jane Doe, and she crossed her arms in front of her for warmth.

"Look inside the purse," Lefcourt urged her. "I think you may have a surprise in store."

Owen's eyebrows drew together in a straight line. He didn't like the sound of that, and he *definitely* didn't need any more surprises this morning.

Mariana stared down at the purse in her hands. She'd already opened it, and now she examined it more closely.

It was a wine red leather purse. A hand-tooled geometric design still showed in soft relief against the water-brittled, dirt-smudged material. The lining inside was gritty with drying mud that had seeped in through the flap. When she'd lifted the closure moments ago, a fine, dark, powdery residue had sifted down onto her lap.

Mariana wasn't as consumed with curiosity to see the contents as she would have been a day or two earlier. After all, she'd remembered her complete name and where she was from, and she was gaining confidence that she eventually would remember everything. Anselm Brock's comments about Owen's past had been much more riveting than the prospect of seeing her driver's license.

There was a wallet inside the purse. And a pen and pencil. And a small, water-stained pad of blank, chartreuse green self-sticking notes.

Mariana removed the wallet and ran her fingers over it. It did seem vaguely familiar. It was plain black leather, with a small insert of plastic sleeves for holding credit cards, wallet-size photographs and a driver's license.

She flipped open the wallet and looked at the license.

She lifted her gaze and glanced first at Lefcourt and Brock, then at Owen, then back to the license. Disbelief was stamped on her face.

"This can't be," she protested huskily. She shook her head, denying what she was seeing with her own eyes. "This is...me...in the picture," she murmured. "But this isn't my name."

Owen, who'd remained standing while the others had sat down, came to her side and reached down for the wallet to see for himself what had so shocked her.

The name on the driver's license was Maryanice Roualt. The license had been issued by the state of Maryland. That was because Maryanice Roualt's home address was in Maryland, just west of Washington, D.C.

Mariana frowned and slowly shook her head. She looked up at Owen, as if he could explain this new turn of events to her.

He, too, however, was perplexed. He squatted down beside her, so that he could look straight into her eyes.

"The photograph resembles you," he said slowly. He looked from Mariana to the license photo and back to Mariana.

Mariana laughed in dismay and gaped at him as if he'd suddenly misplaced some of his intelligence.

"Yes!" she exclaimed, amazed he'd try to soften that rather obvious news. "But this isn't where I live! And that isn't my name! I've *remembered* those things."

Lefcourt interrupted. "Uh, I believe you left me out of that discovery?" he said.

"Mariana Sands. From somewhere around Phoenix, Arizona," Owen supplied.

Mariana could have hugged him for the firm way he said all that. At least Owen believed her.

"There's an explanation for this," Owen said, tapping the wallet with his index finger. He laid his hand on her knee and looked into her eyes. Softly, he promised, "We'll figure it out."

She blinked at the tears that threatened her. His tenderness undid her, she realized. She swallowed hard and nodded.

"I can contact the Phoenix police and try to get information on Mariana Sands," Lefcourt volunteered. "Have you tried to get a phone number for her?"

"Not yet." Owen straightened and went to the kitchen. He dialed information for Phoenix and asked the operator for any Mariana or M. Sands listings. He jotted down a number and came back to the living room. "She's listed, all right."

Mariana felt a surge of hope.

"I, uh..." Lefcourt cleared his throat. "I called the Montgomery County Maryland police about this late last night. That's where the address on the license is located," he explained. "No one's reported Maryanice Roualt missing," he said apologetically.

"It's certainly disheartening when no one notices that you're unaccounted for," Mariana grumbled with a sigh.

"Would you like me to take you over there to see this address?" Lefcourt volunteered. "I can take you first thing tomorrow morning, if you'd like. Like I said, I have business back at the office that I can't put off today, but I'd be happy to drive you over tomorrow and spend the whole day trying to sort this out with you."

"I'll take her," Owen interjected firmly. He straightened and continued examining the contents of the wallet.

Mariana looked out the window and saw a car pull into the driveway behind Lefcourt's police vehicle.

"Maybe you'd like to do that this afternoon?" she hinted.

He glanced down at her, then followed her gaze to the newcomers.

"The press seems to be here already," he muttered.

Brock straightened his tie and beamed. "How do you s'pose they heard about our finding the purse?" he wondered aloud.

"My office didn't tell them!" Lefcourt emphatically assured them. "We've tried to protect Miss Mariana here from people she wasn't ready to face. We only release information to the press or any nonpolice inquiries with Mariana's, er, Ms. Maryanice's, consent."

Mariana smiled at Lefcourt reassuringly. "I thank you from the bottom of my heart for that, Sergeant." She grimaced. "And please, keep calling me Mariana. I'm sure that's my name. Maryanice—" she shrugged and looked at them all in consternation "—Maryanice doesn't sound..."

She'd been about to say that Maryanice didn't sound like a name she was accustomed to using, that she didn't know a soul

by that name. However, as the name had rolled off her tongue
that last time, suddenly it did seem familiar. There was an echo
of that name buried in her past. A face. A person. It didn't seem
like it belonged to her, but to someone else, someone very much
like her. As she focused on that sense of familiarity, searching
for the memory attached to the name of Maryanice, the illusion
evaporated like fog in the warmth of the sun.

Mariana frowned, wondering what lay hidden in her past that
was connected to the name of Maryanice. She looked at Owen.
He'd seen the peculiar expression chase across her features and
he was watching her carefully. She smiled a little and shook her
head. She held out her hand and closed her fingers. She smiled
ruefully, shook her head and shrugged.

"Couldn't quite catch the memory?" he guessed softly.

She nodded.

"If your office didn't intentionally or accidentally let slip my
discovering the purse, why are the ladies and gentlemen of the
press sniffing at the front door?" Brock drawled, getting them
back to the issue most of interest to him at the moment.

"An interesting question," Owen agreed. "Why don't I ask
them?" He smiled, but his eyes were narrowing in a predatory
manner at odds with the gleam of his teeth. "Why don't I talk to
the reporter while you two finish up with Mariana?" Owen suggested.

"Good idea," Lefcourt agreed.

"If they want to talk to me, I'll be too happy to oblige," the
insurance investigator offered amiably. Seeing the sharp frown
taking form on Lefcourt's features, Brock hastened to clarify his
statement. "Of course, I won't talk about the purse or the accident. Just the value of insurance investigation. In general."

"I'll keep that in mind," Owen promised, smothering his sarcasm with great effort. "But when I finish with them, I assure
you, they'll be leaving."

Mariana wondered what he could possibly say to guarantee
that, even if they were here to talk to him about his legal problems, rather than her indefinite dependency on his charity. She

was reasonably certain that was the source of the reporter's arrival, even if Brock and Lefcourt had no reason to suspect that motive.

Owen returned the wallet to Mariana.

"We'll talk later," he said firmly. "After our visitors leave."

Then he turned away and headed for the people leaning on his doorbell.

He opened the door and stepped outside, forcing the reporter and photographer to move back and give way to him as he went outside. He was still barefoot and tousled looking, Mariana realized. Although, with Owen, that somehow it didn't seem like much of a disadvantage, she thought, half smiling.

Mariana turned her attention to Lefcourt and Brock.

"So exactly what did you two want to ask me?" she asked.

Lefcourt needed to make sure he recorded any returning memories that Mariana had experienced since the last time he'd interviewed her. While she could remember some things about the drive through the mountains and Owen's pulling her to safety, there was little she could add to the accident report.

Brock was focused on the same topic. When he asked where she had been going that night, Mariana still wasn't certain she knew. There was just the overwhelming urgency of getting to that church and phoning someone. That had begun to crystallize.

"Are you sure that you remember that intention?" Lefcourt asked cautiously. "Could you just be accepting what that guy, Kelton, told you? Kind of creating a memory because it's easier than not knowing?"

Mariana shook her head. "I'm sure I was going there. And I'm sure I was running away from that man in the drawing," she said. She looked at Lefcourt anxiously. "Can you find out who he is without his being able to come back and find me through you?" she asked worriedly. She shivered, just thinking about it, feeling foolish being afraid when she didn't know why she should be afraid of him.

Lefcourt smiled at her reassuringly. "We'll be careful. Don't you worry, Miss Mariana. If we can find out who he is and where he is, we'll check him out without his knowing we're asking about him." He looked a little chagrined. "I just hope we can identify him, ma'am. With just a face to go on, and trying to keep this discreet, he may be hard to tack a name on...unless he's a well-known criminal in one of the neighboring states."

Mariana nodded. "How long will it take for you to hear anything back from the police in Phoenix?" she asked hesitantly.

"That's hard to say, but if I get hold of someone this afternoon, they may be able to get back to us in a few days, if we're lucky. That'll give them time to check around, organize a report and phone me. It depends on how many more urgent problems they've got," he added apologetically.

"Of course. Well, that's really helpful. I'll just hope there's no crime wave in Phoenix this week," Mariana said, smiling with what optimism she had left.

"Now...how about those things in the purse?" Brock said, looking pointedly at the contents spilling across the purse on her lap.

Mariana opened the wallet and fingered the health-insurance card in the plastic sleeve.

"Maybe I'll be paying my medical bills sooner than I'd thought," she observed humorously.

"You will if you're Maryanice Roualt," Brock offered, eyeing her speculatively.

"Yes. *If.*" She didn't think there was much possibility of that. Still, the name was more familiar every time she heard it. Mariana frowned in worry.

"What about the other things?" Lefcourt prompted.

A credit card. Two small photographs. One was a picture of a beautiful, Mediterranean-style, whitewashed building with a blue sea in the background.

"It looks like a tour-guide advertisement photograph for the Greek islands," Mariana said thoughtfully.

"Ever been to Greece?" Brock prompted.

"Only in my dreams," Mariana replied. She looked at the insurance man. "As far as I know."

"What about that other photograph?" Lefcourt asked.

Mariana flipped the sleeve and removed the other photograph for a closer look.

A small child was standing beside a small red tricycle. Her stuffed doll was sitting on the vehicle seat. The little girl was staring directly into the camera lens, her eyes wide and serious, seeming much older than her tender years. And she was clutching the stuffed doll's hand, as if it were a desperately trusted friend.

"She looks terrified. All alone." Mariana whispered, a ripple of recognition sliding across her. She knew that child. And that child knew her. Mariana was certain of it. They were connected, she and that little girl.

"Mariana?" Lefcourt nudged her.

"I do recognize something familiar in that little girl...but I'm not sure what it is...."

Mariana knew what it was, but she didn't want to say it out loud. Not to Lefcourt and Brock. Not yet. Not until she'd sorted the facts out. She heard Owen's footsteps approaching and she looked up at him quickly.

"That didn't take long," she said.

"It doesn't take long to say 'no comment,'" he admitted with a shrug. "They got their pictures. Asked their provocative questions. Left with my lawyer's name, address and phone number."

"Did they want to hear about my finding the purse?" Brock asked hopefully.

"We didn't discuss the purse. They haven't heard about it."

Lefcourt and Brock looked surprised.

"Huh. I guess New York needs a few country mystery stories to fill up the out-of-town pages now and then," Lefcourt offered.

"Nah. They're just picking up the trail on Portia and her poor, tragic protégés, aren't they?" Brock guessed astutely. He glanced at Mariana. "That Jane Doe angle is going to be the theme, isn't it, Owen?"

"Probably," he reluctantly replied. He glanced at his watch. "Look, if you two have finished asking Mariana questions for now, I'd like to drive her over to the address on that license."

Lefcourt and Brock stood up and nodded simultaneously in agreement.

"I'll get back to you if we get word on the man in the sketch or Mariana's connection to Phoenix."

"Thanks," Owen said, maneuvering the two men toward the door firmly but politely.

After Lefcourt and Brock had left, Owen returned in search of Mariana. He discovered her standing in the kitchen rubbing her temples with her fingertips.

"Headache?"

She nodded.

He went to his bedroom and its connecting bathroom suite. Mariana could hear a cabinet open and close. Then Owen returned holding a bottle of nonprescription analgesics.

Owen handed her a glass of cold water and silently watched her take two pills.

"Do you want to see a doctor?"

"For a headache?" She glanced at him in surprise. He looked uncertain. "I think it's stress," she explained, realizing he might wonder if the headache was a symptom of something more serious related to her head injury and subsequent coma. "I, uh, keep remembering things." She took a deep breath and slowly let it out. She was hoping it would help her relax. Mariana didn't notice any change, unfortunately. "It's like seeing another jigsaw puzzle piece. But I can't get enough of them to make a sizable portion of the whole picture." She pressed her fingers to her throbbing temples and closed her eyes. "It's so frustrating...."

Owen came closer.

"Like the name on the driver's license..."

"I do know that name." She opened her eyes and turned to him urgently. He was only a couple of feet away, coming nearer, reaching out to drape his arm around her shoulders. "It's bizarre...but I'm sure I know Maryanice. As well as I know myself. But I don't remember meeting her. And none of the things coming back about growing up include her. And I'm getting back more of that all the time...."

He drew her back toward her bedroom, bending his head close to listen.

"I remember my first day of school. The building and the school yard and the sweet young woman who was my teacher. I remember my mother and father attending school events in the evenings and summer vacations and—" she stopped when they were inside her bedroom and turned to look up at Owen "—that photograph of the little girl and her doll on the bike."

He put his hands on the tops of her shoulders and gently began to knead the tension-knotted flesh. He gazed into her anxious green eyes and reluctantly resisted the urge to lower his mouth to hers and distract her with a kiss. They needed to untangle the truth.

"What about the photograph of the little girl, her doll and her bike?" he dutifully asked with a somewhat amused smile. "I'll bet you looked a lot like her at that age." He found that he just couldn't resist. He brushed a soft, tender kiss across her parted lips.

Mariana half closed her eyes and slanted her mouth against his without thinking. For a moment, she was suspended in the pleasure of the intimacy. She slid her arms around his neck and stood on tiptoe, pressing herself against his warm, muscular body.

Reluctantly, she pulled a little away and gazed into his half-closed eyes. His hands kneaded their way down the tense muscles along either side of her spine.

"What about the photograph?" he said, raising an eyebrow and smiling lazily at her.

"You're right," she finally managed to say. "I looked a lot like that. As a matter of fact, I looked *exactly* like that."

She stared at him.

His hands drifted down to her hips. They stilled. He frowned and looked at her questioningly.

Mariana nodded slowly and very deliberately. "That is a picture of *me* when I was very little," she whispered fiercely.

"What makes you so sure?" he demanded.

"I looked like that."

"Small children don't have strongly defined physical features. Maybe the kid just resembles you."

"Like the face in Maryanice's driver's license resembles me?" Mariana challenged him.

"Yes."

"No." Mariana shook her head vigorously. She immediately regretted it and closed her eyes against the reinvigorated throbbing of the headache. She pressed the heels of her hands against her temples. "No," she repeated calmly. "I think I must know Maryanice Roualt. But I'm sure that's *my* photograph in her wallet. I had a doll just like the one in the picture. I kept it on my bed for years. I still have it, back in my house in Arizona. It's on the shelf with family keepsakes." She hesitated. "It's my oldest, dearest childhood toy."

"It couldn't be that Maryanice had one just like it?" he suggested, for the sake of argument. He had no idea who the hell Maryanice Roualt was...assuming she wasn't Mariana Sands, which, objectively speaking, he had yet to prove.

"I remember the tricycle, too. And..."

He maneuvered her over to her bed.

"Lie down," he murmured. "I'll fix your headache."

She looked a little surprised and blushed.

He grinned and pressed her down onto the bed. Laying the palms of his hands on either side of her shoulders, he lowered himself just enough to press his mouth lightly against hers. A long, slow, languorously sensuous moment later, he lifted his lips from hers.

"This wasn't what I meant when I said I'd fix your headache," he teased her huskily. "But I'm willing to try this method, if that's what you think will work."

She laughed and felt the heat of embarrassment rush to her cheeks. "I like your kisses," she admitted shyly.

"And I," he murmured, kissing her lingeringly, "I like yours."

He tried to remember what they were supposed to be doing. Something about fixing her headache and traveling to Maryland. He heard Mariana sigh his name, and suddenly the other things didn't seem nearly so urgent.

Chapter 11

The scent of her skin filled his senses with every breath he drew. Soft and light and clean, like the mountain air in early spring. He was intoxicated by her. Each drugging kiss compounded her dizzying effect on him. He tightened his arms around her, and his entire body savored the increased closeness to her. He reveled in the sensation of pressing against her shape, of inhaling her unique and inexplicably enticing essence. Her soft and yielding form silently admitted to him that she was feeling much the same toward him as he was toward her. A fierce rush of male satisfaction surged through him. That she wanted him was the sweetest part of this moment. If there was such a thing as pure, unadulterated pleasure, he was feeling it wash through him now, Owen thought lightheartedly.

The taste of her mouth made him hunger for more kisses. Deeper kisses. Longer kisses. Endless, rich, warm, wet kisses. Where mouth mated with mouth and tongue entangled lovingly with tongue. Where his arm held her close to him, breast to chest, abdomen to belly, thigh to thigh. He moved his mouth against hers, and she followed him hungrily, unwilling to ease the fiercely tender assault.

He murmured reassurances against her lips. Nuzzled her neck. Sucked air as he felt her lips caress his earlobe. Grasped her head firmly and found her mouth again.

His tongue traced the entrance, teasing the inner surfaces, incrementally sliding closer and closer. Teasing. Probing. Retreating. He smiled as she surged toward him, opening hungrily to his threatened invasion. He swept across the moist warmth as she instinctively yielded to him.

Her warm and honest response cracked some of the shields he had encased himself in long ago.

"Mariana," he whispered against her soft lips. He wanted to say more than her name, but what could he truthfully say to her? That he ached for her. She knew that already. That he burned for her? She was kissing the hot skin of his face. Surely she felt his heat. In the end, it seemed more honest just to reverently murmur her name. And Owen prized honesty above all else in life. "Mariana…" he murmured, rubbing his lips across her cheeks in tender awe.

Mariana looked into his eyes, and all her swirling, chaotic feelings swam there in the dark green depths. She looked at him as if she'd just discovered him, had never really seen him before, as if he were some Greek god come down to awaken her and bring her to life.

Owen had never been the recipient of that kind of look, and for a moment he was stunned. Then she half closed her eyes and kissed him with all the tender, trusting, overwhelming feelings that he aroused in her. When he kissed her back, she moaned softly in welcome and showers of hot fireworks shot off all over his skin, from his mouth, across his chest and arms, rocketing through his hips and thighs and deep into the depths of his loins.

Owen slanted his mouth against hers, adding then easing the pressure in slow, rhythmic fashion. He wanted to go on forever, but dimly he was aware of the hardening bite of desire.

He broke off the kiss suddenly. Gasped for cool air. And for some faint hope of cool reason.

"I should have known better than to have touched you again," he whispered, his voice harsh from the effort he was exerting to crush his biting frustration upon releasing her.

"I let you...." she said shakily, then laughed unsteadily. "I *helped* you."

"I don't remember kissing having quite this effect on me," he observed, trying to inject a little humor in an effort to dampen his eagerness for her. The humor did nothing to soften the hardness of his contours, she quickly realized.

Mariana laughed, but she was trembling with reaction and the laughter sounded strained.

"Well, that's what I was thinking myself," she admitted. "We just must be particularly biologically well matched," she murmured.

He looked at her in surprise and then, slowly, grinned. "Yes. I think you could say that."

Mariana blushed and lowered her gaze to his chest. Against her own better judgment, she succumbed to the desire to look at his face one more time. She gently traced the line of his jaw, the slight creases in his cheeks and beside his eyes.

Her fingertip was infinitely gentle. And tender. Cool against his heated skin. Owen exhaled a slow, painful breath. When she laid her palm against his cheek, he turned his face into it, kissing its center. He felt her small tremor of response. That small gesture fanned the flames that had never cooled in spite of his determination to douse them.

Groaning, Owen buried his face against her neck, trying to recall where in the hell he'd buried the rational elements of his brain. They'd gone missing in action the moment he'd kissed her. He wondered if this was some form of early-onset dementia. His wits had never completely deserted him before with other women. Then again, he'd never felt like this about other women. Not any woman.

He inhaled and the indescribably seductive scent of her skin filled his nostrils once again. Every red-blooded cell of his utterly male body surged to attention. He became excruciatingly aware of the delectable imprint of her feminine form against his. Stretched out, they were shoulder to shoulder, belly to belly, thigh to thigh. Every inch of him pulsed with awareness. Although she was wearing clothes, he was tantalizingly aware of the shape of her breasts, the curve of her hips and the hidden valley between her thighs.

"We've gotta cut this out," he murmured unconvincingly.

"Uh-huh," she barely managed to whisper.

Somehow, he couldn't quite find the strength to take his hands off her.

"In just a minute..." he promised, caressing her with slow, sweeping strokes that went the length of her body and back.

She wriggled beneath him, snuggling against him with her whole self. Owen gritted his teeth against the heavy surge of ecstasy that rocked through him.

Mindlessly, he slid his hand between their bodies, cupping the soft shape of her breasts, stroking one then the other, as she helplessly twisted, trying to follow his touch.

He tugged her shirt loose from the waist of her slacks, fumbled momentarily with the back fastening of her bra and then gently pushed it aside. He covered her bare breast with one hand, stroking the sensitive skin with his thumb. Beneath his palm he could feel the stiffly pouting nipple, awaiting his fingertip's featherlight caress, which he unhesitatingly supplied.

Mariana moaned and moved beneath him. He urgently found her mouth again with his.

She wrapped her arms around him, holding him close, desperately aching for even more intimate closeness, although she knew that it would be a big mistake to succumb to the demands of her heart and body. She slid her hands beneath his shirt and ran them slowly, lovingly, up and down his sinewy back. She felt the muscles flex and bunch. She felt the burning heat of his skin. Owen, she silently cried out. Oh, Owen, what is happening to me? What are you doing to me? My heart is breaking, and yet I feel like I'm being born again. Owen...Owen...

He pushed his knee between her legs and captured her thigh between his. He squeezed her tightly and rolled over, pulling her on top of him, without ever losing contact with her mouth. His tongue swept through the dark, sensitive regions, conquering and being conquered in return.

She had been well aware of how aroused he was becoming, but now the unyielding tumescence pressed against her crotch demanded a choice.

Owen made it for both of them.

With a long, painful, very regretful sigh, he broke off the kiss and pulled her head against his shoulder.

"Do you suppose a man can die of frustration?"

She hugged him tenderly. "I hope not," she replied fervently.

They lay there a few moments, letting the warmth of each other's arms ease the slowly receding pain of unsatisfied passion.

Finally, Mariana propped herself up on his chest and looked down into his storm-darkened eyes.

"Do you know how you make me feel?" she asked him softly.

"How?" He looked at her lips, then he dragged his gaze back to her eyes by sheer force of will.

"You make me feel fully, completely, irrevocably alive."

She kissed him tenderly on the lips, but lifted her mouth before either of them could surrender to the almost irresistible temptation to assuage their desire in the age-old way.

"When I'm with you, I feel my heart beating," she said softly. "I feel the breeze on my skin. I'm aware of my own existence, something I used to take for granted and never gave any thought to." She laid her hand on his cheek and gazed lovingly into his hard, chiseled face. "When you kiss me, lights go on all over. When you touch me, it's like turning on the electricity inside my heart. Everything sizzles." Color blushed attractively across her cheekbones, and she laughed a little in embarrassment. "You make me feel like a woman, Owen. Vibrant and alive with all kinds of possibilities in life.'' She swallowed and looked at his chin. ''I hope...I'm not embarrassing you by telling you this.''

He captured her chin with his hand and forced her to look into his eyes. They were serious.

''How could I be embarrassed?'' he asked her huskily. ''You make me feel the same way.'' He grinned a little. ''Only, in my case, you make me feel like an electrified *man*.''

She giggled and lay down on him, relaxing as he held her loosely in his arms again.

''We seem to be connected to the same high-voltage circuit,'' he murmured, resting his chin against her head.

Mariana felt the slight tremor in his body as she gently rolled off him and curled up against his side. A similar tremor passed through her. She was still shaking with desire for him, she realized.

''I'm sorry, Owen,'' she whispered, unexpectedly fighting back tears that unaccountably threatened. ''I'm not teasing you.''

''I know,'' he sighed. ''And I'm not teasing you.'' He glanced at her.

She brushed away the tears and smiled at him reassuringly.

''I know.''

''I should have kept my hands off you,'' he said evenly, although he was having a very hard time regretting it. Hell. He didn't regret it. He just regretted the circumstances that were making it impossible for him to handle this like a normal— He stopped and frowned. A normal what? Courtship? Was that the word he'd almost said?

Owen sat up and rolled off the bed. He rubbed the back of his neck, thinking, trying to shake off the lingering feelings of unslaked passion, and pacing back and forth across the room. Finally, he came back to the bed and squatted in front of Mariana.

''When we came in here, I was going to give you something for your headache, if I recall correctly,'' he said dryly.

Mariana laughed. ''You mean making love wasn't for my headache?'' she teased.

He sighed and looked at her like a starving man. He shook his head regretfully.

"No. That just created new aches, it would appear," he noted in wry apology.

She looped her arms around his neck and kissed him on the lips.

"Some aches are worth it," she whispered sympathetically.

His eyes darkened, but this time he resisted the urge to throw her back down on the bed and make love to her.

"In spite of your siren provocation," he noted gravely, wearing a pained expression, "I'll ignore that invitation, and give you the cure for your headache."

"Is that so?" she said, laughing a little dubiously.

"That is right. Now, sit up on the edge of the bed, and I'll show you how it's done."

Mariana did as he asked. He placed his fingertips on her face, and she trustingly closed her eyes.

Owen pressed his thumbs against the small indentations in the occipital bones over each eye. He held the pressure for a few counts, producing incredibly deep pain. Then, just when Mariana thought she would scream from the agony of it, he released the pressure. He repeated the procedure twice. Next he pressed his thumbs just above the points where her jawbone connected to her cheekbone. He pushed down very firmly, until pain welled up almost unbearably beneath the points of contact. Then, as she squirmed beneath the torture, he released the pressure. Then he repeated the treatment. Again, twice. He paraded his thumbprints across the centerline of her skull, from front to back, as if marking a trail for a Mohawk hairstyle. There were several other spots that received his special treatment, too. Each side of her jaw. Behind each ear. Two points at the base of her skull on either side of her spine. And between the V made by the thumb and forefinger of each hand. Each spot was tremendously painful and knotted when he first applied pressure. Each was languid, its discomfort miraculously vanished by the time he concluded his final release.

Owen sat back on his heels and rested his forearms on his

thighs. He searched her eyes deeply, looking for any remnant of the headache's pain.

"Better?" he asked softly.

Mariana's eyes widened. She nodded her head in surprise.

"Yes. Much better." She tilted her head from side to side and examined herself mentally. She looked at him in admiration. "All better. How do you do that?" she demanded with childlike curiosity.

He grinned and slowly stood up.

"I'm not telling you all my secrets right away," he told her. "But if you need another treatment...let me know."

She laughed at his flagrant teasing.

"Why Owen, are you flirting with me?" she challenged, getting off the bed and straightening her significantly rearranged clothing.

"I think you could say that," he admitted. He looked her up and down, a wolfish admiration in his still dark eyes. "We'd better get going," he warned.

"Uh-huh." Mariana looked at him innocently. She concentrated on refastening her slacks. If she continued gazing into his eyes, he'd realize what she'd much rather be doing at the moment. And they'd never make it to Maryland this afternoon. Which wasn't a good thing, she told herself sternly.

She heard the padding of his bare feet on the floor as he walked back to his bedroom to put on his shoes and socks and grab his wallet and keys.

Mariana collected her own things, including the purse and its contents, and waited for him by the front door. The tingling of her lips, however, remained a lingering reminder of their electrifying kisses.

"We're here."

Mariana opened her eyes and looked at the two-story brick house. She'd fallen asleep in the car, but now she was wide-awake.

"Look familiar?" Owen asked as he parked in the two-lane driveway in front of the double garage.

"I...don't know. It's not exactly *un*familiar," she said slowly. She saw the big black front door and its huge golden door knocker. A memory flashed into her mind. "I've been here before," she said in a deathly still voice. A chill passed over her, and she rubbed her arms to ward it off.

Owen frowned slightly and turned in his seat to study Mariana's worried profile.

"Do you want me to go in?" he asked. "You could sit here, if you'd feel safer...."

She smiled wanly and glanced at him. "You read me very well, Owen," she acknowledged. "I *would* feel safer here. But I think I should do this." She tried to be optimistic. "Maybe fear is the key to my memory. Maybe if I see some things that heighten this fear, I'll remember what's causing it." She opened the car door. "And if I remember what's causing it, maybe I won't have to fear it much longer."

Owen got out and followed her to the front door. He was thinking she might not be able to escape her fear quite that easily. He wasn't going to advise her to cower in ignorance, however, so he just hoped that whatever was scaring her wasn't as bad as her nightmares made it seem.

As Mariana walked along the flagstone path leading to the house, memories began filtering back into her consciousness.

"I've come here before," she said, feeling a little shocked. She glanced back at Owen. "Several times. In the month before the accident." She looked at the carefully mulched and pruned plants and the mowed and raked yard. "It always looked like this. They have a contract with a landscaper to do the yard work year-round."

"They?" Owen asked cautiously.

"Louie and Maryanice Roualt." Mariana stared at the large black-painted door with the huge gryphon's-head brass knocker. The image of the man in the sketch came back to her full force.

Louie Roualt. It was Louie. Of course. How could she have forgotten that? she wondered.

"Mariana?" Owen asked, becoming concerned as she stood in front of the door, staring at it as if she were in a trance.

She reached up and lifted the door knocker, then struck the door firmly three times with it. Her hand trembled when she released the brass gryphon's head. She sensed Owen's presence close behind her, and she clenched her hands to hold the chilly swell of fear momentarily at bay.

There was no sound from inside the house. No approaching footsteps.

Mariana reached for the small button at the side of the door frame. She pressed it firmly, ringing the doorbell. No one replied to that call, either.

She opened the purse and withdrew the key from the change pocket of the wallet. She stared at it for a moment, holding it in her fingers and studying it for the first time since Lefcourt had given her the purse.

"It's the front-door key," she murmured.

Owen remained silent, but his eyebrow lifted when she slid the key in the dead-bolt lock and opened the door.

"You're remembering a lot," he remarked, impressed. He followed her inside the house.

Mariana stopped in the middle of the foyer and turned to face Owen.

"I feel like I'm trespassing," she confessed somewhat anxiously.

"We tried knocking on the door," he said reassuringly. "And you obviously have a key to the place."

"But I'm *not* Maryanice Roualt," she whispered fiercely.

"All right," he said, offering her a half smile and the comforting touch of his hand on her shoulder. He sobered and asked, "Who is Louie Roualt?"

Mariana shivered.

"The man in the sketch. This is his house. Maryanice is his wife. She asked me to come here. I was supposed to..." Mariana stopped. The memory faded out before she could recapture the details. "I was supposed to do something for her. Get something. Or put something back. Or..." She shook her head and sighed bitterly. "I can't remember the rest!" she wailed, balling her hand in a fist of frustration.

She wanted to stamp her foot and hurl furious complaints, but there was no one to blame, and therefore, no convenient target to receive her anger.

"It'll come back to you, Mariana," Owen said, his soothing baritone doing more to calm her than his actual words. "Your memories are getting richer, more detailed, more complete every day," he stated, using the same even, reasonable tone.

"You're right," she agreed, nodding her head. She was glancing around, reacquainting herself with the cool, modern, chrome-and-glass decor, when another memory burst vividly into view. She gasped and threw Owen a desperate look. "And I've just remembered another little detail!"

"What little detail?" Owen shouted at her back as she ran toward a room farther into the interior of the house.

"The security system!" she declared over her shoulder.

Owen cursed under his breath as he trotted after her. There had been no warning sign around the front windows. He'd checked. Too late to argue with Louie Roualt about that little oversight, he thought. When he reached the kitchen, he found Mariana anxiously turning the room upside down.

"It's inside one of these," she explained, flinging open another cabinet door. Two cabinet doors later, she found the one with the security master-control panel. She frowned and closed her eyes. Seconds later, she opened her eyes and shot Owen a triumphant glance. "The code's written on a piece of blue paper."

"It's definitely coming back to you," he said wryly.

"But is it fast enough?" she muttered as she desperately searched the contents of the wallet. "I know it's here some-where," she murmured anxiously. "I think I have two or three minutes after opening the front door to get it turned off before the alarm sounds...." She riffled through the paper currency. "Here!" she exclaimed triumphantly.

Mariana snatched out a receipt, printed on end-of-roll, blue-striped cash-register paper. There were numbers scribbled on the back. Mariana quickly punched them into the security console's keypad.

For a moment, the numbers stared back at her from the small liquid crystal display. Then, finally, the system acknowledged its having been successfully disengaged.

Mariana raised her hands and exclaimed, "Yes!" Grinning victoriously, she turned toward Owen, who was looking suitably impressed.

"I'm certainly glad that you were here before," he drawled. "And that you remember the most critical details about the visit," he added. "Otherwise, we'd be standing here, hoping that the police who normally respond to this alarm wouldn't book us for burglary before we could convince Lefcourt to vouch for us."

"I can't tell you how wonderful it feels to remember how to rescue myself!" she said. She sighed in profound satisfaction.

Owen grinned. He could relate to that.

"Besides," she said, touching him lightly on the shoulder, "after all the problems you've been bailing me out of, I'd be a poor friend if I failed you when you needed me."

"Somehow, I doubt any of your friends have ever felt that you failed them."

Mariana thought about that. Maybe it was the strangely charged ambience she always felt when she was with Owen. Maybe it was the adrenaline-saturated experience of shutting off the security alarm. But Mariana realized that she suddenly remembered lots of friends. People she'd known in art studios, in commercial galleries, in schools and social gatherings. From her childhood, and her adolescence, and her young adulthood. She hugged Owen and just as quickly released him.

"What was that for?" he asked, bemused, as she turned away and went back into the living room.

"I don't know," she confessed. "I just felt so happy I had to share it with you."

He was tempted to tell her to feel free to do that any time she wanted. But before he blurted that out, she had changed direction. Something in the determined way she was striding down the hallway alerted him that she'd remembered yet another important fact.

"What is it?" he asked.

"I remember what I brought here."

Mariana pushed open the half-ajar door, flipped on the light switch on the wall and entered the large master bedroom.

A huge bed dominated the room. It was covered in a thick satin, bloodred comforter. Along the sleigh-style mahogany headboard, there were eight hand-made pillows. Each was covered with a different brightly colored section of fine silk Persian-rug fabric. A large Oriental carpet covered most of the floor except for a small frame of polished wood peeking out around the perimeter. There were two large ornately carved mahogany dressers. Floor-length mirrors on opposing walls. Matching brass floor lamps. And the biggest walk-in closet Mariana could ever recall seeing. Through its partially opened sliding door, she could glimpse a small dressing room with mirror, valet and makeup table, as well as a wall-length rack of clothing. Men's clothing and women's clothing.

Mariana walked over to one of the dressers and pulled open the top drawer. She removed a four-inch-square velvet jewelry box, opened it and turned to show it to Owen.

"Maryanice wanted me to return these to Louie," she explained haltingly.

Owen came close enough to see.

"Her wedding and engagement rings?"

Mariana nodded.

"They look like they cost about as much as that car I'm driving," he noted dryly.

Mariana smiled sadly. "I don't think Louie was ever short of cash." She looked at the sparkling diamond solitaire and its diamond-studded gold-band mate. "It was love that Louie never had to give."

"You seem sure of that."

Mariana nodded.

"Have you met them?"

"I... I've met Maryanice. I keep having this surreal memory of her standing in my studio...and sometimes I see her, like a reflection in my mirror back in my house in Arizona. But I don't remember coming face to face with Louie...except in my nightmares."

"But you sketched him...." he reminded her softly.

Mariana frowned. She shook her head. "I...can't make sense of that yet."

Owen lifted the engagement ring from the velvet, removed the box from her hands and placed it on the dresser. Then he took her left hand in his. He looked at her, and although his gaze was steady, there was a questioning expression in his eyes.

She looked at her left hand and the ring he was holding and realized what he wanted to do. She nodded her head.

He slid the ring onto her finger.

"It fits," he observed.

"Like it was sized for me," she weakly agreed. She watched as he slid on the wedding ring. "So I wear the same size that Maryanice Roualt does," she rushed to explain to him. She pulled the rings off, not liking the feel of them on her finger. "She's probably the same size. It's a common ring size. Lots of women wear it."

Owen watched in silence as she put the wedding set back in the velvet box and then into the dresser drawer.

She closed the drawer with a little more force than necessary and whirled, keeping her back to the drawer, as if to keep it closed and the contents permanently within it.

Owen watched her, a slight frown indenting his brow.

"I'm *not* Maryanice Roualt!" she cried out desperately.

"I didn't say that you were," he said quietly.

Mariana wrapped her arms around herself, as if to hug the truth close and keep it alive. Her eyes were large and vulnerable as she looked into his shuttered expression.

"But that's what you're thinking, isn't it?" she demanded, her voice unaccountably shaking.

"I'm thinking that you still haven't entirely unscrambled all your memories," he said carefully.

"But the ones I have remembered are very clear to me," she argued. Owen didn't say anything, but there was the slightest change in the color of his eyes and she knew he was keeping his thoughts back. "What?" she demanded, her skin flushing with anger. "You don't think I'm telling lies about what I'm remembering, do you?" she asked, horrified.

Owen reached for her, but she quickly stepped beyond his reach. A muscle twitched in his jaw, and his expression became a little grim.

"Memories are sometimes unreliable, Mariana. They're unreliable even when people haven't had head injuries and been in a coma."

She stared at him, and a horribly cold sensation crept over her skin.

"I thought you believed me," she whispered. "I've been pouring out these chaotic, irrational, unconnected pieces of my mind in the raw and nonsensical form they come back to me. I've opened my mind to you...not to mention my heart and..." She blushed, recalling the feel of his hands on her, the imprint of his body, the heady taste of his mouth.

Owen's eyes darkened, and his whole body tensed.

"Damn it, Mariana, I *do* believe what you tell me," he insisted angrily. "I'm trying to help you remember everything. But I'm getting the impression that there's something that you may not want to remember. If that's true, it can warp your interpretation of the facts. And you may unconsciously repress facts because they're just too painful to face."

Although he'd begun speaking with anger in his voice, as he'd talked, that emotion had faded. At the last, he was speaking to her so softly that it brought tears to her eyes.

Annoyed with her weepiness, Mariana quickly brushed them away. She paced across the room.

"I guess it does seem peculiar," she conceded. "I mean…my name is almost exactly like hers. I'm carrying a purse full of her identification when I crash and get knocked unconscious. Her license photo is a dead ringer for me. Although," she hastily said, "her hairstyle, makeup and expression are different."

Owen lifted a brow as if to say that he didn't think those differences were insurmountable.

Mariana grimaced at him and continued her review.

"She's got a preschooler picture of me. That's hard to explain," she conceded with a sigh, then rallied and added, wagging her finger at him. "But I have a life on the other side of the country! Don't I?" Suddenly she was confused. What *was* the truth?

Chapter 12

Owen wanted to fold her in his arms and tell her everything would be all right. But Mariana needed a reason to believe that, not some emotional oath from him. So he suggested a plan instead.

"Would you like me to take you on as a sort of pro bono client, Ms. Sands?" he asked seriously. His steady gaze reminded her that hers would always be a very personal case as far as he was concerned.

"You'd sort of come out of retirement, or semiretirement, to help me find the loose ends in this mess?"

He nodded.

He was just standing there. Calm. Rational. Arguing with her but still letting her make the big decisions. Mariana felt all the trust and love for him filling her heart to overflowing.

"You're quite a guy, Owen," she said softly. "Why hasn't some woman put a ring on your finger?"

"I never met the right one."

That reminded Mariana of the story that Anselm Brock had told about the first Jane Doe. Mariana chewed on her lip, wondering when to bring that subject up. Maybe later tonight. After they finished here.

"I'd be very grateful for your professional services in this matter," Mariana said, accepting his offer. She lifted her chin a little defiantly. "But I want to be billed at the normal rate. Whatever that is."

"Right. The normal rate for this kind of thing," he agreed. He straightened up and walked slowly around the room, examining the few items displayed. "Let's walk through the house and see if anything provides some useful information, or makes you remember anything else."

Mariana nodded and joined him.

"After we leave here, we can use my cell phone to see if Lefcourt can help us."

"Help us with what?"

"The names and addresses of the handful of people who owned cars like the one you were driving. One name in particular interests me." Owen frowned, recalling that one had lived in this county. He had died the night Mariana had been run off the road by that truck. But perhaps he had friends or family who might recognize Mariana...or Maryanice.

Mariana dug in her heels and grabbed his elbow.

"And we should call Phoenix and try to get hold of Cryssa Roberts. My agent. I told her I had personal business on the East Coast, but she must be wondering why I haven't checked in with her. She needs to know when I'll be delivering the pottery I promised her for the Las Vegas Southwestern art show." Mariana blinked. "Las Vegas..."

"What about Las Vegas?" Owen asked, going into the living room and slowly sweeping the room with a glance.

"Maryanice found me through my art there." Mariana stared at him, but she was seeing flashes of bright lights and neon signs and night turned into a carnival of iridescent colors. "She saw one of my collages, and the image of a woman in it reminded her of her own past. She saw my name on it. I sign my pieces 'Mari.' The piece was on display and for sale. So she asked the casino and hotel managers if they knew who I was and how she could reach me.''

Owen stopped in front of a small table and picked up the framed photograph on it.

Mariana saw his expression and went to see what he was looking at.

It was a photograph of a man and a woman on the porch of a whitewashed, Mediterranean-style building. The sea and sky behind them were pure blue. The woman looked very much like Mariana, but about ten years younger. She was slender and beautiful and barely wearing a string bikini. The dark-haired, saturnine man she was draping herself on had his hand proprietarily on her hip. She was wrapping her thigh around his and gazing into his face in absolute adoration. Her lips were slightly parted. There was a glow about her that came from more than the healthy tan they were both wearing.

It was the look of a woman in love.

Mariana slowly shook her head. She glanced up at his face and saw the grim line of his jaw, the ember glow of anger in his eyes.

''That's not me!'' she said emphatically.

Owen glanced pointedly at the small inscription that had been penned in by a delicate, elegant hand in the lower right corner. It said Mari And Louie's Perfect Honeymoon.

Mariana felt as if she'd been hit by a huge wave. She stared at the words, then at the picture, then at Owen's grim face.

''There has got to be an explanation for this,'' she whispered.

He put the picture down and shoved his hands in the back pockets of his jeans.

''Believe me, Mariana,'' he said, measuring his words carefully, ''nobody wants to believe that's not you in the picture more than I do.''

She ran to him and flung her arms around him, holding him tight. His arms came around her immediately, like a strong, protecting castle wall.

He bent his mouth close to her ear.

''We need to know if you're free or not,'' he whispered. ''I will not add to your problems by getting you tangled up with a charge of adultery. The way things are going between us, you know damn well that could happen.''

She nodded her head. Beneath her cheek, she felt the steady beat of his heart. And the pounding of her own.

Owen tightened his arms around her possessively. Then he forced himself to loosen his hold. He'd never gotten involved with a married woman. It was absolutely against his personal code. If Mariana was wrong and somehow she was possessed of a husband... He gritted his teeth against the acid pain of jealousy that thought brought.

Mariana gently disengaged herself.

''Let's finish looking around here and then get to your car phone.'' Mariana grimaced. ''The sooner I can prove to you that I'm not suffering from multiple personalities or some sort of fractured psyche, the better!''

It certainly couldn't be too soon for him, Owen brooded.

They thoroughly surveyed the living room, examining everything from the glossy, upscale architectural magazines ostentatiously placed on the hand-made, stone-and-glass coffee table to the discreetly placed cordless telephone nestled inside a decorative, hand-carved pecan box. Since the room had large furniture and few drawers, containers, and no closets, it didn't take them very long.

Owen was relieved to leave the room and its photo of the besotted honeymooners. He tried to believe there was going to be an explanation for it that would make him a very happy man. It wasn't easy.

They methodically investigated the remaining rooms. There were two other bedrooms. Since neither contained any personal items, they assumed these were guest bedrooms. There was an office with a desktop computer, monitor and printer, also a filing cabinet, a Rolodex and a writing desk with a multiline telephone console on it.

''They must get a lot of phone calls,'' Mariana said in surprise.

''Or make a lot.''

He turned on the computer.

"I'm looking to see if there's anything under your name. We won't read other files."

"So we don't get thrown in jail for invasion of privacy?" Mariana guessed, wide-eyed with admiration. "I knew it would help to hire an experienced professional."

Owen grinned but became serious again as he pulled up the list of files on the system's hard drive. There were a lot of items that sounded like financial dealings. The modem contained phone listings for Internet access via several different local and commercial communications links.

"I'll bet it knows some very interesting secrets," Owen murmured regretfully at the computer. "Unfortunately, there's nothing here that suggests Maryanice Roualt used any of these programs. To search all the files in detail, we'd need a lot of time. We don't have much of that left this afternoon."

"You don't want to see how long we can hang around here before a cleaning person, groundskeeper, security guard, business associate or long lost friend of the Roualts stumbles onto us?"

"Not particulary. Besides, we may make faster progress using this afternoon and this evening interviewing people on our list of folks to call."

Mariana nodded. "I agree."

"Look at the file names on the monitor one last time, while I scroll through them. If any of them do seem familiar, we'll take a closer look."

Mariana read the names as they rolled up the screen. It took several minutes, even though Owen was scrolling through them at a fairly rapid rate. When he reached the end, he glanced over his shoulder at her. Mariana shook her head and gave him an apologetic look.

"No. None of the names mean anything to me."

"It was worth a try." Owen turned off the equipment and rose, turning to look at her. His features eased into the faintest hint of amusement. "Don't look so woebegone," he teased her. "We're just getting started with our investigation."

"By the way," she said, trotting after him as he strode out of the room. "Did you ever quote me the going rate for your services?"

"I don't believe I did." He smiled rakishly. "But don't worry about it, Ms. Sands. I'm sure we can work out terms that you'll find completely satisfying."

Owen stopped abruptly in front of the kitchen doorway. "Do you know how to reset the alarm?"

"Unless someone's changed the procedure," she qualified as she set about resetting the system.

Owen closed his eyes. That hadn't occurred to him earlier, when she was disengaging the alarm. It was probably just as well. He didn't need anything else to be anxious about. He'd already parried more than enough stress in the past month. To his great relief, Mariana did know how to reset the security system.

As he slid into the driver's seat and reached for his cellular phone, he wondered if he was too emotionally involved with Mariana to conduct an objective investigation for her. After all, he was trying to believe her explanation for the facts, but Owen thought most investigators in his position would not.

They'd be inclined to see Mariana Sands as a woman with two identities, for reasons not yet clear. She could be abused and using an alternative identity to protect herself from her abuser. She could have been abused as a child and developed dual personalities. The Mariana Sands personality might have been unaware of the existence of the Maryanice Roualt personality.

He stared at his cellular phone, thinking of the alternative explanations that more objective investigators would be meticulously exploring.

"Owen?"

"What?"

"You look grim," Mariana murmured. She hesitantly touched his knee.

He smiled slightly and pushed the Power button on the phone.

"Well, maybe our old friend Buddy Lefcourt can improve my outlook."

Mariana didn't pay very close attention to Owen's conversation with the police. His call was forwarded from one person to the next within the small law-enforcement office as they tried to locate the busy sergeant. Mariana stared through the car window, willing her scattered lost memories to return. As she gazed pensively at the Roualts' house, something familiar clicked inside her brain, and miraculously, the last of her lost memories did begin drifting back.

The sound of Owen's voice faded into the background. Mariana recalled the first time she'd seen the house, walking up to the front door, the key trembling in her hand. She remembered following the procedures she'd been told about to disengage the alarm. She remembered returning the wedding and engagement rings. And searching the dressers for the safe-deposit box key. A key she never found. She recalled making the phone calls to Louie. Talking to him. Listening to his self-absorbed ramblings, his manipulative praise and his sly inquiries about how she was spending her time.

And she remembered calling Cryssa from a pay phone at a nearby shopping center. And later from the pay phone in the hallway at the AA meeting where Kelton had seen her.

Then Mariana felt the sun rise within her mind. Everything came flooding back in a rainbow of vivid colors. Her childhood. Her parents. Her youth and adulthood. Moving around the Southwest. Living outside Las Vegas. Moving to Phoenix.

And Maryanice. *Maryanice.*

She saw her own face staring back at her as she stood in the glass-enclosed foyer of a rehabilitation program's reception area.

Maryanice...how could I have forgotten you? You and I are two halves of a whole. Of one blood. Of one past. Maryanice...forgive me for not remembering....

Then she thought of Louie. His charm. His engaging smile. His silvery wit. His unexplained wealth. His worldwide travels. And his iron control over Maryanice. Lovely, insecure, fearful Maryanice.

Mariana's mouth went dry, and her blood froze in her veins as she recalled Louie's whispered, silken threat, reverberating as distinctly in her mind as the remembered feel of the telephone pressed against her ear as she listened to it.

"I always return for you, Maryanice, my sweet. Surely you realize that by now. I always expect you to be there, waiting for my return with open, welcoming arms. I'll be home next month. You can play the casinos all you want until then. Entertain yourself, my pet. Drink like a little fish. Deck yourself in new diamonds. Enjoy the Vegas shows. Do what you please till I return, within limits, of course. You know what those limits are. Make certain that the men you stimulate to hover around your honeyed little self keep their hands off you. Of course, I don't mind them admiring you. I like it, as a matter of fact," he'd explained with a self-congratulatory laugh that had made her shudder then, as the memory of it did now. "It's a compliment to my taste in women, wouldn't you agree? Any man swells in pride watching other males hunger after what he already has claimed as his own."

Mariana had cringed at the cold, proprietary description Louie was giving. He was talking about his wife, not his chattel, she had wanted to scream at him. But she had not screamed it. She could not. Maryanice would not have spoken to her husband like that. Not then, anyway.

"Your admirers can look, *but they must not touch,*" Louie explained. Then he had paused significantly. In a deathly soft voice, he had added, "If any of my...acquaintances—and remember, I have many—sees you going into a hotel room with another man, you won't have to worry about where you'll be sleeping next year. And neither will he." He let the effect of his threat sink in. "Do I make myself clear?"

He hadn't needed to spell out the fatal consequences in any more detail. Mariana had gotten the message. Dry mouthed, she had whispered, "Very clear, Louie. Don't worry."

"I never do," he assured her in the same smooth, silvery voice. "Remember, Maryanice...I love you."

The softly hissed words had curled around her like a serpent's tongue. Mariana shuddered at the memory. Love. What did a man like Louie Roualt know of love?

Mariana closed her eyes, fighting against an unexpected spike of panic. Louie's not here. He doesn't know where I am. He doesn't know who I am. I'm safe. Maryanice is safe. We're both safe. He was probably furious that she hadn't been phoning him regularly in the past few weeks, but as long as he couldn't find her, she wouldn't have to confront that danger. But Maryanice...Maryanice didn't know what had happened. She had to tell her...she had to warn her...she had to reach her. As soon as possible. Slowly, Mariana opened her eyes and reached down deep inside her soul to the wellspring of her own personal courage.

Remembering the truth hadn't been quite the liberating experience that she had expected it to be, she realized. Be careful what you ask for, she thought wryly.

Owen's voice drew her back to the present.

"Thanks, Buddy. I'll get back to you later."

Owen turned off the cellular phone and pulled out the map that he'd brought along.

"The guy who owned that car lived here," he said, pointing to an old, established neighborhood on the outer fringes of the county.

Mariana looked at the spot he was pointing to and nodded.

"Yes," she said. A small brick rambler, she thought. Built back in the late 1940s.

The way she spoke instantly caught Owen's attention. His head snapped up and he stared at her through narrowing eyes.

"What is it?"

"His name was Fred Lowe," she said, staring sightlessly ahead of her. "He loaned me his car that night, because I needed to get to the AA meeting, and I had no car of my own. You see, Louie leases cars or rents them. He'd turned in the last one when he left for Suriname last month on business. That way, anytime Maryanice went anywhere, there could be a record of it. A cab record. Or a rental-car record. She had to spend money to leave the house.

She left a paper trail every time, one that he could follow. That's why she used Fred's car. When Fred realized what was going on between Maryanice and Louie, he'd offered her the use of his car to attend those meetings in West Virginia. She had to go to another state to feel safe in an AA group," Mariana said, shaking her head in disbelief. "Can you believe that? What kind of husband treats a wife like that? What kind of person treats another human being like that?"

Owen laid down the map, his gaze riveted on her.

"So you remember Fred Lowe," he said slowly. "And borrowing his car?"

Mariana nodded.

"Fred was not a handsome man. He was gaunt and wore clothes that had once been expensive but were gone shabby from too many years of use. Years of alcohol addiction had left him with no family, no profession and broken health. He'd hit bottom after losing everything. But then, he joined AA and slowly built a new life. It was tough, but he was succeeding. And he was loved and respected by the new friends he made. He was a reliable employee at a small photocopying shop. And he was a volunteer with the local AA chapter here. He was manning their information and referral phone line when Maryanice called them months ago. She was desperate for help, but she was terrified her husband would discover what she was doing. You see, Louie encouraged her to keep drinking. I think he knew that he couldn't continue dominating her if she sobered up and got a life."

Owen wished to hell he knew whether Mariana was remembering the truth or the fractured version of the truth that a tortured woman had constructed to save her sanity.

"Go on," he murmured encouragingly.

"There was something about Fred Lowe that made Maryanice trust him. She told him everything, eventually. And he used the AA network to locate a group she could meet with, one her husband would have trouble finding and separating her from."

"Kelton's group up in the mountains."

"Yes." Mariana swallowed and tried not to cry. "They were

very supportive. When she flew out to Nevada, trying to find me, it was partly due to the strength she'd found talking to them. They helped her *want* to stop drinking. They helped her want to believe in herself. They showed her it was possible to rise from the ashes of your worst nightmare and begin again.''

"She flew out west to search for you?" he asked in surprise. "Why?"

Mariana sighed and smiled sadly. "She's my twin sister."

Owen dubiously lifted an eyebrow. "Your twin sister."

Mariana felt her cheeks redden with embarrassment. Defensively, she lifted her chin and stared directly into his night gray eyes.

"My twin sister," she repeated, separately emphasizing each word. "From the way you repeated what I said," she noted, a little angrily, "I assume you don't believe me."

Owen sighed and ran a hand through his hair in frustration.

"I'm trying to believe you," he hedged.

"Trying?" she exclaimed.

"Look at the situation objectively, Mariana," he argued. "This tale sounds more like imagination than reality. People who have been abused have been known to repress reality and create a fantasy explanation for their life that is easier to live with...."

"You still think I'm both Mariana Sands and Maryanice Roualt?" she said in dismay.

"I don't know what to think," he said evenly. "But that is one obvious explanation for your memories and your being in possession of Maryanice Roualt's purse, wallet, house key and identification at the time of the accident. If Louie Roualt is as manipulative and terrifying as you think he is, it's understandable that you'd try to create another personality, an entirely new life, in order to escape him. Maybe the concussion triggered a dual personality. Maybe it was there before the accident."

His jaw tightened stubbornly as he saw the growing hurt and disappointment reflected in her eyes as she gazed at him. "I don't particularly want to believe this," he said irritably. "I told you earlier...I don't relish the possibility that you have a husband.

And it has nothing to do with Roualt's nasty disposition. It has to do with the way I feel about you."

"How do you feel about me?" she challenged him. "Are you sure you're not confusing me with the woman that Mr. Brock was talking about this morning? The first Jane Doe?"

He frowned. "What the hell are you talking about?"

"I've been wondering why you stuck around at the hospital after the accident. You didn't know me. It was a lot of trouble to drive back and forth, and to stay at Madge's." Mariana drew in her breath and forced herself to tell him what had been worrying her. "Did you stay with me when I was comatose because you were making up for what you couldn't do for that other woman, the first Jane Doe in your life?"

Owen's face was hard to read. The frown had smoothed away, but a mask seemed to have replaced it. His lack of expression would have been the envy of any high-stakes poker player.

Just when Mariana began to think that she had hit him so close to a vulnerable spot that he would refuse to answer her, he began to speak.

"Yes."

Mariana almost flinched from the pain.

"Well, that makes perfect sense," she said, her voice thin and wispy from having the wind knocked from her lungs by the shock. She'd been hoping he would deny it. She hadn't realized just how much she'd been hoping that until he confessed the truth.

"That was part of the reason, in the beginning," he continued. "Have you ever lost someone dear to you like that?"

Mariana thought of Maryanice. And their parents. It wasn't quite the same, she decided. Especially their parents.

"Not exactly," she admitted. She looked down at her hands. "What was the first Jane Doe's name?" she asked unhappily.

"Madelon Hurst."

There was another awkward silence. Mariana broke it first.

"How did you meet her?"

"At one of Portia's dinner parties, like Brock said. For once, the newspaper accounts got it right," he added with a bitter smile.

"Did you love her?"

He looked at her for a long moment.

"Are you sure you want me to answer that?" he asked huskily.

She lifted her chin, bravely looked into his eyes and nodded in the affirmative.

"Yes."

Mariana wished she hadn't asked. She hadn't expected the fiery hurt in the region of her heart that his admission ignited.

"I wasn't ready for a permanent commitment," he said reluctantly, as if the words were being dragged from him against his better judgment. "She was. She'd been trying to convince me to go to a cabin in the mountains with her that weekend. She thought spending time alone together, away from the city and my work, would give her a chance to bring me around to her point of view."

"You were going to go with her the weekend she disappeared?"

Owen nodded.

Mariana began to understand.

"The last time I saw her," he said, his cheeks flushing with embarrassment and self-recrimination, "she begged me to come with her. I refused. I told her I knew what she was hoping for and that I wasn't ready to give that to her. There were tears in her eyes when she got into her car."

"I'm so sorry, Owen," she whispered unsteadily, her heart aching for his long-ago pain.

"I felt very guilty about it," he said evenly. "I did everything I could think of to try to find her. But it was too late. While she was missing, I didn't know what to think. I didn't know whether to imagine her kidnapped and raped and tortured to death by some maniac or injured and alone and suffering for days on end from some accident. It was a relief to finally know what happened to her," he said, his voice tinged in bitterness. "Seeing someone that I loved tagged as a Jane Doe, with no one there when she was found, that hurt."

His eyes flashed angrily, and his gaze bore into Mariana's without apology. "So, yeah, when I realized you were a Jane Doe, that brought back a lot of bad memories. And, yes, I tried to make up for what I hadn't been able to do for Madelon by being there for you while you were unconscious. And later, when you were awake but didn't know who you were, I wanted to keep your spirits up, because I knew your friends and family would have given everything they had to be there for you, if they only knew where you were."

Mariana looked away and nodded. "It was much more than most of us do for a stranger," she said thoughtfully. "And if doing those things for me helped you heal the pain and lessen the guilt you felt about not being there for Madelon—" she turned her steady gaze back to his and smiled slightly, although not too happily "—I'm glad. Perhaps that repays a little of the debt I owe you."

He reached out and yanked her half onto his lap.

"You don't owe me a damn thing," he growled. "And while I may have been there in the beginning partly because of what happened to Madelon Hurst, the most important reason I kept driving up there, kept calling about you, kept finding excuses to keep involving myself in your life has nothing to do with her at all."

Mariana felt the tension rippling through his body as she sat wedged between him and the steering wheel. The gray in his eyes was illuminated with the angry sparkle of dark green now. His lips were flattened, and a small muscle worked in his jaw.

He moved the palm of his right hand up across her cheek and ear, then sank his fingers into the luxuriant softness of her hair. She felt the pressure pulling her closer to his mouth, and as she closed her eyes, his lips touched hers.

It was not kind. It did not plead for understanding. It was not gentle or hesitant in any way.

The kiss was one of anger and frustration and a touch of anxious despair. It quickly melted into the heat of burning desire. Moving back and forth across her mouth, easing the pressure and then increasing it, he demanded and returned in full measure profoundly intimate pleasure.

He lifted his head slightly and looked into her passion-dazed eyes.

"Does that feel like guilt to you?" he demanded roughly.

His mouth sought hers, and he renewed the onslaught. His tongue glided along the sensitive ribbon of inner lip. He suctioned hers into his own mouth. He slid his mouth warmly across the tingling flesh of her neck until she moaned out loud and tilted back her head, yielding in ecstasy. Breathing unevenly, he lifted his head.

"Does that feel like a man repaying an old debt?" he growled.

Mariana tried to make her eyes focus, but the world seemed to be swirling. She shook her head in a daze.

"Not really," she had to concede.

He wrapped his arms around her and buried his face in her hair.

"I may not be absolutely sure whether you're Mariana Sands or Maryanice Roualt," he confessed huskily. "But I know damn well you're *not* Madelon Hurst." He leaned back and looked into her eyes. "The only thing that's worrying me now is whether or not you have a husband."

Mariana smiled at him and placed her hand tenderly on his cheek.

"In that case," she said softly, "you have nothing to worry about."

He didn't say anything, but he didn't look completely convinced.

Mariana pushed away from him firmly but gently.

"I hired you to investigate," she reminded him firmly. "I think the sooner we've gathered the facts, the less you'll have to worry about."

Owen sincerely hoped so.

"Tell me about this twin sister of yours," he suggested, attempting to get his mind off the lingering imprint of Mariana's body. "Why didn't you remember her relationship to you earlier?"

Chapter 13

As they drove toward the late Fred Lowe's house, Mariana explained.

"Maryanice and I lived with our parents until we were three years old. We lived in western Colorado in a little town where the houses were tumbling down and most people had moved away to find work in other places. Remember that snapshot in Maryanice's wallet that I said was of me? It was taken when we went to visit my mother's brother in Durango. Maryanice had one taken at the same time with the same tricycle but with her favorite doll, which was a different color and style from mine. About two months later, our parents were killed in a flash flood while they were driving into the mountains to talk to a rancher about hiring out as a cook and a ranch hand." Mariana smiled a little and glanced at Owen. "You and I both had humble beginnings."

Owen flickered a glance at her, then returned his gaze to the highway.

"Anyway," Mariana continued. "Maryanice and I were orphaned, and our uncle took us in but asked a local lawyer to find homes for us to go to. Our uncle was a single man and he had just signed up to go into the infantry. He couldn't raise a couple of children. He didn't want to, either."

Owen felt a very personal surge of anger against Mariana's uncle, who had refused to shelter and care for her as a child. His hands tightened on the steering wheel.

"The lawyer had contacts in a lot of big cities. Lots of people wanted to adopt babies or toddlers or young children. We were healthy and not too bad to look at," she said modestly.

She still wasn't too bad to look at, he thought.

"Unfortunately, the lawyer didn't know anyone looking for two small children. He did know of two couples who each wanted one child. So, Maryanice was placed with one family and I was given to the other."

"Were the two families living in the same town?" he asked.

"No. Maryanice's family lived in the Texas panhandle, My family lived in eastern Nevada."

Mariana looked at the passing countryside and tried to get a grip on her feelings. This was always a hard part of the story to tell.

"Our uncle left me with a baby-sitter and took Maryanice away. When he came back, he told me I was going to go live with the couple who had come to see me at the lawyer's office and who had taken me to play at the park several times. That was the last time I ever saw my uncle or Maryanice. Before my new parents arrived, my uncle told me that something awful had happened to Maryanice, that she'd been hit by a car and was dead."

"How the hell could an adult lie to a child like that?" he demanded angrily.

"I don't know. I was distraught. Crying my eyes out. Completely inconsolable. My new parents were quite shocked to see me in that condition when they arrived to pick me up. They had been told that my sister had died in the crash with my parents. Mom and Dad, my adoptive parents who raised me, were good-hearted people. They would not have wanted to separate us, if they'd known about Maryanice. But they couldn't have taken both of us. The lawyer knew that, so he kept the truth from them. And they were left to soothe me and comfort me for months. When I told them about playing with Maryanice at our uncle's house, they assumed it was childish fantasy that comforted me in my loss of my twin and my birth parents. Eventually, I moved on with friends and school and my new home. I dreamed about Maryanice at first, but after a while, it was hard to remember her. I couldn't quite make out her features in my mind's eye. Maybe that's what my uncle had hoped for when he told me she was dead.''

"They didn't leave you with any photos?"

"My uncle had mistakenly given me Maryanice's photo and Maryanice had been given mine. He couldn't tell us apart, and he didn't recognize which dolly belonged to which child. So we each had a photograph. I believed that Maryanice was dead.''

Owen nodded, guessing what was coming next.

"But Maryanice knew that you were alive?" he said.

"Exactly. Unfortunately, her new parents weren't very happy people. They took out the fears and disappointments in life on Maryanice. She was never submissive enough for them. She was too pretty. Too lively. Too artistic. They wanted a shy, studious, plain daughter.''

"That sounds like a recipe for adolescent rebellion," Owen noted dryly.

"And that's what happened. Maryanice ran away from home when she was seventeen. She got a bus ticket to New Orleans and worked there long enough to earn bus fare to New York City. When she arrived in New York, she got herself a job waiting tables in a restaurant, and shared a small, overcrowded apartment with several aspiring actors she met there. She went to their modeling agency and was offered a few low-budget advertising jobs. That's how she met Louie Roualt.''

"New York?"

Mariana grinned. "If she'd met you, her story would have had a happier ending.''

Owen gave her a quizzical look, but let the comment pass.

"She was ripe for someone like Louie," Mariana mused. "He flattered her, bought her nice things, took her to fine restaurants and generally swept her off her feet. As soon as she was nineteen, they got married.''

"But her prince turned out to be less than charming after the honeymoon,'' Owen supplied.

"Much less. As the years went by, Maryanice realized that some of his friends were...crooks. She had no higher education, no job skills of any particular importance, no money. All she had were her looks and Louie's willingness to support her.''

"So she looked the other way when he philandered, gritted her teeth when he badly used her and told herself there was nothing she could do when he bent the law in his business dealings.''

Mariana gave Owen a startled look.

"Do you know Louie?'' she asked in amazement.

"No. But your sister sounds a lot like mine. So, I just guessed that my sister's disreputable husband behaves a lot like Louie Roualt.''

"Unfortunately, it seems that they have that in common,'' Mariana agreed, grimacing.

"You said that your sister went to look for you.''

"Yes. Poor Maryanice,'' Mariana murmured pityingly. "She'd been married for ten increasingly hellish years. She'd wanted to leave him for close to five years, but Louie...'' Mariana felt the familiar wave of fear ripple over her. "Louie sensed her withdrawal from him, and began tightening his control over her.''

"How?''

"He kept her on a cash allowance, insisting that she account for her expenses. He became suspicious if she refused his advances.''

"His advances? In bed?''

"Yes. If she seemed unenthusiastic or...reluctant...he questioned her relentlessly about other men in her life. The more she tried to move away from him, the more he tried to tie her to him.''

Owen frowned. "That kind of possessiveness can be dangerous.''

"Oh, it was. Louie's the primary reason that she developed a serious drinking problem. I'm sure of that.'' She glanced at Owen. ''And by the way, *I* don't have a drinking problem. I distinctly remember having an occasional margarita with my dinners back home. And white zinfandel wine. Light beer. But just a glassful with a meal.''

Owen's mouth curved into a slight smile. She was sounding quite confident, downright zealous, about her identity and lifestyle.

''So your sister decided to search for a relative to flee to.''

''Basically, yes. Her parents had moved away, and she wouldn't have known what to say to them, anyway. Asking them to provide her with a room to stay in while she battled alcoholism was more than she could ask for. She was sure they'd reject her, and condemn her for having the disability.''

''But you were safe to approach.''

''Yes. But she didn't know where I was. She remembered hearing her parents discuss the adoption proceedings with a neighbor who was considering going through a lawyer for a private adoption. She remembered the lawyer's name and the name of the town where our uncle lived. So she made inquiries, and searched the court records for that period. To her delight, she found the court order making permanent our respective adoptions.''

''Which led her to your parents' surname and place of residence.''

''Right. My parents were in their early fifties when they adopted me, and their health had begun to fail several years ago. They died within a year of each other.''

''I'm sorry,'' he said softly.

''I had time to prepare for the inevitable,'' she said, still feeling the sadness of the loss. ''But their selling their home and disappearing from phone lists made it very difficult for Maryanice to try to locate me. I used Cryssa's phone listing for most of my business, and until recently, I avoided having a residential phone of my own. It seemed I was constantly inundated with unwanted sales pitches. That was really disruptive for me. I needed long periods of peace and quiet to concentrate on the work. I got a cellular phone and a pager, so people could page me and I could call them back. It worked very nicely.''

"But made you invisible for your sister. She couldn't even use the Internet phone-directory search throughout the West to locate you.''

Mariana made a face and nodded. "Exactly.''

"But we got a listing for you in Phoenix this morning," he pointed out, frowning. "Or is that some other person?''

"No. That's me. I finally broke down and got a residential phone line installed. Actually, I did it because I thought it would make it easier for Maryanice and her doctors to reach me after she went into the hospital.''

"Hospital?''

Mariana noticed that they were getting close to Fred Lowe's house.

"Fred's house is on that street on the left. The second house down.''

"I guess I'm not going to hear what a hospital has to do with your getting a phone line," Owen said dryly, pulling into the driveway.

"Later. There's a For Sale sign up on the property," Mariana observed. "Maybe it's part of his estate settlement.''

Owen turned off the engine.

"Let's see if anyone in the neighborhood can tell us about you and Maryanice and Fred," he suggested.

Mariana got out of the car and cast a sly smile at him.

"You're thinking of Maryanice and me as separate persons, aren't you?''

He hesitated in midstride.

"Yes," he conceded with a pained grimace. "But I *want to*, Mariana. *That's* the *problem*.'' He tried to focus on fact gathering. "Come on. Let's canvass the neighborhood and see if we can get some objective corroboration for your tale.''

Two hours later, they returned to the car and backed out of the driveway, somewhat more informed than they had been when they pulled in. Lowe's house was vacant. The bank had been appointed by the court to manage the inventory, accounting needs, bill paying and tax filing for his estate. That included selling his house, the neighbors had explained. Some of them recalled seeing someone who looked exactly like Mariana on one or two occasions in the past, although not on the day Fred Lowe drove off and died in a Virginia motel room. They knew he was alone, estranged from his family for the most part.

And there had been a strange car prowling in front of his house the day before his death. But the police knew all that, the neighbors had assured them.

Owen was frowning as they drove back to his home.

"Call Lefcourt," he suggested, handing her the cellular phone so he could concentrate on the rush-hour traffic. "Ask him if the authorities have determined Fred Lowe's probable cause of death."

Mariana punched in the numbers. She had a bad feeling about Fred Lowe's death. She'd been having it ever since she regained the rest of her memory. Lefcourt was at his desk, and he had lots of information for them.

"Oh! Sure glad you called!" he exclaimed heartily. "The police in Phoenix verify that a Mariana Sands lives in an adobe-style house on the outskirts of town. She's an artist. Sells pottery, paintings and other kinds of artwork. Cryssa Roberts runs a gallery and also serves as an artist's agent, brokering consignment sales all over the Southwest. No one answers M. Sands's phone. No one answers her door. Her home is locked up, and it appears no one's there. Ms. Roberts's answering machine was on. She's apparently gone on a business trip for a few days, according to the people who operate a shop next door to her gallery."

Mariana had held the phone up between her and Owen so they both could hear Lefcourt's reply. She raised her eyebrows and smiled at Owen, as if to say *I told you so.* He could tell what she was doing out of the corner of his eye, although he was still watching the traffic ahead of them. He shrugged, indicating that it was great news but was not definitive proof.

"Funny you should ask about Lowe's cause of death," Lefcourt said in surprise. "I told Owen they weren't sure how to classify it at first. They thought it was suspicious, but it could have been natural causes, accidental or some intentionally inflicted injury. He hadn't checked into the room. No one saw anybody else coming or going from the motel room, not even the dead man himself. There was no obvious signs of foul play in the room itself—"

"Sergeant," Mariana interrupted, momentarily bringing the phone back to the side of her face so she could speak into it. "I'm sorry to interrupt you, but for weeks I've had to face all the things I didn't know. Would you mind sparing me all the things these poor detectives don't know and get to what they *do* know?"

"Oh, sure. I understand, Ms. Sands," Lefcourt replied apologetically. "The coroner put the time of death sometime on the Sunday afternoon that you had your car accident. He thinks the cause of death was a drug overdose. It appears Lowe swallowed a fatal amount of black-market tranquilizers. The autopsy lab analysis identified the substance. Apparently it's something you can get from a pharmacist without a prescription in some of the Latin American countries. Works fine, if you take the right amount. Which Mr. Lowe, unfortunately, didn't."

"Why aren't they calling it a suicide?" Owen demanded.

"No suicide note. No threats of suicide reported by any of his friends. No reports of his being despondent. No known failed love affairs. No financial problems. As a matter of fact, his neighbors and friends at AA all thought he'd been happier this year than any time before. His doctor had seen him recently and declared him in good physical and mental health. It just doesn't seem like this man had any reason to end his own life. And then—" Lefcourt cleared his throat awkwardly "—when they heard from me about the car inquiry, they began looking into the possibility that his death had something to do with Jane Doe's driving off with his car, assuming it was his car, which it now sure does appear to be."

"Wasn't there any evidence of foul play on his body?" Mariana asked.

"Some. The coroner thought it looked like he'd been restrained. His wrists and ankles were a little bruised, like he'd been tied up. When the lab chemistry came back with the overdose, it didn't answer where those bruises came from, but it certainly made homicide a possibility. It could be that someone restrained him, then forced him to swallow a fatal drink laced with tranquilizers."

"Drink?" Mariana said, her heart sinking.

"Yep. He'd downed nearly a pint of vodka."

"But they didn't smell that on his body at the scene?" Owen asked in surprise.

"Nope. 'Course, vodka doesn't smell that strong. And the guy wasn't breathing when they got there. The liquor was all inside him. Not spilled on him. Oh, yeah...they haven't found the bottle anywhere."

"Maybe someone took it with them after they force-fed him his last nightcap," Owen suggested.

"That's a mighty popular theory among the investigators on that case right now," Lefcourt confided with a short laugh. "It's still considered a suspicious death, but they're working on probable homicide. Unfortunately, they've got no suspect, no motive, no obvious clues to point them anywhere in particular to look for a motive or a suspect. The only suspicious thing about the motel where he died is the question about how the man got into a locked room all by himself. They're doing the usual legwork and hoping for a break in the case, but they're stumped for now and open to suggestions."

Owen took the phone. "Well, take this one. Suggest they check on Louie Roualt's whereabouts at the estimated time of death. They could also trace the movements of Roualt's associates," Owen said grimly. "They might want to discover what countries Louie's been in recently, and whether customs has ever found any of those tranquilizers in excess quantities in his baggage."

"Louie Roualt?" asked a clearly perplexed Buddy Lefcourt.

"Louie Roualt. Maryanice Roualt's husband."

"Her *husband?* Then he lives at that address on the driver's license Anselm Brock found?"

"You got it, pal," Owen muttered.

Lefcourt whistled under his breath in consternation.

"Okay," Lefcourt agreed. "I'll call if I get any news. If you think of anything else, give me a buzz."

Owen turned off the cellular phone and glanced at Mariana.

"Have you always led this adventurous a life?" he asked in consternation.

Mariana laughed and shook her head. "No. This is the most adventure I've ever had."

"I'm relieved to hear it," he muttered. "How about stopping at Rafael's Café for dinner on the way home? With all this investigating, we somehow forgot to eat lunch." He shook his head, unable to explain how that could happen.

"If I had my credit card, I'd treat," she said gamely, offering an apologetic grin instead.

"Lucky for you, I haven't lost mine yet." Owen turned onto the road that would take them toward the town. "You can explain the rest of this adventure to me over dinner...beginning with that comment you left dangling about your sister and the hospital."

Mariana nodded and absentmindedly agreed.

"You know," she said thoughtfully. "It's much easier to accept your financial kindness now that I know I have money and can return the favor. I'm going to have to get duplicates of my driver's license, bank card and credit cards, but I actually do have accounts." She leaned back against the seat and relaxed. "I have enough money to take care of all the bills we're running up."

"What happened to your wallet and identification?" Owen asked curiously.

"It was in the back seat of the car. Unless Anselm Brock finds it, it's probably lost somewhere in the mountains."

"Too bad he couldn't have found yours instead of Maryanice's," Owen observed. "She already had a roof over her head and a known identity."

"Gosh, I should call her," Mariana said, frowning. "She was supposed to be isolated from outsiders. It's part of the rehabilitation program. But she would have expected me to call every Sunday, or in case of an emergency. She must be very worried."

"Use the cell phone," Owen said.

Mariana punched in the numbers. When the rehabilitation center operator answered, she explained who she was, gave them the confidentiality number that authorized them to speak with her about the case and asked to speak to Maryanice.

"Are you sure?" Mariana asked, shocked. "She hasn't finished the program yet. I'm sure it's too soon... I see. No. Thank you. Uh-huh. Goodbye." She turned off the phone and turned toward Owen. "She checked out."

"When?"

"Yesterday. She left with Cryssa. They think they were going to Las Vegas." Mariana's voice trailed off.

Rafael's Café was more than half-filled by the time they had been seated and had placed their orders. The after-work crowd had been drifting in for more than an hour, and families looking for someone else to cook their dinner were filing in, one after the other.

Mariana sipped her margarita, watching Owen over the top of the salt-rimmed glass. He was tipping back a long-neck bottle of Texas beer and taking a long, satisfying swallow of foamy brew. She'd never noticed how sexy that was, she realized, feeling as if her mind was becoming strangely fogged. She absentmindedly turned the rim of the margarita glass, letting the citrusy iced tequila flow over the salt and into her mouth. She watched Owen's Adam's apple move as he swallowed some more of his beer, saw the slight sheen of moisture on his lips, the ruddy hue of his neck and cheeks....

And the distinct gleam of male amusement in his eyes.

Mariana choked on her drink. She hastily put down the drink and picked up her napkin, coughing a few times to clear her windpipe.

"I don't normally stare," she hastily defended herself.

"Does your staring at me mean something's wrong with me?" he asked.

Mariana thought he looked suspiciously poker-faced, but she vehemently blurted out her reply before considering why that might be.

"No! Nothing's wrong with you," she assured him, still feeling flustered and not knowing precisely why. She frowned and looked at the margarita. Maybe she shouldn't drink after all. She raised her eyes to his and felt herself enfolded in a mysterious and exciting warmth. "There's nothing at all wrong with you, Owen Blackhart," she murmured. "I was just...admiring you...admiring your appearance...as an artist...." And as a woman, she thought with an inward sigh.

"Then I'll take it as a compliment," he said, a slow grin curving his lips. He touched his bottle to her glass and proposed a toast. "To mutual admiration."

"To...mutual admiration," she murmured in a thready voice made peculiarly weak by his steady regard.

They each drank in honor of the toast. Then for a long, silent, moment, they gazed at one another.

"Why don't you tell me how your sister finally found you and what the hell a hospital has to do with her? You may have remembered everything and feel very illuminated. I, however, am still significantly in the dark."

In between bites of spicy grilled chicken, savory sautéed vegetables and freshly cooked, soft tortillas, Mariana provided him with the answers he wanted.

"The neurologists at Cleary Hospital said that the memories acquired immediately before a traumatic head injury are sometimes lost...or slow to return. I lost my identity, memories of my entire life. The last ones to return are those that occurred during the months just before the accident, and the least related to my past."

Owen nodded, conceding that often happened.

"Every time I remembered something, it jogged a new memory into being, Owen. The memories were linked together in an endless chain. Tug on one, and it pulled another into view." She looked at him. "That domino effect of memories falling into place turned into an avalanche when I sat in your car and looked at the Roualts' house this afternoon. It felt like a barrier had disintegrated. Suddenly memories began cascading back so fast I was overwhelmed by them." She pushed a piece of grilled pineapple around a roasted-green-pepper slice. "I think it was Louie that was the barrier."

"Louie?"

"I think you were right when you said I was avoiding some things too painful to recall." She frowned, trying to analyze her own behavior. It was difficult, being both doctor and patient at the same time. "I remembered his face, and my fear of him and that somewhere a woman was desperately depending on me. All those things came back in my dreams fairly quickly. And I was fairly sure they were memories, not just fantasies. They didn't make sense in the beginning, because I hadn't remembered that Maryanice was my twin sister."

Owen's expression didn't change, but Mariana knew he wasn't completely convinced that there actually was another person named Maryanice. He was going along with her explanation, partly to encourage her returning memory, and partly because he wanted to believe that Mariana Sands and Maryanice Roualt were two separate people. She smiled at him reassuringly, knowing that he would soon be able to lay the last of his doubts about that to rest.

"I had only learned that Maryanice was still alive a few months before I lost my memory. She was a *recent* memory. And she was a *traumatic* memory. She brought back the deep pain from my earliest childhood about the death of our parents, our uncle's giving us away and his lying to me." She blinked away the moist stinging of tears. "I guess the brain tries to protect you when you're vulnerable. I guess I wasn't able to handle all that at first, especially the old grief on top of the new fears. So my mind bought me some time to recover by smothering Maryanice's identity, and with her, Louie's. Maryanice's marriage was a nightmare. When she told us what it was like, we were all afraid of Louie ourselves. Afraid for Maryanice's safety...and our own.''

''We?''

''Cryssa, Fred Lowe and me.''

Owen's expression hardened. He hoped he ran into Louie Roualt under circumstances that allowed him to repay the man for the torment that Mariana and her friends had suffered.

''Have you fully recovered your memory and remember everything now?'' he asked casually, trying not to pressure her.

''I think so. I remember why I came here. I was masquerading as Maryanice.''

Chapter 14

Owen grimly stared at her.

"Let me see if I have this straight," he said slowly. "You impersonated your twin sister to protect her from her maniacally possessive husband, a man with more than enough money to destroy you and no known scruples that might deter him from that goal if he found you out?"

Mariana's eyes widened, and for a moment she questioned the wisdom of being scrupulously candid with Owen about the plan she had concocted with her sister. Owen definitely did not look pleased.

"Well—" she said. "Yes."

"Why the hell did she involve you in this? Why didn't she deal with it herself?" he demanded, radiating disbelief at the risk Mariana had taken.

"I'm getting to that," she promised, trying to remember why it had seemed like a perfectly reasonable plan to her at the time. She had to admit, her memory was getting a little foggy on that point. Owen's furious glare wasn't improving her recollection at all. She hurried on with her explanation.

"We planned it so that I wouldn't run into Louie...."

"And just how the hell could you be sure that he wouldn't surprise you?" he demanded, sublimating his anger with sarcasm.

"All I had to do was be at the house to phone him on schedule...."

"He left a schedule for Maryanice to use to check in with him?"

"Yes."

Owen rolled his eyes heavenward, seeking divine assistance for his self-restraint.

"What if he'd arrived at home unexpectedly?" Owen asked, his voice hardening and his eyes turning the color of billowing black smoke.

"He rarely showed up unexpectedly," Mariana retorted defensively. "We picked a time when he was committed to a big series of meetings with his business contacts in Suriname, Colombia, Mexico and several island gambling resorts in the Caribbean. For the past several years, he made that trip in the late fall, and he never came back in less than a month."

"Did it occur to you that he might kill you if he realized you weren't his wife?" Owen demanded furiously, completely dismayed that she had put herself in such a dangerous situation.

"Of course," she hissed, looking pointedly around the room. "Keep your voice down, please! I don't want this mess to be the newest piece of gossip for everyone to chew on."

"That's the least of your worries, Mariana," he muttered, but he did lower his voice. "Did you ever come face to face with him?"

"No."

Owen breathed a soft sigh of relief.

Mariana took the opportunity to seize control of the conversation again.

"You asked me earlier how Maryanice ended up in the hospital," she reminded him. "I'm trying to get to that."

Owen closed his mouth and nodded for her to continue.

"Well...Maryanice finally located me when she was in Las

Vegas. Louie likes to stop there when he has business in Los Angeles. She used the visits as an excuse to search for me, pretending to go shopping or gambling or sight-seeing. She happened to see one of my collages hanging on the wall of a coffee lounge in her hotel. It was the image of a young woman that looked a lot like us. She was drawn to it, and when she saw the way I'd signed it—'Mari'—she asked how she could buy the piece.''

"The hotel management referred her to your agent, Cryssa Roberts," Owen guessed.

Mariana, wreathed in proud smiles, nodded her head happily.

"God must have smiled on her, Owen. She had done everything she could think of, as discreetly as possible, since she didn't want Louie to know what she was up to. She had persevered for months and months, but that piece of art was a gift from heaven, pointing her toward me."

She looked at Owen, and her expression became very vulnerable.

"Sort of like when he smiled on me that night on the mountainside, and maneuvered you behind that truck so you could put your hand in mine and pull me to safety."

Owen felt the strange sensation swirling around him that he always felt when he looked into Mariana's eyes.

Maybe you were a gift to me, he thought. Would she be willing to hold on? Would he?

"Just don't test the limits of the Almighty's generosity," he warned her.

Mariana disregarded his annoyance for the moment and picked up the thread of her story again.

"Maryanice had begun searching for me in earnest over a year ago. She desperately needed to find someone to trust. Someone she could turn to for strength so she could break free of Louie's psychological hold over her. Someone to love her. Someone to believe in her. She'd lost all faith in herself. She wanted someone to tell her she could make something of her life. That her life was worth struggling for." Mariana looked at him anxiously. "Can you understand how she felt, Owen?"

Owen steepled his fingers and stared at them thoughtfully. He knew from personal experience how difficult it could be to withstand the determined manipulations of a rich and powerful person. How much worse it could be for a young woman virtually alone in the world being toyed with by an older, more sophisticated man who lacked a conscience.

He lifted his steady gaze to Mariana's worried eyes.

"Yes," he assured her evenly.

Mariana reached out and covered his strong hands with one of hers.

"And can you imagine how I felt? Here was my twin sister, whom I believed dead, given back to me. It was like a miracle. And it was like a nightmare. She was trembling and frightened and she needed me, Owen. Can't you understand why I would want to help her escape from the man who was destroying her?" She pleaded silently with her eyes when at length she fell silent.

Owen covered her hand with his and stared at the strong, supple fingers. They were slightly roughened from work. The strong, expressive hands of an artist who worked with clay.

"I can understand the impulse," he said at length. "But why didn't you just keep her with you and let her file for divorce from long distance?"

"First she needed to get into a rehab program," Mariana said fiercely. "There's a really good residential program that Cryssa knew about. Maryanice agreed to go in. She needed money of her own to pay. And she didn't want her husband to come and interfere. We thought we could buy her a few weeks of uninterrupted therapy there if someone kept talking to Louie for her. That would keep him from suspecting that she was actually laying plans to leave him for good. We hoped by the time he returned, she'd have a support network in place. It would give her a fighting chance to divorce him."

"But you said you returned her rings. Wouldn't selling them have generated cash for her?" Owen asked, frowning.

"She didn't want anything to do with those rings. It might have made financial sense, but...they were symbols of bondage to her,

Owen. She'd have scrubbed toilets for years to pay her bills rather than use money raised from those."

"Well, then, what assets did she expect to use?"

Mariana sighed. "I was supposed to find a safe-deposit box key that she had left taped underneath the top dresser drawer. But it wasn't there when I showed up at their house. I maintained the pattern of life that she led, going to the AA meetings on Sunday. Being bored out of my skull all week long..." She grinned. "Picking up liquor at the store and pouring it down the drain at the house, so some bottles would pile up."

"Until the accident," he amended.

She nodded.

"Well, that explains why Kelton thought you looked pretty strung out when you first came to the AA meetings, but seemed much healthier recently. There were two of you—Maryanice in the beginning, and you later on."

Mariana nodded.

Owen frowned. "So why isn't your sister in the hospital now?"

Mariana frowned worriedly. "I wish I knew."

"Where's Louie Roualt?" Owen asked more pointedly.

"He...might be back by now." Mariana gulped when she saw the angry dismay in Owen's eyes. "I didn't know that when we went there this afternoon, Owen!" she exclaimed heatedly. "If I'd remembered all this, believe me, I wouldn't have gone back there. Not without talking to Maryanice first."

Owen closed his eyes. When he opened them, he seemed to have found an iron core of self-control.

"We're calling Lefcourt and letting the police sort this out," Owen said. By the tone of his voice, he made it clear there would be no debate or argument about this point. "Domestic power struggles are dangerous situations. Marital combat can be fatal. You've done as much as you can for Maryanice with that—" he was about to say *hairbrained*. "—misguided masquerade. You will *not* pretend to be your twin sister in dealings with Louie Roualt again."

Mariana withdrew her hand and straightened in her chair, her cheeks reddening in angry embarrassment. Part of her was deliciously gratified that Owen cared deeply enough for her to say something so transparently proprietary. However, the rest of her had been independent far too long to meekly acquiesce to such an unvarnished command.

"I have been looking after myself for almost thirty years, Owen Blackhart!" she briskly informed him. "That last comment of yours sounded more dictatorial than anything I've heard directed toward me since I got out of kindergarten!" Her eyes flashed defiantly.

Owen gritted his teeth and glared at her across the table of dirty plates.

"I simply want you to live *another* thirty years," he growled. "And considering the way I feel right now, you should consider my choice of words to be extremely diplomatic!"

Mariana gaped at Owen. Before she could reply, however, a shadow fell across their table. She looked up to see Seymour Rushville beatifically beaming down at her. She smiled weakly.

"Mariana!" he said, his voice booming. "And Owen!" He bent in Owen's direction conspiratorially. "I'm surprised to see you two are still in town, what with all the reporters crawling all over us all day long here. Sweet Aunt Annie's fan," he swore, grinning. "I think just about every last person in town today got taken aside and interviewed."

"Great," Owen muttered sarcastically. He motioned for the check and sat like a man stoically awaiting the next unseen blow to fall.

Seymour leaned toward Owen and lowered his voice. "Bye the bye, Owen, Averson's been looking for you this evening. He called me about a half hour ago to ask if I'd seen you."

Owen frowned. "Did he say what he wanted?"

"No..." Seymour hesitated. Then he sheepishly added, "But I figured it was probably something to do with the court hearing the judge set for tomorrow morning in the matter of that challenge to Portia's estate settlement."

"I haven't heard about any court proceedings being scheduled," Owen said in surprise.

"Probably because you haven't been home to check your mail or answer your phone calls from your lawyer," Seymour suggested cheerfully. "I have it on very sound authority that there'll be a hearing, all right."

"What authority?" Owen challenged.

"The court docket manager is my stock boy's aunt," Seymour confided with a hearty grin.

"That's sound authority," Owen conceded fatalistically. He looked at Mariana. "Maybe you'd like to help Seymour redecorate his store tomorrow, Mariana? Looks like I'll be sitting on a bench most of the day." A rustling sound drew his attention to a figure weaving through the now packed restaurant. Averson Hemphill, Esquire. Looking very relieved to have spotted Owen.

"There you are, Owen! I've been looking for you everywhere!"

"So I hear."

In all the excitement, Owen hadn't noticed a man approaching him from behind.

Mariana had. Her eyes grew big, and she cleared her throat, trying to get Owen's attention.

"Mr. Blackhart?" called out the newcomer, who was pointing a camera at them.

Owen turned to glower at the man and was greeted by a bright flash of light. Then another. And another.

Then the photographer grinned at them and hastily headed for the front door. He was in a waiting car and driving away before Owen could stop them.

"Looks like you two will be seeing your faces in tomorrow's newspaper," Seymour said, finding it all greatly amusing. "Autograph a few at the store, if you have some time, will you?" He heard his name being insistently called from a raucous corner table. "Uh, sorry, folks...it's my turn to buy the beer. Good luck in court, Owen. And holler if you need anything, Mariana. You know my number."

"Owen, we need to discuss what's going to transpire in court tomorrow," Averson was saying. "Could you come by my office after you're through with dinner?"

"Would right now be soon enough for you, Averson?"

The lawyer was taken aback, but he quickly recovered.

"I'll just pick up my take-out order and meet you at my office. I hope you don't mind if I eat dinner while we talk?" Averson said with an apologetic smile.

As the lawyer went to the back of the restaurant to pick up his food, the waitress returned with their check and began clearing away the plates.

"Was everything okay tonight?" she asked automatically.

"No," Owen muttered darkly.

Startled, the waitress looked from Owen to Mariana.

"Don't mind him," Mariana told her soothingly. "The photographer didn't shoot his good side."

The waitress looked from Mariana's solicitous expression to Owen's mildly outraged one.

"I don't like having my picture taken, neither," she heartily assured him. "Both my sides are not good," she added with a little too much sincerity to be believed.

"Come on," Owen said, rising to his feet and turning to leave. "We've got too much to do to sit around Rafael's Café looking photogenic."

Mariana grabbed the purse and hurried after him.

Owen spent over an hour with Averson Hemphill, listening to the description of what was likely to happen in court the following day. Pleading sleepiness, Mariana had curled up on the somewhat worn leather couch in the reception room and tried to catnap.

She soon realized that she couldn't fall asleep while Owen was pacing slowly around Hemphill's office, discussing what could become a very serious problem for him.

The door that connected the reception area to Hemphill's office was made of a beautiful light oak. Its oil-rubbed finish looked like it had been done by hand, she thought, admiring the warm wood tones.

For some reason, Hemphill had installed a large pane of glass in the upper portion of the door. While it afforded less privacy than wood, the intricately etched designs and shadows made by frosting the glass permitted more light to pass through from one room to the other, and made each seem more open. Hemphill had another, adjoining office which had a solid wood door, so he had seclusion when he or his clients required it.

Mariana was glad he was using the etched-glass-and-wood door's office tonight. She could watch Owen through the pane to her heart's content. Every once in a while, he seemed to sense her wistful regard, because he would turn and glance back at her. She'd smile at him sleepily, and she'd see something flicker in the depths of his North Sea eyes.

It was late by the time they returned to Owen's stone house in the country. The frail crescent moon provided only a hint of light. Except for the pools of man-made electrical light, the house and its surrounding grounds were blanketed in darkness. Mariana hadn't realized she'd dozed off in the car until she awoke with her cheek nestled against Owen's shoulder.

"Why don't you go on to bed," he said huskily. His gaze roamed over her face, as if he were carefully committing every lovely feature to his memory. Slowly, he caressed her cheek.

"I'm going to take a look around, make sure everything's locked," he said finally, letting his hand fall away from her face and dragging his gaze from her lips.

They went into the house, with Owen leading the way and checking to make sure nothing had been disturbed.

"I thought crime was almost nonexistent around here," Mariana commented, sleepily smothering a yawn with one hand.

"Normally that's true." He prowled through their bedrooms, bathrooms, and all the other sections of the old stone house. When he returned to the living room, Mariana was still standing there, watching him thoughtfully. "I'd feel a lot better if we knew exactly where Louie Roualt was and what he was doing."

Mariana felt a strange premonition at the mention of her brother-in-law's name. She told herself she was overreacting. She shivered nevertheless.

"Nobody has reported seeing Louie around here," she argued, trying to be logical and reasonable. "If a stranger had come around asking questions, I'm sure the word would spread like wildfire," she added dryly, having great faith in the town's ability to gossip fast and furiously.

There were strangers around asking questions, though, Owen thought. Roualt could let people assume he was another journalist, hiding his identity. Since the media circus was likely to continue, he could still use that ruse in the future. Owen decided not to alarm Mariana with that scenario just yet. Maybe he was over-reacting. Maybe he just felt too fiercely protective of her to think straight.

"We didn't see any sign of him at Maryanice's house today," she further noted. "If Louie didn't connect Maryanice with the reports of the amnesia accident victim, he probably doesn't have any more information now than he had a few days, or a few weeks, ago."

"Unless he's returned and decided to make finding you his top priority." Owen argued seriously. "It's dangerous to underestimate a man like Louie Roualt." His concerned gaze fused with hers. "I'm going to check around the outside of the house."

He locked the door on his way out.

There was no evidence that anyone had tried to tamper with any of the entrances. It was far too dark to see if the ground bore any unexpected footprints. The ground was a little soft, and it would have shown the marks. Unfortunately, there'd been so many reporters covering the story, he couldn't be sure any prints didn't belong to house-peeping members of the press.

He went back inside, locked the door one last time and stopped in front of Mariana's bedroom. She had taken off her sweater and shoes and was standing by the bed in her shirt and slacks, staring at him with a questioning, vulnerable look in her eyes.

"I want you to stay at Averson's house tomorrow while I'm in court," he said slowly.

Mariana wasn't opposed to the idea, but she didn't reply. She was focused on where she was staying tonight. Tomorrow seemed a long time away.

His gaze caressed her from head to toe and slowly back up again. And yet, he made no move toward her. Mariana wondered why.

He could see the question in her eyes, the uncertainty as she wondered if she had misjudged their relationship. He ran a hand through his hair and expelled a long, frustrated breath.

"There's nothing I'd rather do right now," he said huskily, "than lay you down on that bed and make love with you. But you've just remembered your life, Mariana. You're still thinking of me as the man who saved you from the brink of death. Believe me, it's hard not to take advantage of that," he admitted, smiling faintly at that monumental understatement. "I don't want you falling into my arms out of some sense of gratitude. Or while you're still in a state of confusion."

Mariana walked toward him, stopping when their bodies just began to brush. She tilted back her head and looked into his eyes for a long, tender moment. Then she slid her arms around his neck and drew his head down as she raised herself up on her toes. Their lips met, and she kissed him.

Owen closed his eyes and pulled her up against his chest. The world began to revolve slowly around them, and all he was aware of was the joy unflowering from their kiss.

The softness of her lips, the sweet wine of her mouth, the tender yielding of her body made him forget everything he had sworn to remember. All he wanted was to make her entirely and irrevocably his own. His hands moved over her restlessly. He slanted his mouth against hers and deepened it.

Moments later, when he lifted his head and gazed down at her, feeling stunned by the explosion of feelings between them, he realized she was smiling at him tenderly.

Mariana laid her hand on his hard cheek and looked seriously into his eyes.

"Did that feel like gratitude to you, Owen?" she asked him softly.

His eyes darkened.

"Surely, it didn't feel like confusion, did it?" she gently challenged.

His gaze fell to her soft lips.

"This is your last chance to escape, Mariana," he whispered.

"I have no desire to escape," she assured him, looping her arms around his neck and brushing her lips provocatively across his. "I know who I am. There's no reason to worry about this. I know it sounds hopelessly romantic, but I think you and I were meant to be, Owen."

He lifted her into his arms and carried her back to his bedroom. When he laid her down on his bed, he looked down at her.

"You're sure?" he asked as the last vestiges of his conscience sank beneath the rising sea of his need for her.

Her eyes were wide-open. Her lips trembled a little. She felt shy of him, lying on his bed, having to so nakedly admit the truth. And yet she wanted him so fiercely that all those worries dissolved beneath the radiant warmth of her love for him.

She opened her arms to him and nodded, too moved to speak.

Owen's eyes darkened and he lowered his mouth to hers, sealing her unspoken answer with his own silent promise. He slid his arm under her hips and pulled down the covers beneath her with his free hand. He cradled her face in the darkness and brushed feathery kisses along the delicate line of her throat.

"I don't have anything with me, Mariana," he whispered. "We've got to be careful." He sighed as he felt her lips against the hot skin of his throat. "I haven't needed to worry about protecting anyone," he explained wryly. "There hasn't been anyone to protect for a long time." He covered her mouth with his and felt the hot rush of desire well up from deep within him. He groaned softly and stood up long enough to peel off his clothing.

The bed sagged a little as he rejoined her. He didn't waste

time, now, though. Mariana felt the need in his hands as he quickly undid buttons and loosened her waistband. Tugging clothing down. Shoving it off her and covering her bare flesh immediately with his own warmth.

In the darkness, they found each other. Sighs of pleasure mixed with the hurried rustle of bedcovers being pushed back and remaining scraps of clothing hastily being pulled off.

His mouth trailed across her throat and followed the path his palm took, tracing the swell of her breasts. Softly he caressed the delicate skin, first with his hand and then with his lips. The caress continued down the length of her body. Across the pale skin of her waist, over the gentle curve of her hips and down the sensitive skin of her inner thighs.

His hands laid the kindling. His lips warmed the coals. And his tongue ignited the fires. Little fires. Everywhere. Mariana moaned and writhed and arched. She pulled him close, but he kept a little away, leaving room to touch all the secret places he hungered for. Tingling followed the tip of his tongue like inner fireworks. She pulled his head back, and he kissed her harder this time. He forced open her mouth, and her hands clenched in his hair as the dark red depths of passion slowly unfurled within her.

She ran her hands over his muscled shoulders and back, feeling the coiling tension within him everywhere she touched. His hips were hard, his buttocks smooth beneath her hands. She felt him try to pull to one side, as if to remove his weight from her, but she wrapped her arms around him and caught his leg with hers.

She felt the satiny hardness of his proud male flesh pulsing against her inner thigh. She knew why he had tried to pull away. She knew she should let him. Should help him. Should pull back herself.

She opened her eyes and looked into his. He looked as tormented as she felt. She kissed his lips. Gently. Tenderly. Longingly. Each kiss clinging a little longer. Their bodies relaxing again. Moving slowly and lovingly against one another. His hard thighs sliding against the soft inner skin of hers. His arms around her shoulders. His hands splayed against her back. His fingertips marking ten points in her smooth back.

She heard his breath coming more harshly and she ached to ease his pain.

He felt her arch up and he instinctively lodged himself against the petaled flesh that yearned for him.

"Mariana," he whispered, gritting his teeth and trying to find the will to pull back.

"I love you, Owen," she whispered, unable to hold the words back, as her heart overflowed. At the same time, her body spoke the same words silently, opening to him, yielding to him, embracing him completely.

Owen groaned and kissed her deeply. She was fire and light in what had become a lonely, disillusioned life. He wanted to make her his own. He hadn't realized how desperately he had wanted her until the last of his iron control melted in the heat of their embrace.

He caught her hips with his hands and surged into her warmth.

And suddenly the light of a hundred galaxies burst into the darkened room.

His whole body stiffened and shuddered. His back arched, and he felt her cry out in joy.

The starlit waves of exquisite happiness pulsed over them. Again and again.

Owen cradled her in his arms and rolled over, keeping them intimately joined. Silently, he rocked her in his arms.

Don't ever let me go, Mariana thought. Her face was pressed against his neck. She could feel the damp sheen of sweat on both their bodies. She closed her eyes and absorbed it all.

"I may forget who I am again some day," she whispered dazedly. "But I will *always* recognize you."

He laughed. It was a deep, rumbling, masculine sound of pleasure arising from deep within his chest.

"If this made a lasting impression," he teased her in a low, husky voice, "maybe we can immortalize it."

She felt him harden within her, felt her own body tingle in

response and giggled in astonishment as he drew her head down for another deep, soul-wrenching kiss.

The second time should have been slower, more leisurely. But it was just as hot and firecracker fast as the first time had been. The second time not only matched the hot new flames, but its culmination was even more spectacular than the first.

As the last ripple of pleasure finally subsided, Owen stared at the ceiling of his room and folded his arms around Mariana's damp body, still draped on top of him. Complete. That's how he felt, he realized. It was disconcerting. Maybe she was made of his rib, he thought whimsically. Maybe that's why reuniting their bodies felt like two pieces of a whole being put back together. And why there was a certain loneliness as the intense, climactic pleasure faded, leaving them two separate people again.

He gently caressed her hair. Forget me not, he thought wryly. What hell that would be, he mused. For Mariana not to recognize him.

"Are you okay?" he whispered drowsily, when he knew he was about to fall asleep.

She smiled against his shoulder.

"I am much better than *okay*," she mumbled against his muscled chest.

"Good," he murmured, a satisfied male smile slowly spreading across his face. "That's very good...."

Then sleep gently stole them both away.

Chapter 15

Mariana snuggled up against the warmth. Unfortunately, it had gone. She opened her eyes and blinked sleepily at the empty spot in the bed next to her.

"Good morning."

Mariana looked at the doorway, where the voice had come from. Owen was standing there, leaning against the frame, barefoot and tousle haired. And looking rather moody, she thought.

She sat up, shyly clutching the bedcovers across her breasts.

"I don't know what to say, Mariana," he said solemnly. "I've never done that before."

She looked at him in surprise. Her certainly had behaved as if he'd known what he was doing, she thought, feeling a little breathless at the memory. But he looked really remorseful, she realized. He couldn't be talking about making love, she decided.

He came over and sat down next to her, brushing a light tangle of red hair away from her eyes.

"If there are any consequences from last night, I think we should face them together."

Mariana nodded but was a little at a loss to know what to say.

He was talking about not taking precautions, she realized. It wasn't as if they'd actually made plans to share their lives. She had thought of it, of course. But she knew they hadn't discussed it.

"There's no excuse for what I did," he said, frowning and mystified that it could have happened. "Hell, I'm thirty-six years old, Mariana. More than old enough to know better."

"Hey, it's okay," she assured him. "I'm old enough, too," she said with a shaky laugh. "You were being responsible and I...held you back," she reminded, a light flush brushing across her cheeks.

Owen looked at her as if she'd lost her mind.

"You couldn't hold me back, Mariana," he said dryly. "It wasn't a wrestling match. And you didn't drag me against my will."

Mariana got up on her knees, not knowing whether she wanted to hug him for feeling worried or box his ears for insisting on shouldering all the responsibility himself.

"Next time we'll be better prepared," she said blithely. "We'll probably have nothing to worry about. If not...we'll talk about it when the time comes."

"Would you consider marrying me?" he asked bluntly.

Mariana sat back down. She felt as if the wind had been knocked out of her. At least he no longer was worried about her already having a husband, she thought, wondering how her life had gotten this crazy.

"An unplanned pregnancy isn't a very good reason to marry," she argued stubbornly. She'd always hoped her husband would be marrying her for herself. Somehow, that seemed a little petty to blurt out right now.

"A large percentage of marriages start off for just that reason," he said dryly. "They always have.

Mariana turned away. It had never occurred to her that Owen might feel obligated to marry her. She wanted to kick herself for not foreseeing it. But she'd been so blinded by her love for him, she hadn't thought that far. She licked her lips and searched carefully for a reply. Slowly, she turned to gaze at him.

"It isn't a reason that I would use for something as important as marriage." She saw his slight frown, but wasn't sure what he was thinking. "I have a comfortable life. I can support myself, unlike many women who've found themselves facing an unexpected bundle of joy. I'd want you to know our child, if we had one," she assured him, clutching the covers with one hand so she could cover his hand with hers. "I think you'd be a wonderful father, Owen." And a wonderful husband, she added silently, too shy to say it.

Owen was staring at her as if he couldn't quite believe what he was hearing. He rose to his feet and paced back and forth. He looked at her and hesitated, as if about to ask her something else. But he decided against it.

"Do you have to leave for court soon?" she asked, not wanting to be the cause of a contempt of court charge.

"Yeah," he sighed, and ran a hand through his hair. "We'll have to talk about this some more later."

He remembered her words of love, her passionate response and the incredible joy he'd found in her arms last night. Why the hell was she balking at the idea of marriage? he wondered. He'd thought the possibility of pregnancy was worth their seriously talking about the future. And instead, she was telling him she could handle it. He didn't have to worry. Worry! All he'd done was worry about her since the day he hauled her out of that car. Well, maybe that wasn't *all* he'd done. Hell, he didn't have time to untangle this latest knot in their unconventional relationship, he thought, irritated that Portia's nephew was proving to be such a roadblock in his love life.

Owen strode back to the bed, hauled Mariana up into his arms and kissed her until her knees began to buckle and his groin was throbbing against his fly. He lifted his mouth just enough to murmur against her lips, "There are occasional compensations to being married, Mariana. People don't do it just for the benefit of the kids."

He released her, jutted his jaw out in an unconscious gesture of defiance, turned on his heel and left.

Mariana stood there, naked and trembling, staring at him as he stalked out of the room like a spurned suitor. Male pride was such a touchy thing, she thought in dismay.

"*'People don't just marry for the kids,'*" she echoed to the empty doorway. "That's my point exactly." But he was too far away to hear her shaky retort.

Mariana snatched up her clothes and hurried back to her own bedroom to shower and dress. She didn't recall her life being so complicated before. She was quite sure that she would have remembered that. Nothing was wrong with her memory anymore.

Now the problem was her heart.

Averson Hemphill's red-haired wife warmly welcomed Mariana when Owen dropped her off. She smiled reassuringly at Owen, who was standing in the foyer and regarding Mariana as if he hadn't quite concluded an important discussion with her.

"You'd better get going, Mr. Blackhart, if you're going to make it to the courthouse on time," Lyn Hemphill warned him, smiling knowingly. "It's not a good idea to keep a judge waiting, as I'm sure you know. But showing up tardy to Judge Hammer's court is—" she rolled her eyes delicately "—legal suicide." Seeing the worry and frustration deepen in his eyes, she patted him on the arm and added kindly, "Averson explained your situation with Mariana." Her genteel smile grew warmer as his face darkened slightly in embarrassment. "You aren't used to having a woman living with you, are you?" she asked softly.

"No," he admitted, his brows wrinkling with annoyance. Mariana wasn't exactly just "a woman living with him."

"I'll take good care of her. Don't you worry," she soothed. "So just hurry on along to court, and we'll see you late this afternoon."

Lyn Hemphill's attention was captured by the drumroll clatter of young footsteps descending the nearby stairs.

Two children stampeded down the curling staircase and raced

past their mother en route to the dining room, whooping at the top of their lungs.

"No running in the house! And you'll be late for school if you don't get in the car in five minutes!" she called out to them. She sent Owen an apologetic look. "Excuse me..." She hurried off to corral her children and herd them toward the door connecting her kitchen pantry with the attached garage and its waiting car.

Owen turned back to Mariana, going over all the things she needed to be prepared for during the day. He knew they'd reviewed the possibilities until they were both becoming numb from the repetition. Still, an ingrained checklist was sometimes the difference between success or failure in emergencies. So, at the risk of infuriating her, he repeated one thing that was uppermost on his mind, one last time.

"If the police call you with information, or if Roualt or anyone suspicious should show up here, get word to Hemphill at the courthouse," Owen told Mariana. That way, word would get back to him. Quickly.

"I will," Mariana agreed, patiently ignoring the fact she'd already agreed to this several times in the past hour. She smiled at him optimistically. "Good luck with your case, Owen. I hope you win. And I hope the judge brings this to a close today."

Owen smiled slightly. "Thanks. Miracles happen," he conceded with a philosophical shrug. "But I doubt that a case like this can be disposed of in the space of a single afternoon in court."

Owen was opening the door to leave, but turned back for one last time. He had been uneasy about leaving her like this, with him being gone for most of the day and not easily within her reach if she needed him. The expression on Louie Roualt's face in the honeymoon photo haunted him, as did Mariana's description of his psychopathic behavior. Realizing he wouldn't be able to protect her personally for virtually the rest of the day was eating away at him.

Mariana had followed him to the door and stood a few feet away, watching him wistfully.

"I wish I could go with you...for moral support," she said, trying to smile.

He reached out and took her hand, holding it gently but firmly in his.

"And I wish I could stay with you...for the same reason."

He drew her close and folded her in his arms, lowering his head, finding her mouth with his and kissing her one last time before leaving. When he reluctantly drew back, letting her arms slide away from him, he whispered, "Watch your back, Mariana Sands. I'm counting on you to be here when I return."

She grinned at him, locked her hands behind her back to keep from flinging them around his neck.

He sighed and left, checking the door to make sure it was locked after him. Then he went to his car parked in front of the house and drove off to face Judge Hammer's court.

Lyn Hemphill took her two kids to school a few moments later. Mariana, saying she felt perfectly safe in the Hemphill home, stayed to drink a cup of coffee and read the morning paper.

The Hemphills took a local paper, a national daily newspaper, three major city newspapers and an internationally respected financial-news daily. It was a lot to read, she thought, astounded at first by the stack of papers in a floor rack beside the kitchen table. Mariana guessed that Averson Hemphill believed it was important to keep abreast of the major stories in order to be well informed for his clients.

Mariana poured herself a cup of coffee, added some sugar and light cream and sat down to scan the headlines. She was startled to discover an article on Owen a few pages into the first daily she read.

Mariana swallowed her coffee before she choked on it, gulping down the mouthful of warm drink in an uncharacteristically unladylike manner.

Before finishing the story, she picked up another paper. And another. Then another. She was gaping at the last one, still trying to come to grips with the fact that Owen Blackhart's legal battle with Portia Willowbrook's nephew was close to front-page news from coast to coast in major newspapers.

The articles did not just cover Owen's court hearing today, either. They also resurrected years of society gossip about him and Portia, as well as offering snapshot biographies of both Owen and Portia's nephew.

There was an intriguing summary of an earlier court scandal in which Owen had been awarded an unspecified, but apparently large, amount of money for having been libeled. Mariana vaguely remembered Owen's references to his semiretirement and realized why he could afford to be virtually self-employed if he wanted. He'd been publicly accused of covering up an investigation, destroying evidence to protect a client from being charged with insurance fraud, and obstructing justice. The court fight had been nasty and quite dirty. In the end, Owen had been exonerated, the real culprits identified and punished and Owen recompensed for the virtual destruction of his professional reputation.

It all was very fascinating to Mariana. Until she saw the photograph. There were several in each of the articles. But one of them riveted her full attention. And it was in every newspaper the Hemphills had.

It was of Owen and Mariana, having dinner at the café last night. The caption identified her as a friend temporarily staying with Owen at the home whose ownership was being challenged in court. They all made some mention of the fact that Owen had helped save her life and was nurturing her back to full health as she regained her memory.

Mariana shut her eyes and closed the last paper.

What if Louie Roualt saw one of these papers? What if he thought she was Maryanice? What if he made good on his threat to enforce retribution if his wife spent the night with another man?

Mariana folded the papers and put them back. Her hands were shaking as she poured herself a fresh cup of coffee. When Lyn Hemphill pulled into her garage, closing the electronically controlled door with a hand-held device, Mariana hurried to the door to confront her with this new, unfortunate development.

Lyn put down her purse and removed her coat, laying them both on a kitchen chair. She frowned thoughtfully.

"My dear, if that's a problem, why haven't you already heard from or seen this man you're concerned about?"

"Why would we have seen him?" Mariana asked, perplexed. "The papers were just delivered this morning."

"Yes, but this was on the television news channels last night."

Mariana gripped the back of a kitchen chair and gave Lyn Hemphill a totally stunned look.

"I suppose you weren't watching television last night?" Lyn said hesitantly.

Mariana shook her head. No. They were locking up the house and falling into bed. She bit her lip. Turning on the late news hadn't crossed their minds. A shiver of fear danced across her flesh, leaving a wake of goose bumps.

"Did they show my picture?" Mariana asked, afraid to voice the question.

"Oh, yes. It was a long, telephoto videocam shot. You and Owen were leaving his house yesterday morning, getting into his car." Seeing Mariana pale, Lyn hastened to her side and put a comforting arm around her shoulders. "It looked perfectly respectable. I don't think they mentioned your name, dear."

"They wouldn't have to," Mariana murmured fatalistically.

Louie Roualt didn't need her name. He wouldn't have believed it, anyway, if they'd used her real name. He probably would have assumed she'd taken an alias to conceal her identity. But a photo of her with Owen...

"Maybe you should sit down, Mariana," Lyn said, concerned by Mariana's sudden pallor. "Do you feel faint? Maybe you should lie down, instead of sitting...." Lyn put her hand under Mariana's elbow in a gesture of support.

Mariana smiled wanly and shook her head. "I'm not going to pass out," she assured her, struggling to put as much of a smile on her face as possible. "I promise. I just wasn't expecting this kind of exposure. It's...a shock."

Mariana paced back and forth across the kitchen, thinking hard.

But with Owen tied up in court and still no word on the whereabouts of her twin sister or her agent, she wasn't certain she could do anything but wait.

And then the telephone rang.

Both women looked at it. Then they looked at one another.

The phone rang again.

Lyn reluctantly lifted the receiver and said, "Hello?" She stared at Mariana, listening to the caller. Her expression relaxed a little, but she looked as if a whole new set of questions was occurring to her. "Yes, she is, Sergeant Lefcourt. I'm sure she'd like to hear this from you herself."

Lyn Hemphill handed the telephone to Mariana and leaned back against her kitchen counter, curiously waiting for the next act of the drama to unfold.

"Sergeant Lefcourt? This is Mariana Sands."

"I'm glad I caught up with you, ma'am. I imagine you know how much publicity you and Blackhart've gotten in the last twenty-four hours?"

"Yes."

"Well, it's helped you with one problem, I'm happy to tell you."

"Oh?" Mariana felt her breath catch. "Which one?"

"Locating your sister and your agent."

Mariana's whole body unclenched, and her eyes brightened as she glanced at Lyn. "Where are they? Have you talked to them? Do you have a number—"

"Whoa," Lefcourt interrupted, chuckling. "They went to Las Vegas, intending to look up an old friend of your agent's who's a retired police officer turned private investigator. They told him you were missing and they were scared something'd happened to you. They also said they were afraid to make a public missing-person report until they'd checked out as much as they could...'cause they were afraid of your sister's husband and what he might be up to. If he were responsible for your disappearance, they didn't want him to locate them. And if he had nothing to do with it, they wanted to find you before he caught on to what had happened.''

Mariana felt a wave of relief. "They're all right, then?"

"Right as rain. They'd just talked to this private investigator a few days ago. When the national news started broadcasting photos of you, they had no trouble figuring out where you were. The investigator called me to explain who they were, and to find out what he could from us about her husband. That didn't take long,'' Lefcourt said with a short laugh. "The man hasn't been around, doesn't know what's happened, as far as we know.'' He hesitated. "That's still correct, isn't it, ma'am?"

"So far...." Mariana said, without a great strength of conviction that it would be true for much longer. "Where are Maryanice and Cryssa?"

"The investigator said they're catching a plane this morning for Washington.''

"They're on their way *here?*"

"That's right. They should set down at Dulles International late this afternoon. They have to change planes in Chicago, and that's slowing them down some.''

"Thanks, Sergeant," Mariana said, feeling a little dazed. "Do they have Owen's phone number?''

"No. Uh, I was going to ask you about that...."

"Are you sure this investigator is the real thing?" Suddenly, she remembered that it could be prudent to be suspicious.

"Yeah. We checked him out. And we also confirmed the hotel reservation at one of the airport hotels for Cryssa Roberts for two people. Want me to give him Blackhart's number?''

"Please do, Sergeant," she asked fervently. "And Cryssa or Maryanice, too, if they should contact you.''

"Happy to 'blige ma'am," he said with a good-humored drawl. "I'll leave a message at Hemphill's office down at the courthouse about all this.''

"I'm forever expressing gratitude, it seems," she stated in tired amusement. "But my thanks are as sincere as can be...."

"Don't mention it. I like bein' the bearer of good tidings, and frankly, ma'am, I don't get to do it as often as I'd like." He paused. "Uh, since you've got your memory back, the police investigating Fred Lowe's death are mighty interested in talking to you."

"Oh. Of course." Mariana smiled faintly. "I'll tell them what I know."

"They'll probably be callin' soon. I gave them Blackhart's number, Hemphill's office number and the Hemphills' home number."

Mariana swallowed. The police were obviously quite anxious to see her. "Do they have a suspect yet, Sergeant?" she asked.

"Not officially. But I think they've got a real short list and a name at the top they'd like to build a case around. Uh, I've got to go now, Miss Sands. You take care."

They said goodbye and hung up. Immediately, Mariana dialed the courthouse number that Hemphill used to collect messages when he was at court. She left a message on his voice mail, explaining to Owen about Cryssa and Maryanice...and the police's intention to question her about the late Fred Lowe. When she hung up the phone, she breathed a sigh of relief.

Mariana looked at Lyn.

"My sister and my agent are coming to see if I'm still in one piece! They were hiring a private detective to find out what happened to me." Mariana laughed shakily. "I guess my newspaper notoriety did serve some good purpose."

Lyn came forward and hugged Mariana briefly.

"I just know things are going to work out for you," she said fervently.

Mariana's smile firmed. She was encouraged by this recent turn of events. However, she wasn't as sanguine as Lyn Hemphill that her life was about to smooth out. After all, Louie was still unaccounted for. And he could be a formidable obstacle. That thought sent a light shiver of apprehension across her skin.

"How 'bout another cup of coffee?" Lyn suggested, curving her elegantly shaped brows upward in a question.

Mariana nodded.

"While I'm making us a fresh pot, I'll tell you all my favorite tales about Portia Willowbrook. You never met her, did you? Well, she was one of a kind, I'll tell you. And it was obvious that she loved Owen. Not in a lustful way, of course, but like a...well, almost like a long-lost prodigal son that had miraculously come back to her fold. By the way—" she glanced over her shoulder at Mariana and smiled dryly "—did you know I witnessed the signing of her will?"

Mariana shook her head, her eyes wide in surprise.

"I was in Averson's office the day she came in to sign it. I was between errands, and the person they'd been planning to use as a witness was stuck in Washington with a stalled car. So I became a witness. And I can tell you she was tickled to death to be spreading her estate around the way she'd decided. She even asked me if I thought Owen would enjoy the people here and settle down when he discovered he'd inherited the house and lands on Algonquin Road...."

"What did you say?" Mariana asked curiously. How would Owen have felt about it? About the town?

"Oh, I told her he might think it slow and uneventful after such a full life in busier, bigger cities, but by the time Ms. Willowbrook passed to her reward, I expected he'd be more appreciative of the riches found in our calmer, more relaxed environment here."

"Poor Owen. He may never have the chance to find out, if the court rules in the nephew's favor."

Lyn Hemphill gave Mariana a curious look.

"You really care for him, don't you?" she asked in sympathy. She patted Mariana's hand and poured them each a cup of freshly brewed Kona coffee. "Don't you worry just yet. I think Averson can cut that out-of-town lawyer off at the county pass." She grinned and sat down. "Virginia isn't just for lovers, you know," she declared, scrambling the state's advertising slogan. "Our lawyers are pretty sharp. And Averson drew up that will for Portia. Averson's shrewd, even for *our* lawyers. As his wife, I would know if he weren't too bright, now wouldn't I, Mariana?'' she asked, laughing softly, her eyes glimmering with amused wisdom.

"Surely you don't expect me to reply to that?" Mariana demanded, struggling not to choke with laughter.

Lyn shrugged that it made no matter, and she smoothly continued, letting Mariana off the hook for a reply.

"Furthermore, it's hard to disregard the wording of a will in our courts. Around here, people don't often overturn the wishes of the deceased. We still have respect for the dead."

For Owen's sake, Mariana fervently hoped so.

Mariana spent the rest of the morning talking with Lyn about life in the small town and raising children and the challenges of love and marriage. She found Lyn Hemphill to be a gracious, honest woman. She was a little older, and she was definitely more settled down and burdened with domestic responsibilities. Still, there was a vibrance and sense of humor in the lawyer's wife that warmed and illuminated everything she did or said.

"Your husband's lucky to have you, Lyn," Mariana said as they cleared away their lunch dishes.

Lyn laughed, but she gave Mariana a measuring look. "I've been thinking that you and Owen seem to have found a lot to be thankful for in your recent friendship." She ignored Mariana's ambiguous smile and discouraging silence. "I would say you've made a big impression on him."

Mariana murmured something noncommittal. Maybe they *had* made a distinct "impression" on one another. But how lasting would that impression be? she wondered. Cynically, her anxious fears tried to smother her gossamer dreams of love.

Mariana had just agreed to help Lyn clean away some of the last fall leaves cluttering her backyard gardens when the phone rang.

Lyn answered it and turned to Mariana a moment later, looking completely dismayed. "Yes. Of course. Tell the judge I'll be there as soon as I can drive over to the courthouse. Of course I'll bring Mariana with me!" she exclaimed tartly. She glared at the phone as she replaced it on the receiver. "As if I'd leave you on your own."

"Do they need you in court?" Mariana asked.

"Apparently Judge Hammer wants me to testify in front of him regarding Portia's state of mind when I witnessed her will. Averson warned me that I might be called at some point, but normally, it wouldn't be until things were a little further along." She grinned as she put on her coat. "I can't say that I'm surprised. Judge Hammer always had the highest respect for my mother and father, and his middle son was my steady beau in high school. I spent many a Sunday afternoon playing poker or pinochle or bridge with the Hammers and staying for supper."

Mariana tried to cover her laughter behind her hand. "No!"

"Oh, yes indeed, honey. If you ask me, he's just hunting for some good solid reasons to send that money-grubbing, never-met-her-didn't-know-her nephew out of town with a one-way ticket on the next bus."

Amid Mariana's laughter, Lyn telephoned a neighbor whose children attended the same school that the Hemphills did. After a few moments of explanation, Lyn had arranged for the other parent to pick up her children and keep them until the Hemphills had returned from court.

Lyn sailed through her kitchen door that connected to the garage, pressing the remote-control device to lift the garage door. Mariana, still struggling into her coat sleeves, grabbed her purse and hurried after her.

Everything went just fine until they got to the courthouse. There was no place to park. It was a small town, with very few parking meters and no parking lots. People normally parked along the curbs. Today every curb was lined as far as the eye could see.

All the media interest in the trial had stirred up local interest. More journalists had arrived in town to cover the court proceedings, and they all apparently had driven a car and parked it downtown. It looked like a huge overnight population boom had swamped the place.

After the third time around the courthouse and the eight adjacent blocks, they saw Averson's law-student intern standing on the courthouse steps, madly waving his arms at them. From the urgent way he was gesturing for Lyn to come inside and the terrified look on his face, it was obvious Judge Hammer was losing patience.

"You go. I'll park the car," Mariana said firmly.

"No!" Lyn exclaimed in alarm. "We're trying to protect you."

"What could possibly happen to me in broad daylight, driving in a car near the courthouse?" Mariana asked reasonably. "I'm scared of him finding me in places that have been mentioned...or tracking me down at Owen's house on Algonquin Road in the dark when I'm alone. This is not a problem, believe me," Mariana insisted confidently. No one in his right mind would assault her or kidnap her off a public street in broad daylight. "Go on!" she urged Lyn. "Hurry and tell the judge what he wants to know. Maybe you can speed up Owen's escape from this headache."

Seeing the panic on her husband's assistant's face, and in light of Mariana's persuasive arguments, Lyn regretfully agreed that it was her only option.

"But you keep the doors locked and hurry straight into the courthouse, and if anyone comes near you, scream like Pickett's Charge."

Mariana raised her palm in solemn oath. "I swear I will."

Lyn hopped out of the car and ran up the steps. She spoke to the assistant, trying to get him to go to Mariana, but he shook his head, indicating he was needed in court, too. He literally dragged Lyn Hemphill by the arm into the building, while she looked worriedly over her shoulder at Mariana driving off slowly in the Hemphills' car.

Not far down the street, a dark sedan pulled out of a parking spot. Mariana, hardly able to believe her good luck, quickly drove up and parallel parked in it. She'd just gotten out of the car and locked it when she noticed that the sedan hadn't driven more than a few lengths away. Now it was backing up, stopping parallel to the Hemphills' car. The driver got out, leaving the door open and the engine running.

Mariana had already started through the space between the front of her car and the back of the car parked ahead of hers. The driver was now blocking her exit. She looked up. And froze.

Louie Roualt was smiling at her. She had never seen such a chilling expression, nor such icy fury in a man's eyes.

She started backing away and looking around frantically for someone to yell out to. No one was nearby. And before she could take more than two steps, he'd reached out and grabbed her arm, yanking her into his body.

"Don't run away, my dear. That isn't the way to greet your husband. You know that."

Chapter 16

Roualt grabbed her wrist, twisted her around in front of him and shoved her roughly into the front seat of his car. He pushed her to the passenger's side and swiftly climbed into the driver's seat, slamming his door shut after him. Then he stepped on the gas.

She grabbed her door handle, intending to jump out of the car.

Roualt pressed down the driver's master switch, locking all the doors. "You're not going anywhere," he said angrily.

She was trapped. Locked in. Her heart pounded faster. She turned and beat her hands on the window, screaming as loud as she could, "Help!"

The courthouse was fading in the distance behind them, but she was still close enough to recognize the man who came out of the building and stood on the steps, looking around. It was Owen.

"Owen!" she screamed, trying to lower the window. It dropped a couple of inches, and she thought he must have heard her because he suddenly looked straight at the car.

Roualt yanked her away from the window as she shouted Owen's name again, yelling for help like a desperate banshee.

"Shut your mouth or I'll shut it for you right now," he snarled.

He used his master switch to raise her window. Unfortunately, having to control the locks and windows and Mariana made turning down the short and oddly angled old streets difficult.

He nearly sideswiped one parked car. Then he overcompensated and barely avoided hitting a pedestrian in a crosswalk.

Mariana reached for the wheel and pulled it hard, making the tires squeal and forcing Rouault to brake quickly to avoid wrapping the front end around an old-fashioned stoplight planted smack in the middle of an intersection.

He backhanded her face hard, snapping her head back and stinging her lips as they were cut against her teeth. She felt dizzy and tasted the rusty, salty flavor of blood on her tongue. God, how had Maryanice ever fallen prey to this monster?

"You really outdid yourself this time," he said, as if it were so profoundly offensive that it was unbelievable that she had actually done it. "Until last night, I was angry because you haven't been keeping me informed of your comings and goings. I told myself that you're beautiful, but you gamble and drink, sometimes going for days without really sobering up. When I had the time to travel with you, it was entertaining. But I'm too busy with expanding business opportunities..."

His voice drifted off. He never explained the businesses he dabbled in. Never.

"As long as you're beautiful and faithful...well, I've looked the other way. But now...now you've crossed me, Maryanice."

He shook his head slowly. He was looking straight ahead, weaving his way through the crisscrossing streets. He glanced at her as if measuring her for her funeral casket.

"I warned you..." he said, his baritone soft like a hissing snake. "But here I fly back to my loving wife after many weeks of business travel over three continents, and she's not only gone with no forwarding address, but I find her face in half the major newspapers...and stories about a man in her life." His voice had become quite hard. "That's a serious no-no, my love. I'm going to have to do something about it. I warned you."

Mariana, gingerly touching her bleeding lip and trying to wipe away the blood, had never heard such detached, cold comments made by such a seductively even voice. He was a devil, she thought bitterly. He'd mastered the art of seducing women and giving them the masculine attention and possessiveness that so many craved. Unfortunately, it was a very shallow version of the real thing. Beneath that handsome, hypnotic veneer lay a man without any genuine depth of feeling, who knew all the right things to say, and how to say them and when. But none of them held any true meaning for him. Everything was an award-winning performance, but the stage he played on was real life, and the other players didn't imagine themselves to be in some psychopathic theater performance. They thought they were living their lives.

They were leaving the thinning outskirts of the town. Roualt would be able to pick up speed. He could turn off onto a country road. And then she would be isolated. Alone.

She reached for the keys and turned off the engine. Roualt instantly grabbed her hand in a bruising grip and yanked her free. He'd kept his foot on the accelerator, however, and when he tried to turn on the engine again, it had flooded. As the car coasted, and he repeatedly tried to restart the engine, he cursed Maryanice viciously. It was awkward to try to hit her again, however, since he needed the hand nearest her to turn the keys in the ignition.

Mariana leaned on the door and unlocked it at the same moment. The door flew open, and she sailed out on the hard dirt shoulder of the two-lane paved road. Pain smashed into the bones and joints of her shoulder and hip.

She heard Roualt skid the car to a halt and crank the engine again. While it turned over, she scrambled painfully to her feet and stumbled back in the direction they'd come. Ignoring the piercing fire shooting through her injuries with every jarring step, she ran as fast as she could.

Behind her, she heard Roualt's car engine take hold. Tires squealed. She knew he was turning around or backing up. He was coming closer to her every second. Her lungs hurt as she desperately dug for more speed. Would he just run her down on the road? she wondered, terrified. The outlying houses and businesses were within sight. But was anyone watching them? Probably not.

Then she heard an approaching car. Coming fast, the engine screaming. It was Owen. In his car. Mariana didn't waste energy or add wind resistance by waving her arms. He obviously was coming for her and had probably seen her about the same moment she saw him.

Unfortunately, the sounds behind her were horrifyingly close. She didn't dare turn around to look. She needed all the forward motion she could squeeze out of the next few seconds.

Then she felt the heat of the approaching metal and she leaped as hard to her left as she could, diving into the heavy grass and sloping runoff at the side of the road.

He caught her lower leg and foot, spinning her into a half flip. She landed on the same side she had just moments ago. This time the pain was blinding, and she screamed, but the breath whooshing out of her left her with nothing to make sound.

And then she heard the sickening crash of metal against metal. She shoved herself off the ground, tears coming to her eyes from the hurt, and looked fearfully toward the source of the sounds.

All the blood left her face, leaving her paper white with shock.

Owen had plowed his car straight into Roualt's before Roualt had been able to evade him or turn himself around to attack Mariana a second time.

The cars weren't moving anymore. Owen's was smashed in and quarter-turned in the road. Roualt's had flipped and skidded after the collision. Dark smoke was beginning to billow from somewhere inside it. There was no sign of either man.

Mariana limped toward Owen's car, fearing to see what had happened to him, desperate to help him if he was hurt. She prayed someone had heard all the noise and called for emergency help.

That prayer had already been answered. Wailing sirens were approaching fast.

Mariana reached Owen's car just as the fire engine came roaring into view. The windshield sported a dense display of spider cracks. The front end was snubbed two feet shorter than it had been. There was steam rising from under the hood, and the air bag had deployed on the driver's side.

Owen was slumped under the bag.

Mariana tried to open the passenger's-side door, the one closest to her approach. It protested with a metallic creak, but yielded to her and fell open.

Mariana crawled up on the seat and felt for Owen's hand and arm. Found them. Slid her fingertips down to his wrist.

"Come on, Owen," she murmured, choking back tears of fear and anger and painful exhaustion. She felt a pulse. Her breath slid out of her lungs, and she laid her other hand ever so lightly on the back of his head.

"Owen? Can you hear me?" she murmured.

The rescue squad, fire truck and police car all careened to squealing stops around the two vehicles.

"Here!" she cried out to them. "He's not responding.... Help!" She laced her fingers between his, holding on to him and murmuring, "They'll get you out of this and to a hospital, Owen. Hold on, Owen. Owen..." she murmured, her voice cracking in anguish. "Owen, hold on...."

His fingers tightened, and his eyes flickered open.

For a moment, she was certain she saw the old flame of recognition that was in his eyes only when he looked at her. Joy leaped in her heart. His eyes slid closed, as if it had taken a great effort to keep them open even that short amount of time.

"You're going to be all right," she said fiercely, as if no force in the universe would be so cruel as to take him from her. As if she would not permit it.

She swallowed hard. "Oh, Owen, I'm so sorry. I've caused you so much pain."

She felt the hot tears sliding down her cheeks, but she couldn't seem to stop them now. She leaned her face close to his and gently kissed his cheek. His fingers tightened on her hand, and he said something, but it was so faint, she couldn't make it out at first.

"What?" she said softly, speaking close to his ear.

"You...okay?" he whispered hoarsely, his voice raspy and just barely audible.

"Fine. Thanks to you," her voice caught on a sob. She gently stroked his cheek with her fingertip. "This is the second time you've saved my life, Owen Blackhart."

She thought his lips were curving into the faintest memory of a smile. He managed to open his eyes a crack.

Before they could say anything else, the rescue personnel descended on the cars. One paramedic firmly steered Mariana away from the car and examined her from head to toe. While her bones were being checked for fractures and her body for evidence of internal injuries, the police began questioning her. Since she was the only fully conscious person at the scene, they relied on her to supply an initial description of what had transpired.

Mariana kept leaning and stretching to see what they were doing with Owen, much to the annoyance of her paramedic and the policeman who kept repeating questions for her.

From the cluster of emergency medical techs swarming around Louie Roualt, she assumed he must be in bad shape. It wasn't long before the sound of helicopter rotors announced that he needed to be flown to a shock-trauma center. Mariana swallowed hard. She felt awful about being involved in such a serious accident, but she found it very hard to feel any real empathy for that conscienceless man who had misused her poor sister for so many years.

Louie's car also had an air bag, but unlike Owen, he hadn't bothered to fasten his seat belt in his haste to kidnap Mariana. As a result, Louie had gone halfway through the side window when he ran into Owen's car.

Mariana watched the emergency medical techs carefully settle Louie on a stretcher. It was a relief to know he wouldn't be trying to hunt any of them down for a while, she suddenly realized. If he didn't survive the crash, they'd be free of him forever. Mariana couldn't help but feel a little guilty for being so cheered at the prospect of Roualt's death. Such an unworthy thought made her feel very small. Before she could feel too sinful, however, she was surrounded by people inquiring after her health, asking for a description of what had happened and taking snapshots.

Mariana wanted to stay by Owen's side, but the technicians kept hanging on to her, insisting they needed to examine *her* and promising her she could see Owen back at the hospital later, where both of them were most likely going to be getting X rays to look for smaller, harder-to-diagnose fractures.

Mariana was feeling stiffer by the moment, too, which slowed her down considerably when Owen's stretcher was raised to its normal height and wheeled to the waiting ambulance.

She thought his eyes were open and his head turned, trying to see her. She ached to run to his side, but the ankle and leg that Roualt had hit with the car were beginning to feel more seriously hurt than she'd believed at first. She looked down and was startled to see the amount of swelling.

"It isn't broken," she said, looking at the nearest emergency techs. They weren't so sure. "It can't be!" she exclaimed, thinking of all the things she needed to do in the next few days and weeks.

One of the techs shrugged and said, "You get what you get. It's the luck of the draw."

Mariana rolled her eyes and sat down on a stretcher brought for her. She was beginning to feel pretty woozy, now that she was starting to relax and could leave the crisis management to the paid professionals.

"Wake me when we get to Owen's hospital," Mariana murmured. She didn't even feel her eyes close before she passed out.

The following evening, Mariana and Owen were discharged from the hospital and driven back to Owen's house by Averson Hemphill. With all the hustle and bustle at the hospital, there had been little time for them to talk. In the medical center, it had been hard even to find one another's room and make sure the other was healing and nothing serious had suddenly raised a threatening head.

It seemed someone was always in the room with them. A nurse.

A doctor. A medical technician. Friends. Family. A virtual stream of reporters generating a constant demand for access and interviews. Someone delivering a meal. Someone selling get-well balloons and cards, or newsstand-quality reading material.

Staying in the hospital was quite exhausting.

Owen had finally confronted his doctor and said he was leaving—with or without medical permission. The doctor looked over the chart and shrugged. "If you want to nurse the aches and pains alone at home, Owen, go right ahead." He'd glanced over his reading glasses and with some effort maintained a poker face. "I could arrange for someone to stay with you twenty-four hours a day for a few days, just to keep an eye on you...."

Owen shot him a look that could have boiled water.

"Pardon me," the doctor murmured in sly amusement. "I assume that nasty look means you don't want any company, er, paid company."

"Get a life, Doc," Owen warned him without subtlety. "I certainly intend to."

As soon as he could sit Mariana down and talk to her.

Maryanice and Cryssa had arrived at the hospital, and Mariana had embraced both of them with great joy. Maryanice was quickly submerged beneath Louie's problems, however. As his wife, she had to authorize procedures and fill out forms. That required her returning to their home in Maryland and their bank to get information. And the police wanted to interview Maryanice as part of their ongoing investigation into Fred Lowe's death. That had really hit Maryanice hard, since he had been a close friend at a time in her life when she had truly needed one.

The police were working on the theory that Louie was responsible for Fred's death. It would take them awhile to make the case, since a man with Louie's underworld connections could get false passports, hire personal jets or boats, and enter and leave the country without being detected, if he put his mind to it. Being abroad was a great alibi. However, he'd had people watching his wife, and reporting to him. So the authorities hadn't ruled out the

He held Mariana's chin gently in one hand. "The man must have damn poor eyesight. Along with all his other major problems," he growled.

Mariana laughed again, reveling in the fierce expression burning in his eyes. Owen's arm tightened around her, and he swayed slowly from side to side, as if they were dancing to a tender ballad. Mariana felt no pain. She smiled into his eyes and looped her arms around his waist.

"Do you like to dance?" she asked curiously.

"I never did," he confessed. His gaze wandered over her. "Until now." He slid his hands down her back, gently cupping her hips, molding her bottom, drawing her abdomen and thighs closer against his.

"Maryanice called me at the hospital, just before I left my room to meet you," Mariana said quietly.

"Oh?"

"She was on her way to the hospital where Louie was admitted. They'd called her. His condition deteriorated rapidly this afternoon. He didn't make it, Owen."

Owen rested his chin on the top of her head. "Is your sister okay?"

"She's busy. I think she and several investigatory agencies will be trying to unravel Louie's so-called businesses for months, if not years. However, she does have a lot of assets, and most of all...some control over them, finally."

"So she'll be living in their house?"

"For now."

"I'm impressed with your business manager. She certainly hung tough," Owen remarked in amusement. "I like her, too."

"And Cryssa was positively smitten with you," Mariana teased him. Then, a little nervously, she added, "She had to return to Phoenix tonight." Mariana hesitated. "She volunteered to cook for you if you ever came that way and found yourself in need of a meal."

Owen thought Mariana had more than a little difficulty delivering that message. She sounded jealous. He smiled slowly. He put his hands on her shoulders and held her a little away from him so he could watch her expression.

"Tell her I appreciate the thought."

"If you insist."

Owen's grin broadened.

"And what are your plans, Mariana?" he asked softly.

She looked away, trying to escape the intensity of his gaze. He captured her chin gently, forcing her to face the truth with him.

"I'm not interested in eating with Cryssa unless you're with me," he declared. "I won't stray, Mariana. We will fight about something someday. Most couples do, sooner or later. But it won't be about another woman. You have my word."

"Oh." Mariana stared at him, feeling weak in the knees from the determined expression in his eyes and the rock-solid conviction in his quietly spoken promise. Mariana blinked. "We're talking about something more serious than dinner with Cryssa."

"Much more serious. Much more long-term."

"We hardly know each other," she forced herself to protest. There was no point in being coy. They'd been through too much together to bother with that now.

"That's why people spend their lives together," he murmured, his voice roughened with emotion.

"To get better acquainted?" She couldn't believe the words were actually coming out of her mouth. She could barely breathe. Her lungs had stopped functioning. Her mouth was dry. And all she could do was stare at him. She felt weak and giddy and hot and cold all at once.

"It appears that I do indeed own a house," he said dryly. "You're welcome to stay in it as long as you like."

How had his eyes become so silvery? she wondered, dazed.

"But...I have a house of my own," she murmured. She half closed her eyes when she felt Owen's lips slide slowly across her throat. She tipped her head back, giving him better access. "I'm glad you won the lawsuit, Owen." She hadn't had a chance to tell him how relieved she was that the court business was over and the judge had found in his favor.

"People can have two houses," he said against the side of her neck, slowly nuzzling his way across its tender flesh.

"Uh-huh..." she said, through a haze of wonderful sensation. She put her arms around him and splayed her fingers across the muscled ridge of his back. She felt the heat and strength of his body through the layers of clothing, and vivid memories of lying against his bare, hard body came rolling back over her in rhythmic, agonizingly sweet waves.

He caressed her in long, sweeping strokes, murmuring something about bicoastal living and two-career families and self-employed people working from their homes. And all she could comprehend was how right it felt to be in his arms. How much she wanted to spend the rest of her life like this.

Mariana snuggled against his chest, listening to the strong beating of his heart. She was drowning in his scent and his warmth and his beautiful, trusted voice. His strong, reassuring touch.

"Are you sure this isn't a dream?" she whispered shakily. "And someday we'll wake up and we'll feel like strangers?"

He looped his arms around her shoulders and swayed with her for a moment, considering her cautiously voiced fear. Then he held her a little away and looked seriously into her beautiful green eyes.

"My life was a dream until I woke up the night that I scrambled down the mountainside and took your hand in mine and told you to hang on," he said quietly. His warm gaze drifted down across her face to her lips. And back to her eyes. "I know there will never be anyone in my life like you. There never has been. And there never will be. You touch something deep inside me, something so hot and so aching that only holding you in my arms takes away the pain."

He rested his cheek against hers and whispered.

"I knew I was falling in love with you, but seeing you nearly killed in front of me kind of speeded up my plans for courting you. I don't want to spend months dating. I love you, Mariana. I want to marry you. I want you in my life, every part of it, every day of it. I want to sleep with you. I want to feel your body in my arms when I fall asleep at night and when I wake up in the morning. I want to be there for you when you need me. If you can't handle that, you'd better brace yourself, sweetheart, because I'm not letting you escape. If you want more time, we can talk about how to work this out. I'm free to come and go as I want. I have enough money to live on from my investments. I can work when I want to, where I want to, for whom I want." He lifted his head and shrugged. "I can just as easily live in Phoenix as here. There are plenty of things I've wanted to do, but never had time to pursue because I was working for a living."

Mariana placed her hands on either side of his face, framing him and holding him still. She searched his eyes, and deep in the innermost depths of their silvery gray, she saw what she felt in her own heart. This was different. This was special. This was a once-in-a-lifetime love.

"This is forever for me, Mariana," he whispered against her lips. "Marry me, sweetheart." His lips touched hers persuasively. "Give me your warmth and your humor and your courage and your love. I've ached for you. Before I ever met you. And ever since. Strike a bargain with me. Share the rest of your life with me, and let me share the rest of my life with you."

His mouth covered hers, and this time he let the urgency, the need show. He needed her. He wanted her with every masculine cell in his body.

Mariana melted into his arms and opened her mouth, sealing the bond with her complete surrender. Since that terrifying night when his voice had brought her back from the darkness of death, she had felt connected to him in a very special way. But now she knew he felt that same incredible sensation for her.

"All right," she agreed, murmuring against his mouth. "I will marry you, Owen Blackhart."

He groaned and held her up in his arms. Until that moment, he had feared she might hesitate, might refuse. He hadn't realized just how deeply he'd feared it until she'd said yes and freed him from the darkness.

Against her soft lips, he achingly murmured the eternal pledge, "I love you, Mariana Sands."

* * * * *

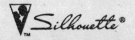

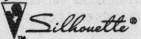